# Vamp

# Vamp

*xxx,*
*Savanna Samson*

THUNDER'S MOUTH PRESS
NEW YORK

VAMP
*A Vivid Girls Book*

Published by
Thunder's Mouth Press
An Imprint of Avalon Publishing Group Inc.
245 West 17th St., 11th Floor
New York, NY 10

AVALON
publishing group incorporated

Library of Congress Cataloging-in-Publication Data is available

ISBN 1-56025-782-2

9 8 7 6 5 4 3 2 1

Book design by Maria Elias
Printed in the United States of America
Distributed by Publishers Group West

*To all my fans: may you find in these pages*
*the pleasure you seek . . .*

# Chapter 1.

When I think of her name, a cold sweat drips down my back. I remember how she fanned through my life like a hot desert breeze before the rains. From the first moment I saw her shining eyes, I knew I was lost forever.

It has been three long years since that hot, humid night. Life was so different then. Now all I can think of is her—and how I yearn to see her again.

Savanna's soul was dark—a darkness that thrilled the senses. Her body was firm, her skin pale and smooth. Her blond hair gave her the face of an angel. Her power was palpable in her gaze. When she cast her eyes upon me, I could feel something inside me melt, and my flesh would tighten like a violin string, yearning to play a duet with a siren. How I miss her.

I close my eyes and can see her standing before me, her blond hair streaming down like a halo, her pale flesh straining against black, smooth, supple leather. Behind her are rows upon rows of candles lighting a hallway. She stands with one hand on her hip and the other playing with a flogger. Her nipples protrude from the crisscross straps of the cupless halter she wears around her breasts. Each nipple is hard as a cherry and pierced with a silver ring. The leather straps cross around her taught abdomen, and her glittering belly ring sparkles in the candlelight. She wears a leather studded g-string that shows off her long, shapely legs. Black stilettos click on the marble floor. She stares at me.

"Franco . . . I am waiting for you."

The words are what I have been longing to hear for so long. In a trance, I step toward her—she snaps her flogger in the air. She points to me like a queen commanding her soldiers.

"Not so fast, Franco. Not so fast. First, you must show me that you deserve to come with the queen."

"I deserve you, Queen Savanna." My words come from some deep place inside my soul. "I have shown you before . . . I haven't been able to eat or drink or even . . . you know . . ."

"Silence. I don't want to hear groveling. Kneel."

I kneel down before her.

"Lower."

I press my forehead to the floor. I can hear the clicking of her stilettos approaching me. My heart races with expectation. My Savanna. She has come for me at last.

I feel the pressure of her stiletto turning my head to the side. She presses down above my ear.

"Is this what you want, little boy?" she asks me.

"Yes, my queen."

"Lower your jeans," she commands. I unbutton my jeans, which isn't easy with a stiletto on your head. I struggle to slip them down.

She pulls her foot off my head and walks behind me. *Click, click, click.*

"I see you're not wearing underwear." I glance back and see she's smiling.

Suddenly I feel the sting of whip on my bare ass. It comes down again and again. I am breathless. Pleasure and pain soar through me.

She stops and kneels down behind me. I feel her hot breath on my neck, and she cups my cock and balls in her hand. She tugs on them; I moan. Her touch is warm and forceful, and I grow hard as she tugs on me again. She teases my ass with the handle of the whip.

"You've been a bad boy," she whispers in my ear. Her words are like dark, liquid honey dripping into my mind.

"I only want you, Savanna, my queen," I say.

Her hand strokes my cock. I moan as she teases me.

"We shall see about that . . ." She stands up, brushing her breasts along my back like a stretching cat.

"Sit up."

She stands in front of me with her legs spread. I can see the full lips of her pussy pressing against the leather. Her fingers deftly untie the g-string, and it falls to the floor.

"Keep your hands behind your back, I want you to do a good job."

She spreads her delicious lips to my face and presses them into my mouth. I suck on her, and she sighs. I nibble from side to side, tugging at her pussy lips. She pulls herself wider so that her clit is protruding enough for me to lick and suck. I greedily help myself as she grinds her hips into my face. One of her hands lets go of her pussy and wraps around the back of my head. She pushes me into her so hard I am drowning in pussy juice. I feel her excitement build as I lick and suck her eager clit. She pulls me to her, her hips now bucking frantically as I try to keep pace. She cries out, and I lick her even harder.

She steps away and rubs her fingers in her pussy. She stares at me as she licks her fingers, a slight smile on her face.

She turns to walk down the hallway, her bare ass swinging. I struggle to pull on my jeans, and the dream disappears.

Every night is the same.

Waiting for her.

Looking for her.

But she has disappeared.

However, I digress.

I need to tell you the story of how I met Savanna, and how she cast her spell over me. This is the type of fantasy every man dreams about but few ever get to experience.

Really, there is nothing special about me. I just happened to be in the right place at the right time. Or at least, that is what I would like to believe. Sometimes I'm not so sure.

I really didn't have much to complain about in my life. Options and choices were all around me—as they are for everyone. We can choose to take options or ignore them. We can build our futures or we can dwell on the mistakes of our past.

Before I met Savanna, my job was going well. I had even gotten a small promotion, so money wasn't and hadn't been an issue in a long time. In fact, I quite enjoyed my work, and it could sometimes be hard for my friends to get me out into the world.

This day, though, it wasn't too hard to tempt me. Halloween was coming, and I loved Halloween. I had been single long enough to want to have some fun.

In my adult life, I was single more often than I ever had a girlfriend. Yes, there have been women who have charmed and entranced me longer than a night or two, but not many. I had an agenda for the right woman, and it was hard for anyone to meet it.

My first real crush had been Rosa Cabini. She was my childhood sweetheart. We had grown up together in the same apartment building. We went to the same school and same church. Our parents often let us play together while they had a few drinks.

As the years went by, Rosa and I became inseparable. It was all childhood innocence and initiation. Looking back on those times, it was all very sweet.

How trusting young love can be.

How naive.

My Rosa inspired me and dared me to do so many things. I guess we were lucky to have each other. Not many people these days live in the same place long enough to grow close enough to have friends for many years. It was rare to watch a girl-next-door blossom from child to woman. We loved doing so many of the same things. How rare to have a childhood friend whose parents were friends as well.

One night we were sitting in Rosa's room, playing a board game. Rosa had been wearing a bra for a few years now. Her breasts were growing into something like you would find in her mother's balcony tomato garden. It was hard to imagine it was the same girl I walked to kindergarten with every day the few short city blocks to the school. All of us were maturing at different speeds. It wouldn't be long until everyone was grown up.

That night, the moon shone through the bedroom window, making Rosa's face glow with a seductive wisdom. Her long black hair fell in loose curls. She wore wire-rimmed glasses that she had to keep pushing up on her nose. I remember looking for the child in her face, but she was gone.

"What do you think they do when we're in here?" she asked suspiciously.

"I don't know." I shrugged. "Have a couple of beers, I guess."

"Do you think they do anything else?"

"Like what? What would they do with each other but have beer and play cards?" I asked.

Rosa pulled a magazine out from under her bed. It was a

women's magazine with lots of enticing headlines on the cover. She opened it up and pointed to a picture of a group of naked people fondling each other.

"You know, a lot of couples are into swinging these days."

"Oh, please. I don't believe you."

"Seriously." Her eyes were wide behind her glasses, as if she were trying to will me to believe her through her stare.

"No. That's only in porn. Real people don't have group sex."

"Oh, sure they do. Don't be such a prude."

"Me, a prude?" I grinned as I wrapped my fingers around her breast. She wore a soft fuzzy sweater and even to this day, when I see a woman in a certain color and texture of sweater, I think of that moment.

She laughed and pushed my hand away. She leaned over and kissed me full on the lips.

"Save it for later. Don't you want to find out what is going on?"

"Yeah, sure." In those days, it didn't take much to bring on an erection. The thought of touching her soft sweater-clad breasts again made me smile. I knew that as long as the parents were happy, we would be happy. They didn't seem to notice or mind that we still hung around together even though we were off to college the next year.

We went into the living room and there was no one there. The stereo was playing loudly as it always did when they were together. There were a few empty beer bottles on the table. I found it strange that no one was there at all, since they were always in the living room. The apartment wasn't that big, so they must have gone to one of the other bedrooms.

VAMP

"How did you know they wouldn't be here?" I asked. I stared down the hallway toward the closed bedroom door.

"I thought I heard the door slam."

"Really?"

"Yeah. Back when I whipped your ass in Monopoly."

"Why didn't you say anything?"

"It isn't the first time, Franco." She rolled her eyes at me. "Tell me, please, that you aren't that naive."

"How do you know what they're doing?"

"Easy. First of all, I read a lot, so I know there's a sexual revolution going on. People are over the fear of disease because they know to wear condoms and take steps to educate themselves. They want to explore. They want to see all that is going on in the world. The idea of monogamy is outdated. It's not even outdated; it's just some in-between kind of custom that someone somewhere thought up. Humans are meant to roam and wander. We live too long to not have variety."

"You're scaring me."

"Really, Franco. Consider all the angles. When this monogamy crap was created, people were dead by fifty. Usually they were in poor health for most of their life from something or another, so who cared about sex? Those who cared found hookers or had mistresses, depending on their kink, if their spouses were too sickly."

"What does that have to do with the fact our parents are in the bedroom together?"

"They still have a life partner, but they are also free to experiment."

8.

I thought about it. I still think about it.

We never really did find out what our parents did behind closed doors. We never asked and they never told us. I don't know what I thought they did before Rosa brought it up; I'd never even considered it. I had noticed the door shut once in a while over the years while I went to the kitchen to get a snack or something. As a child, I don't think I thought twice about it. Parents were mysterious creatures that came and went as they pleased. As I got older, I was usually preoccupied with how to sneak a cigarette or a beer without getting caught. Then there were those times when a shy kiss from Rosa turned into heavy breathing and petting in the closet. I figured the parents might be smoking dope or talking about private things. Heavy breathing and petting didn't take long to evolve into the real deal.

Rosa never said anything, but before the night she pointed at the closed door we had nearly been caught by the parents.

Rosa had been showing me her newest CDs and I had been sneaking peeks down her bosom. That night she wore a black lacy bra. She knew that black lacy bras made me mad with desire. All night she had been teasing me, pretending to fix her socks, or bending over to pass me things. She made certain that I was looking into her cleavage at all times.

It nearly drove me crazy. In my younger, greedier days, I was persistent. Once my hormones engaged, it was a short drive to finding release. Rosa grew to know that about me and was accommodating.

I always thought I would grow up to marry Rosa. That day,

I slipped her sweater up over her bra. I cupped those lacy tits in my hands and kneaded them. I squeezed them together and apart, staring with awe at her cleavage. I buried my face into her cleavage, licking her fair skin. I nuzzled and kissed the flesh that spilled over the top of the lacy bra. Her hands stroked my hair, encouraging me to fondle her tits.

My groin ached. Before the days she let me take her, I used to have to go to the bathroom to relieve myself. She had me so turned on so much of the time. Back in those innocent times, I thought I was in love with her. Now that I'm older and wiser, I know that I was just a regular horny guy who was lucky enough to have a good sexual companion who let me fuck her whenever I wanted.

That night, I was in lust and in love. She pushed me back on the bed and quickly opened up my pants. She pulled out my dick and started to suck on it. I moved her head up and down my shaft with my hands. She sucked and nibbled on the tip. Every time we got together, she grew a little more adept at her dick-sucking skills. She wasn't afraid to try new ideas that she read about in her magazines. I was thrilled to be her guinea pig, much as she was mine. Her tongue swirled around the tip of my dick, tapping at the hole. She pursed her lips, sucking and kissing in alternate rhythm. She lowered her head until my shaft squeezed down her tight warm throat. I moved my dick up and down a few times. She pushed my hips firmly down, taking control. She feasted on my dick as if it were the last dick she would ever see in her life. I thought for sure I was going to shoot into her face. I pushed her off.

"Let me fuck you," I said, buying time before I shot my load.
She stepped back from me with a smile.

"You want to fuck?" She played with the button of her jeans.
"How badly do you want to fuck?"

I put my hand on my dick.

"See how hard I am for you? Tell me you aren't wet and ready
for me?"

She played with the zipper of her jeans, running it up and
down until at last, she slowly lowered the zipper to expose her
neatly trimmed pussy.

She peeled off her jeans and squatted over my dick. Her
tight, hot cunt wrapped around my dick. She sank onto me, gri-
macing a bit as we had only started fucking not long ago. She
told me a few years later that I had ruined her for the average
man. She said that when your hymen is busted by a horse dick,
anything else just doesn't really measure up after that.

This night wasn't our first, nor was it our last. We were getting used to each other, and I was learning more how to please
her. She lowered herself onto me, and I grabbed her hips. I
heard the apartment door slam and I knew that her parents
were home. I slammed into her quickly five or six times and
then I came. She jumped off in the wink of an eye and slipped
her skirt back on. I was zipping up my pants and reaching for
a book when the door opened. Her mother came in, eyeing us
suspiciously.

"Fancy you two inside on such a lovely day."

"Studying for test," Rosa said, her face flushed, trying to
swallow down her panting breath.

Her mother looked at me lying on the bed and Rosa sitting at her desk shuffling papers. Rosa's mother sniffed the air.

"Well, you'd better be passing all the tests in the next month, or there'll be hell to pay," she said. She shut the door again. Rosa giggled as she left.

"What's so funny?" I asked.

Rosa laughed.

"Didn't you see her? The way she was sniffing the air?"

"So let her sniff. We weren't smoking pot or anything."

"I bet she smelled us."

"What's to smell?"

"Why, your hot Italian testosterone, of course. And my hot Italian pussy juice."

"We're zesty," I said as I kissed her. We looked at our books for a few minutes, our heartbeats returning to normal.

"Do you think she knows we fuck?" I asked.

"If she doesn't, she's pretty clueless."

"I guess."

Rosa looked so pretty as she looked over her book, her glasses perched on the end of her nose.

As I kissed her again, I dreamed of the day we would kiss on our wedding day. I knew that our lips would touch and it would be magical. She would always be my treasure, my flower, my Rosa.

Of course nothing is perfect. Nothing lasts forever.

Life throws its twists and turns at you.

What is love? Is it lust? Is it a longing to search for people who fill missing holes in your soul? We can love so many people, because they all fill a certain yearning inside of us. Then there are those big loves. Our soul mates.

We realized as we kissed goodbye, the night before we were to part ways to our separate colleges, that things would never be the same again. We tried to keep our special friendship alive. We wrote letters and talked on the phone. She was so far away. I stayed in New York, but she went to Connecticut. I guess she could have been in Australia or some other distant land, but when you are young and impatient, even a few hours can be too far.

My heart started to fade and hers did too. Our letters grew infrequent. She didn't come home in the summers, opting instead to make jewelry and sell it in a boutique in Cape Cod. She eventually settled in Cape Cod.

It was funny how our lives started off so much alike, and ended up so differently.

I love the hum of the city. The bustle of people. I like looking out of the window of my condo and seeing people scurrying to get somewhere. The yellow cabs all lined up waiting for fares or trying to navigate traffic always gave me a sense of adventure, like there was so much to see and do in the world. Who didn't like to see the colorful strangers on the way to work each morning? I know I loved it.

I had a mild flirtation with the coffee shop lady for the longest time. She always had my double latte ready when she spied me coming in the door, no matter how long the line was. When it wasn't too busy, we'd chitchat back and forth about movies and books and all those things people use for small talk.

One day, on a whim, I asked her out to dinner.

We had a lovely time over red wine and steak. She was a lively conversationalist and had good business sense, too. It was a shame she was trapped in a coffee shop—but we all make choices. I never did ask her why she didn't get a better job.

After sharing a chocolate fudge cake with real whipped cream, we went back to her place. She was a kinky sort of girl. She was the first woman to introduce me to fetish, bondage, and S&M.

I didn't really dig getting tied up by her. I mean, I was open to the idea, which is why I let her do it to me to begin with. But she was so immature. So fumbly. I've seen people with more experience do it since those times, and I yearned to feel the firm hand of a mistress pulling my collar. How I wished for a mistress to show me the ropes.

When the coffee shop girl, Misty, I believe her name was, got undressed, the first thing I did was admire her pierced clit. You couldn't help but notice it. I really noticed it when my tongue was licking her sweet juices later on that evening.

She surprised me when she pulled handcuffs out of her purse.

"A handsome stallion like you needs to be harnessed," she cooed. She led me over to the bed and handcuffed me to the post. She had a four-poster bed and I guess it was to entertain the likes of me. There was assorted S&M gear hanging from the walls. She had an extensive collection of whips and handcuffs. They were displayed floor to ceiling, almost like museum pieces. She plucked a riding crop from its position on the display.

She smacked me with it several times.

When that crop hit my ass the first few times, I didn't feel too much. Then as it started to sting a little more, I began to appreciate the buzz. As she continued to slap me, I grew to understand what the allure could be toward S&M and other rough play. Watching it on porn sites either seemed sloppy and staged or mean-spirited. I had a sense that it was supposed to be fun and exciting and could hurt like hell yet feel good at the same time.

Misty was my first sampling of what these new feelings could entail. We stayed together a few months, until I grew bored. After all, I was a successful sales executive while she was a coffee shop girl. It just wouldn't look right at the parties. I needed to find someone more my speed.

For many months, I searched for a trophy wife. Someone I could flaunt to my superiors. In my mind, not only would I have a beautiful wife but she would be an intelligent conversationalist and be great in bed. There were many women in between who I fancied for a few days, a few weeks. It was hard for me to relax enough to get to know anyone.

I knew that I would find my trophy wife one day. So maybe I may have been a bit hasty to cast off some well-meaning respectable women.

Then again, maybe I knew Savanna had been waiting for me all along. Maybe somewhere in my deep unconscious soul, I knew it was she and she alone who could lift me from myself and along the path toward a vibrant career and exuberant life.

It doesn't seem possible. If someone had teleported back in time to tell me that I would be haunted until my dying day of a possibility that may have existed, I would have laughed in his face.

Tell me—me, Franco, the man who knows what he is looking for—I would pine away over someone I spent a few hours with?

I would have laughed and poured myself another martini.

Franco doesn't fall in love and pine. Not after Rosa. Not after Rosa broke his heart.

I remembered back to another time. Rosa had come back for a week one fall. We hadn't really seen much of each other in two years, but I still thought of her as my girl when she was in town. That was how it had always been. When she came to town, we were together. It was only us. No one else.

Yet, after two years, we didn't spend every minute together when she was in town. In fact, even our parents weren't as friendly as they used to be.

There was a football game on while she was in town and I just assumed she'd be coming with me. That was pretty much how it had always been. Football games were our treasured time to spend together. In fact, for the past three visits, all we did was go to two football games and one movie. We fucked a few times, but we didn't go anywhere.

This visit, I had talked to her on the phone but there was no mention of the game. I didn't think we had to mention it, since it was an unspoken thing for ten years or more. However, she didn't come by for a pregame drink. She wasn't at the front gates when it started. I went to the seats and drank a beer while I looked around. I saw Mark and Tony and waved at them. Then my heart sank as I saw that Rosa was sitting with them.

Back in those days, Mark and Tony and I weren't really friends as we are now. We had been acquaintances during high school and then we all went to different colleges. Well, Mark didn't. He was working at his dad's restaurant and training to take it over one day.

That was how I discovered that Rosa and Mark had a thing. Later on, when Mark and I became buddies after Rosa dumped him, we bonded over how Rosa wasn't really who we thought she was.

While I had visions of marrying Rosa and having her bear my children, she was fucking not only Mark but Tony and Ralph and even Ernie. When she was with Mark, she fucked me again once in a while. I didn't care, I was fucking Misty and a couple of other hot ladies. That was when I started forming my trophy-wife ideal. Each girl I met had a little echo in them of something that I yearned for in one complete woman. There was the lady who loved classical music and the ballet. The other lady who loved to go to the comedy shows. They all had killer bodies in their own way. Each one pleased me on some level and I learned how to please them.

With every woman I tasted, I felt I was preparing myself for my ultimate desire. And it turned out that I really was in training all those many years. The aching that I felt wasn't in my head. There was a reason I never fell in love. I had been saving myself for Savanna.

The seasons changed and still I felt a hollow ache in the pit of my stomach. On the surface, I know I looked jovial and good-natured. Even when I was eating the sweetest of pussy, my thoughts turned toward a yearning. There must be something more. There must be that final thrill. That one person who fills me with a craving that they write songs about. I wanted to love someone.

I wanted to love my mythical perfect woman.

And unlike most mortal men, I was lucky enough to find her, if only for a night. No other woman will engulf my senses the way that Savanna does.

I threw myself into my work. My sales soared and I was one of the top guys at my company. The bonuses flooded in. I felt pretty good about my life. I started to hang out more with my pals, Tony and Mark, since they were both between women too. They both were itching to settle down, or so they said. I didn't really believe either one of them.

Together we explored all sorts of clubs. We particularly enjoyed the fetish clubs and S&M dungeons. They were always good for a party. We sometimes played the games as well, but I was never satisfied. I felt like I could get whipped and fucked all night long and it would never fill the hole inside of me.

Tony and Mark dragged me down to the club that fateful night in October.

"Hey Franco, why don't you come check out Paradise tonight?"

I yawned as I took a sip of wine. I looked around my elegant apartment. Everything was perfect. White. Modern. Crisp. Right down to the two white candles and the white Swiss clock on the mantel.

"Why would I go to Paradise when I can drink a lovely glass of wine and listen to fine music?" I smiled as Vivaldi's *Four Seasons* played in the background.

"They've done it all up for Halloween. Rooms that no one's seen," Mark said with a wink.

"Really?"

"Oh, yes. There are slaves and everything," Tony said.

"They always have slaves there," I said.

"Not like these ones. Not from what I've heard . . ." Tony said.

I took another sip of wine and thought about it. I thought about how hard life had been lately. My job. My broken relationship. It had been a few months since I had last been with a woman. My heart had been briefly enamored with a young executive for a shoe company, but our schedules and lifestyles got in the way. After a few months of dating, we parted company. Since then, I'd been alone.

Although I had been to Paradise before, it wasn't really what I had in mind for the evening. However, seeing the enthusiasm in Tony and Mark's eyes, I wondered if I should give it try. After all, it was Halloween. If there was anytime to get back in the saddle again, it was during this weird and exciting season.

Before I knew it, we were standing outside of the club, waiting to get in. Music throbbed through the walls and spilled out onto the sidewalk beneath my feet. I tapped my foot expectantly as we waited to get in.

"Hey, Franco . . . you look absolutely ghoulish," Mark said, looking me over. I knew I looked hot. I wore tight black leather designer pants that hugged every curve of my muscular thighs and calves. My cock made its own warm curve and I smiled as I wiggled my hips. We had lightly powdered our faces to get into the groove of Halloween. For other accessories, we wore dog collars and wrist cuffs. My black hair was slicked back and I had a dash of black eyeliner to bring out my ebony eyes. My white dress shirt was ripped and showed off the washboard stomach that I toned three times a week at the gym. I ran my hands along it, feeling how tight it was against my fingers.

"I am feeling very ghoulish tonight." I mocked a Transylvanian accent.

A woman behind me in line giggled, and I turned to face her. She was very young, barely twenty-one, and she wore a witch's hat. She giggled again as she held my gaze.

"Good evening," I said in my best Bela Lugosi impersonation. She flushed and turned to her friends. They whispered excitedly as I turned back to Tony and Mark.

"It's crowded tonight," I observed.

"Halloween. A time of magic and mystery."

"Anything can happen at Halloween."

It was our turn and we paid our money to the lady in eye-popping fetish gear. I swear her tits must have been triple-Ds at least. As she stamped my hand she looked me in the eye and muttered the words that I would hear many times that night.

"Savanna is waiting for you."

"What?" I asked, but it was too late. She was on to the next client.

"What did she say to me?" I asked my buddies. They shrugged and shook their heads. The music was already too loud for half-decent conversation. We wandered through the large hallway. This building might have been a bank or a church or some other monstrosity in another life. The stonework was beautiful, and its immense size made it perfect for a nightclub that offered many delights in different areas. There were candles lit everywhere. In wall sconces, along the massive mantelpiece in the center of the hallway, on little tables and railings, there were the little telltale flickers of light in the darkness. People were lined up for the coat check, but we walked on by.

All around us people were dressed in kinky Halloween gear. Some of the costumes were very creative, others were the regular nurses and witches and demons. I admired a savage-looking woman wearing a fur bikini and clutching a giant bone. She growled at me as she walked by. I watched her round, naked ass for a moment, then turned my attention to my friends.

"So, what's the plan, guys?" I asked.

They shrugged.

"Find chicks. Get laid." Tony laughed.

"That shouldn't be too hard to do here," Mark said, staring

at a couple making out in the corner. We weren't even in the club yet and people were necking all over the place.

"Well, let's get in there then. Which way?"

We stood in the hallway, and looked at the options. There were three ways to go. Two were large rooms and one was a hallway that led to stairs and more rooms. Flashing lights leaked out of one room along with pounding music.

"Let's go check out that room," Mark said, as he led the way.

"Sure, I'm game," I said.

As I followed the men toward the doorway, I felt a sense of excitement I hadn't felt in ages. A sense of adventure and lust, as if I was on the brink of a marvelous adventure.

And I was.

# CHAPTER 2.

We stood in the doorway of the first room, trying to get our bearings. It was huge. There were two levels in this room. The main area, where we stood, was mostly dance floor and a few bars. There were stairs going up either side of the room, leading to balconies where people leaned against the rails, staring at the people below. There was a stage where girls were go-go dancing to some electronic beat music blaring over the loudspeakers. The dance floor was packed already, although the night was young. We wandered over to the bar.

Our bartender wore a red devil costume. Huge breasts loose strained against her tight rubber bikini top, and her little red g-string was nearly nonexistent. Her hair was red and curly, tied up in two large pigtails. She had tiny red glittering devil horns on her head.

"Yes?" she asked, leaning over so that we could fully appreciate the depth of her cleavage.

"Three beers, please," I said. "Imported."

She put our beer on the bar and I paid her. We put the bottles to our lips as we turned to face the dance floor.

There was a dizzying array of people. A kaleidoscope of color and flesh swirled in the strobe lights. I could have stood staring all night at the gorgeous costumes and jutting breasts everywhere I turned.

"Do you want to dance?" A cute young lady, dressed in white tight latex, stood staring at me. She blinked fake white eyelashes, her curly blond wig bobbing as her toe tapped to the beat.

"Sure." I followed her out to the dance floor. The view from inside the throng was even more amazing. People danced in chains, in couples, in groups. Many people wore collars and leashes and were led around by stern-looking women with high stilettos and tight clothes. I watched two girls beside me kissing and feeling each other's breasts.

"You come here often?" she asked me.

"No," I said.

"I didn't think so. I haven't seen you around. I think I would recognize you even underneath all that makeup." She smiled.

I grinned.

"Should I be coming here more often?" I asked.

"Well, the club is a great place. Of course, Halloween is even more special. It's the night Savanna picks her slaves."

"Savanna?"

"Savanna knows everything. She sees everything. She is beauty." The girl smiled. She reached over for my beer and took a sip, never missing a beat of music.

"Who is this Savanna? I heard her mentioned before."

"She's a queen. A goddess."

"She's human . . ."

The girl shrugged and laughed. We danced the rest of the song and then parted company as a tall tanned man led her off by the hand.

I saw some great outfits. The ones that truly intrigued me were the pony boys and pony girls. They pranced around, looking like two-legged ponies. The outfits were all quite different but basically consisted of many leather straps wrapping around them from head to toe. There were makeshift saddles and harnesses. They had bits in their mouths and plumes on their heads. Many of the ponies had tails.

"What's with the pony people?" I asked Tony. He smiled.

"They like to be horses. Get a riding crop and watch them go."

The elegance of the pony people was something to behold. The song ended and new one came on. The pony people gathered around the edges of the dance floor and started to stomp their hooves. They shook their heads and pawed the ground. They danced their own kind of jumping, shaking pony dance.

A man went over to a girl pony and boy pony. He took their reins and led them around the room. The ponies pranced, their feet kicking high as if in a parade. The man stopped and then released the reins. He waved his hand and the ponies kneeled, their butts in the air. The man stood behind them and drew a crop from his belt. One by one, he whipped their asses.

A thin man in his thirties pranced in front of us for a moment. He held his hands in front of him as if they were paws and shook his head proudly. His makeshift mane of white braided leather shook playfully as he tossed his head. His entire outfit was created from white leather straps. His tail was braided leather and came from the harness around his back. He walked away from us, shaking his butt.

My attention turned away from the playful antics of the pony people and surveyed the scene around me. The room pulsated with a thick air of decadence. Strobe lights flashed and glittering sequins of light from a dizzying array of disco balls patterned the walls. It was as though we were in a primitive throng of people underneath a layer of champagne bubbles. Above us, from the balcony that looked over the dance floor, people watched.

Well, they may have been people, you couldn't really tell. There were costumes of many kinds, but along the balcony, most people wore feathered masks. It was creepy and erotic at the same time. Flashing lights illuminated the feathered faces, dark holes for eyes, peering out expressionlessly. Almost bird-like, when I thought about it. Birds watch the world go by, their beady black eyes staring. You never know what a bird is thinking until it either sings or swoops. I wondered if the feathered-mask people were enjoying the show. I've never seen so many feathered masks in my life. It made me wonder how many birds were looking for their tail feathers.

I returned my attention to the stage. Three girls were go-go dancing. They wore thigh-high platform boots that looked great with striped stockings and tiny go-go shorts. They had bikini tops on. One girl looked like she needed a bigger top, but that was OK with me. Her cleavage jiggled lasciviously as she bounced around. The girls all had wild green hair and were dancing up a storm. Now and again someone would jump on the stage to dance with them.

"Check it out," Tony pointed to the two pony people and their master. They were standing against a wall, their bums out. Long brown tails were affixed to leather straps. Pretty apple cheeks were firm and appealing. The crop licked their asses, one after the other. The pony girls whinnied and wiggled their tails more. The girls rubbed their butts side by side, like they were four perfect little hills. They quivered as the crop smacked them cheek by cheek.

The short-haired pony girl shook her head. The large feather plume that graced her headpiece fluttered like the wing of a bird. She had a long neck and slender backside. Her breasts were small but pert. Her nipples stood out prominently. When the crop met her buttock once more, she turned to meet my eye. She winked.

I smiled back. She wiggled her butt at me. I put my hand up to signal no thanks.

Three men in feathered masks started dancing with the go-go girls. They all played with each other, laughing and touching.

One man was humping one of the girls, his mask feathers waving wildly as his hands cupped her breasts. She gyrated her hips back into him. Another one of the go-go girls was squatting in front of one of the other men, his dick in her mouth. She slowly licked and savored him as he impatiently thrust into her mouth. The third couple was doing a sort of tango-type dance, dipping and stepping and moving back and forth along the stage.

The man feeling the girl's breasts had now unleashed them from their tight little bikini top. They were large and full and I could see pert nipples from where I stood. The music swelled through the dance floor, and around me, people thrashed as they watched the dancers. The men were licking the breasts of the women. Teasing nipples with playful tongues. The women continued to dance, acting almost oblivious as the men fondled and suckled.

Green-mask man slid his partner's tight little go-go shorts off. She stepped from the clothing, showing nothing but a tiny little g-string. Her taut stomach glittered with a belly ring. The man crawled under her as she crouched over his face. She bobbed her pretty little ass up and down as his tongue found her secret spots. She ground herself harder against him and she smiled.

Another one of the girls was strutting around the blue-masked man. His feathers made him look like a rooster as he watched her walking around him. She knelt before him and unzipped his pants. She pulled out his cock and waved it at the audience. A few people whooped in the crowd. I raised my hand, pumping it to the music. Her lips were pursed as she slid them over the tip of his dick. His rooster stance softened as he tipped his head back. The girl's mouth was busy taking his large shaft down to the back of her throat. She slid her mouth up and down then pulled away. He was half erect and fairly impressive. She nibbled on the end of his dick, circling it with her tongue. Her lips kissed and pulled at his head. She slipped him back into her mouth once more. This time he was harder and she had to work hard at taking all of him. She let him enjoy sweet, warm ecstasy for a moment, and then pulled away again. Her fingers tugged on his shaft and she gobbled the end of his dick like a hungry animal.

The third couple caught my attention. The man was fucking the woman from behind as they danced and gyrated. She reached back to put her hands on his ass and raised her own backside to let him slide in deeper. I could see her mouth open in a moan as she held him in her for a moment, and then released him to his thrusting once more.

I noticed that the first couple was fucking now, too. The man lay on the floor with his dick pointing straight up in the air as the woman squatted over it. She moved herself up and down. I admired the strength of her legs and the glistening streak of pussy juice trickling along her thighs. She perched herself forward, putting her hands on the floor for support.

The second couple was going at it doggy-style. The woman crouched on the floor while the masked man drilled her.

My own dick was getting hard, watching all the marvelous sights. All across the dance floor, people were licking and sucking and fucking. People were sitting in chairs being eaten out. Another woman hopped onto the stage and sat on the edge, her legs spread to show a glistening pussy swollen with lust.

A woman in a fireman's hat kneeled down before her and nibbled on her clit. She howled in ecstasy, kicking her legs in the air.

A small group of people gathered around one round table. Their faces were lit by a dull orange candle that sat on the table. The women all wore black catsuits and black cat masks. They stood around a man, arching their backs and pawing at their little fake ears. Three out of the four catwomen were tall, with thin tapered torsos and large round bottoms. Their catsuits shimmered in the candlelight and their bodies were so smooth they looked like polished obsidian. The fourth cat woman was short and voluptuous. Her breasts were so large they spilled over the top of her catsuit, the areola of her left breast partially visible. Her belly was round like a sensual ball that ached to be stroked.

The man they surrounded was naked and tied to a chair. He was blindfolded and smiling. The cats played with each other, teasingly, and bent over to whisper things in his ear. My view was hindered by dancing bodies gyrating the several feet between the scene and me. The larger cat woman kneeled beside the man. She ran her rubber-gloved hands playfully along his thighs. The man couldn't move his legs or arms, so securely was he affixed to the chair. The throng of bodies that floated in and out of my view intrigued me nearly as much as the scene with the man and his pussies. The girls directly in front of me wore vampire-type outfits. Long black gowns made from gauze and lace, giving a spiderweb effect. They both had trains behind them, as if they were Brides of Darkness or Spanish flamenco dancers. Their hair was covered in black roses. Amazingly, despite the layers of material that fabricated their dresses, their bosoms were out for the world to see. I ventured to speculate that the four perfect orbs dancing in the strobe lights before me were artificial. I didn't mind at all, as I appreciated their firmness.

The man in the chair was very hard as the large cat woman gripped his shaft. She pulled it up and down. His head fell back. Another cat woman ran her rubber claws along his chest as she stood behind him. The other two cat women alternately kissed each other and lavished attention on their victim.

The larger cat woman flicked her tongue at the tip of his dick. He smiled. One of the women saw his smile and batted him with a paw. I can assume that she made some sort of comment to him. Another cat woman wrapped her long tail around his neck. She writhed against him, rubbing her face against his. The woman between his legs was sucking him down in long, deep strokes. With every stroke upward, he grew in size. I was amazed at the lengths to which he grew as she lapped and sucked his rod.

One of the vampire queens stood in front of me.

"Would you like to dance?" she asked me.

"Sure."

I took to the dance floor, adding my steps in with the vampire brides or queens or whatever the hell they were supposed to be. They engulfed me in the fabric sweetness of their wings, then began fluttering and darting around me. I danced with great enthusiasm. The exuberant nature of the people around me propelled my usual moodiness into a sense of hedonism. Despite the trepidations of my past, I welcomed the adventure the night had yet to show me. While I danced, I searched for my friends. They, too, were on the dance floor, letting the primal rhythms of the revelers course through their systems.

The vampire girls danced close and then far, teasing me with locking eye stares and baring fanged teeth. They could have bitten my neck and taken me into a darkness I yearned to taste, but they didn't. When the song melded into another one, they swooped off, leaving me alone on the dance floor.

I looked over at my cat people. The man must have come at some point because the cat women were all lapping at his thighs. Soon he was released from his bondage and sent staggering on his way. The cat women stood staring at the dance floor, searching for another victim.

A woman wearing a yellow vinyl dress, yellow vinyl stilettos and yellow rain hat walked by. Her ass peeked out from under her dress and her shoes made it stick out even more. She looked as though she wasn't too comfortable with wearing such high shoes and gingerly made her way across the dance floor until she found her friends. They too wore vinyl dresses with matching shoes of fluorescent colors and rain hats. One of them carried a parasol with a ruffled fringe that looked odd in one sense, yet in another it added to the weirdness of Halloween. I briefly considered the fact that an open umbrella is bad luck but I put the intrusive thought from my mind. It was Halloween and I was here to have fun. As if a stranger's open umbrella would affect me or any of the other clubbers.

I wandered along the edge of the dance floor, heading toward a bar. Once I approached the bar, I nearly stepped on someone— I looked down and saw a person lying there, probably a man, dressed as the grim reaper. He wore a black hooded robe and was nearly invisible in the dim light except for the fact that I had stepped on him. He clearly didn't mind, as he didn't move or flinch. I imagined he wanted me to step on him again, but I refrained from doing so. Stepping on strangers just isn't my thing.

I ordered a water and looked for my buddies. They were still dancing. Now Tony was with a woman in a military uniform of some sort. She wore high boots and suspenders. Her hat was like a little German army soldier's. Maybe she was supposed to be a Nazi or someone else just as intimidating. She had a crop in her had which she flicked in the air now and again.

Mark was dancing with a girl who might have been a fairy or an angel. She wore a white sheer dress and large feathery wings. Her halo was bobbing in time to the music. Her breasts bobbed against the shimmery fabric in the strobe light. She ran her hands along her body several times as she danced. She locked her eyes with Mark's and danced closer. He stepped closer to her, his hips writhing snakelike in time to the music. They danced with each other, in a mating ritual. I danced alone, watching them.

Over at another table, a girl dressed in a red and black corset was sitting on the lap of a large dark man. In the dim light it was hard to make him out, since he wore a black mask that obscured a large part of his face. She playfully pushed her breasts at his mouth. He licked the milky white mounds of her cleavage with a long pink tongue.

Beside them, a man dressed as a giant teddy bear was shoving his erect penis into a young woman's mouth. I couldn't make out her costume. Perhaps she was trying to be a Greek goddess or something like that, I couldn't see much of her from where I was dancing. All I saw was the fleshy stick of the bear's penis going in and out of her mouth.

The teddy bear costume was pretty impressive, although odd. It had a huge furry head with holes in the cheeks to see out of. The body was like furry flannel pajamas, with long tufts sewn on to the arms. Where his dick hung out, there was a flap that hung down between his legs as he pumped into the woman's mouth. She choked on him and pushed him back. He held on to her head as she took a sip of her drink, clearly wanting more. She gargled and swallowed her drink, then turned back to him. She opened her mouth and he eagerly plunged back inside.

I turned back to Tony and the sergeant. They were still dancing across from each other. I could see the sergeant was eyeing someone else across the dance floor. Tony caught my eye and waved. I waved back. He motioned for me to go over and dance with him. I danced my way over toward them. Just when I got there, the song changed.

The officer stood still and saluted Tony.

"Thank you." She stiffly drew her hand back down and turned away. She marched across the dance floor toward whomever it was she had been flirting with. Tony waved over to the tables.

"Let's go sit for a minute," he said, indicating two empty chairs. We sat down and watched more of the people dance.

Mark and the angel were rubbing their bodies against each other. Around them, other people were running their hands over each other, touching masks and feathers and gauzy pieces of material. The song had a slow sultry beat and reminded me of steamy nights in Argentina. As the beats shifted, people started leaning into each other more, moving in mock-tango fashion. A woman with a bright red, ruffled Spanish dress darted across the dance floor with her partner, a Spanish-looking man in a black hat and black clothes with red brocade. He dipped her, far from us, and then spun her around. They disappeared into the crowd.

The music changed to a raucous big band version of the cancan. A long line of chorus girls dressed like something out of that Sister Marmalade video came on doing the cancan. They high-kicked across the stage in perfect unison, their colorful corseted torsos holding still while their legs stretched impossibly high above their heads. Their skirts flounced, and underneath their skirts they wore fishnets and ruffled panties. They pirouetted around the stage on one leg and then the other. It made me dizzy to watch them. A man came on the stage dressed in a tuxedo outfit and bowler hat. He had a long cane, which he used to point at or stroke the kicking girls. We laughed at his antics and one of the girls kicked off his hat. Another girl snapped away his bow tie. Still another had his cummerbund. All this occurred without the girls missing a single step.

By the time the girls were done with him, he was standing there in his boxer shorts. The girls teased him with their dance until he got a woody. They took turns tapping the woody with kicking feet. He started to stroke it. One girl flounced in front of him and raised her skirt saucily to reveal her lacy behind. She pulled her skirt down and skipped away. Another girl and then another girl did the same. By the time the fourth girl did it, he was prepared and caught her by the waist. With one quick swiff of his hand, he pulled down her panties to reveal her bare bottom. He jokingly played with her bottom for a few beats of the song and then thrust his cock into her pussy. He fucked her in time to the music while the girls danced around.

At last, he was done and he gathered up his clothes in a comical fashion as the girls teased him and danced off the stage in another giant kick line.

When the stage was empty again, there were cheers.

Regular dance music came on again. My friends found me in the crowd.

"Fun times, right, Franco?" Tony said, slapping me on the arm.

"The night is just beginning," I said. "I feel so alive."

"It's anticipation, my friend. You know we're going to get lots of pussy tonight."

"I fully expect it," Tony said.

"I could sure use some tension release," I joked.

Next to us, a girl in a nurse's outfit was riding a doctor. We watched as she rocked on his lap, whispering into his ear. His hands reached around her hips and he pumped her up and down his dick quickly. She moaned and fucked him even harder. Suddenly he cried out and held still as he came. The woman kissed him and stood up.

"Thank you, doctor. I think I understand how to care for my patients a lot better now." She smiled as she straightened her mini skirt. She adjusted her thigh-highs and walked quickly toward the bathroom. The doctor smiled after her as he tucked his dick back into his pants.

His buddies sitting around the table with him patted him and cheered. We raised our beer bottles in admiration.

"How many rooms are in this club tonight?" I asked the doctor.

"I think there are six or seven. Some have dance floors, some are just orgies."

"Been to any of the other rooms yet?"

"I haven't, but Steve here has."

I shook Steve's hand.

"So? What did you see?" I asked.

"Well, I went to a dungeon, where there were lots of cages. And I was hungry so I went to the diner. Boy, the dessert there rocks!" He nodded with a grin.

"Cool. Lot of scenes tonight?"

"Every room is a scene. Except this one. This is like the

carnival of debauchery room or something. They have dancers every fifteen minutes or so. There are all sorts of acts."

As he spoke, the lighting shifted and an old torch song, Garland-style, came on. A drag queen sauntered onto the stage as a baby grand piano was rolled in from the other side. The pianist was wheeled in on a stool, poised to play. The drag queen was an overstated Judy Garland and she warbled her way toward the piano. A touching song ensued as the nurse rejoined the table beside us. She winked as she slid into the empty chair beside the doctor. He put his hand possessively on her knee.

Several girls in leotards were dancing in silhouette in the background as the singer crooned. The shapes of their outlines were fun to watch as they formed different patterns with their arms and legs. As the song drew to the final chorus, the girls danced away.

The audience applauded as the dance music started up again.

"So what do you think?" Tony asked. "Should we finish our drinks and check out the rest of this place?"

"You know it," I said.

We downed our drinks and stood up.

"See ya guys later!" I waved.

They raised their hands and we made our way back across the dance floor to the far side of the hall toward the exit doors. Leaving this room was hard. I could have stayed here all night. Yet, the urge to wander crept up on me. Seeing what was in all the other rooms sounded like a good idea. We had paid our cover. We were in for the night.

"Look." We were standing in the hallway. Mark pointed to a sign: SMOKING THIS WAY.

"We should go for a smoke before we head on. After all, there may be no more smoking tonight."

"True." I didn't smoke a lot but one thing I enjoyed was having a smoke while I was out on the town. Just going to work, to the gym, and home never seemed to call for a smoke. But partying, well, if you were going to hell, might as well take a handcart.

We followed the smoking signs along the hall until we came to some exit doors. We pushed our way through the steel doors and came outside to a little balcony. It wasn't very big, but it could have held about ten people comfortably. Stairs wound from the top of the four-story club to the ground, each with a little landing. We were on the biggest landing by far. There were even big steel ashtrays affixed to the railings.

To my right a man was leaning against a handrail while a devil girl sucked his dick. She was doing a pretty good job of it too, from what I could tell. She suckled and licked, tonguing his head for a moment before engulfing him in her mouth.

We walked over to the far side of the balcony where there was an ashtray and no people. It was not the nicest balcony in the world. It was wrought iron and very old. I imagined thirty or forty years ago the paint would have been fresh on this balcony, not the grungy flaking garbage it was now. There weren't any Halloween decorations out here except for a large jack-o'-lantern grinning by the door back inside. I heard a moan and felt the balcony shaking.

Above me, on the next landing, which was half a flight up, a girl was straddling the corner of the rails, her legs wrapped around her boyfriend's waist as he slammed into her. I hoped he had a good grip on her because it was a long way down to the ground. They weren't quite at the second story, but that was plenty to fall. However, good luck smiled upon them and they continued to fuck for quite some time.

We smoked our cigarettes and watched the other people smoke their cigarettes. People came and went. On the landing below us, leading down toward the old-fashioned basement, there were four or five people smoking dope. The sweet smell of the wacky tobaccy filled my senses. For a moment, I wanted to have some, but then I decided that smoking a cigarette was bad enough. Mark went down to the landing and pulled out a joint. Tony and I watched him. Tony doesn't smoke pot either. For us, it makes us too sleepy to have a good time. Or paranoid. I'm paranoid enough in life without having help.

Mark was soon laughing and talking with the people on the balcony. Every now and again, one of the girls would squeal with an annoying giggle that never failed to startle me every time. Tony and I finished our cigarettes and waved over to Mark. I knew that if we didn't get him out of there right away, he'd be too stoned to want to go anywhere, or he'd wander off on some adventure of his own.

"Mark!" I shouted. He looked over at me and waved. I signaled that we were leaving. He said his goodbyes and hurried toward us. We set out through the big steel door, hearing it slam loudly behind us. The hallway before us was dark and branched off into two directions at the end. One way led back toward the entrance and the dance floor. The other way, well, we determined that it must lead to the rest of the club. Even though I'd been here before a few times, they always blocked off different hallways depending on what rooms and floors they used, so you never really got a good feel for how the place was actually laid out. We knew going back to the beginning wasn't going to get us anywhere, so we proceeded down the hallway.

"I gotta hit the bathroom," Mark said. "Man, all that beer . . ."

"I hear you. I'm sure there's gotta be one along the way. There's at least one per floor here. I'm almost positive."

"I think you're right."

We wandered down the hallway, searching for the bathroom and for a new room to explore.

# CHAPTER 3.

*A*s we searched for a bathroom, we came to another door. There were billows of curtains and streamers hanging over the doorframe so we knew it was a room decorated for this night. We pushed through several layers of curtains that formed a small hallway into a new room. Looking inside, it reminded me of a carnival or circus tent.

The ceilings were draped with thick plumes of silky material. There were glowing stars painted onto the fabric with a gold fluorescent paint. The walls had orange and purple fabric hanging down to complete the giant tent effect. Festive and garish, this room spoke of strangeness and mystery.

Candles were lit on many small tables where people sat in small groups of three or four and drank from pretty little teacups. As we watched, we realized that many of the people were involved in some sort of ritual. One of the ladies, wearing many scarves and beaded necklaces, lifted a teacup and peered inside of it. She turned it, tipping it closer to the candle, talking to the couple in front of her. I realized that they were getting their tea leaves read.

Over at another table, a woman was looking over many stones and holding them up, showing them to the lady in front of her who leaned over with baited breath, apparently hanging onto her every word.

"This is a fortune-telling room," Tony said.

"Yeah, look. There are crystal balls and tarot cards, too." He pointed to the women reading cards and another one gazing into a crystal ball.

"I've never had my fortune told," I said.

"Really?" Tony lifted an eyebrow. "You should try it, it can be very interesting."

"I don't believe in any of that crap," Mark said. "It's all bullshit."

"I don't know. I think there might be something to it," I said. "I've always been too afraid to have my fortune told."

"Why? What's going to happen? Even if someone tells you are going to die, so what? We're all going to die at some point," Tony said.

"True."

"Well, you two can stand here tempting the fates all you

want, I have to hit the bathroom," Mark said, walking back
out the door.

"Hey, wait up," Tony said, "I gotta go too."

"I want to look around this room a little more," I said,
noticing that there were little curtained rooms along one side
of the wall. It gave the illusion of tents within tents. I saw a
man emerging from one of the mini-tents, smoothing down
his costume. Tents with customers had the cloth doors down.
There was one tent at the end of the row where the curtained
doorway was open. It seemed to beckon to me.

"OK, man. Catch up with you in a few," Tony said to me as
he followed Mark.

"Sure." They left me and I walked around the room. I stood
a little way from the crystal ball reader and tried to see what
she might see in that gleaming piece of glass. She stared into
it with enthusiasm, words spilling from her lips. The couple
she spoke to held each other's hands expectantly.

"I see that you will be very happy together, as long as you
learn to communicate with each other."

They both looked at each other and nodded.

"As well, you must beware temptation. It's one thing to agree
to be adventurous, it's another to venture off solo without your
partner's agreement."

"Who will be tempted?" the girl asked.

"You will know at the time. And I would say not to suc-
cumb. Not only will trust be lost, but the person won't be
worth it. The person will make your lives a misery. The person
won't accept fun for fun."

I wandered off. She didn't convince me that she was telling a fortune. Anyone could say that about anyone at any point. We all get tempted. Temptation is as human as fucking itself. Who doesn't look at another pretty face? Especially when you're hanging out in a sex club.

I looked over at the empty tent again. A yellow flickering light glowed mysteriously from it. I wondered if I would discover any mysteries about myself if I dared to enter it. I wondered who was inside and what she would tell me. Was there anything to fortune-telling? Or was it all just a big pile of crap? Were these people just con artists, reading our faces and body language? Or was there truth in the divination devices?

The crystal ball reader was now loosening her robe. It slid down one shoulder, giving her more of a gypsy look then ever before. She shook her long curly hair. The man stood up and slowly unbuttoned his shirt. The lady watched, rubbing her hands along her own breasts.

I turned away from the sight and walked to that lone glowing tent at the end of the room. I stared up at the ceiling, forgetting for a moment that the stars weren't real, and wished for a good fortune-telling experience.

I entered the tent and stood staring at the woman inside. She was beautiful. I didn't know what I was expecting. Maybe because of years of television or something, I thought that maybe there would be something strange about her. Maybe because she chose to be in a tent instead of at one of the little tables. But as I approached her, I saw her beauty emanating toward me. She sat patiently as I darkened her doorway.

"Are you here to have your fortune told?" she asked.

"I've never had my fortune told," I said.

Her eyes brightened.

"Never?"

"No, never."

Her fingers played with the cards on the table, touching and flipping the strange pictures while her dark-eyed gaze was riveted to mine.

"What do the pictures mean?" I asked.

"The pictures tell you everything."

"How? How does it work?"

"No one knows how it works. Just that it does."

She stared at me, the candles on her little table making her eyes dance.

"Are you going to sit down?" she asked.

I shifted my feet.

"I'm a bit nervous . . . I don't want you to tell me any-thing bad."

"Don't worry, I won't tell you anything terrible. I can't imagine there would be anything terrible to tell." She smiled. Her teeth were large and white. She looked like a girl out of a toothpaste commercial instead of a fortune-teller. Her hair was long and dark and curly. She wore a green, flowing shirt and a dark shawl with many colors on it. The candles made our shadows dance against the backdrop of the fabric of the tent.

"Sit."

She indicated the chair again.

This time, I sat down.

"You have a handsome face," she said.

"How can you tell? I have all this paint on it."

"You can tell a man by the shape of his face. And the eyes. Your eyes reveal many secrets."

"What secrets?"

"We'll find out, won't we?"

We looked at each other for a moment. I felt as though the air had thickened between us with some kind of intangible energy. Was this magic? Or was I just hallucinating from incense smoke and fear?

I still felt hesitant about having her look at my cards. I almost seemed like a violation. Maybe we aren't supposed to know what is going to happen. Maybe ignorance is what humans are meant to know and trying to predict through divination is tempting fate.

Besides, what good does it do any of us to know what is going to happen? Can we stop it? And if what is going to happen is bad, how can we change it? Do we just wait as the moment barrels toward us until we have a eureka moment? Or can we change the patterns of the future by knowing what is going to happen? Or maybe, by attempting to change our fate, we create circumstances that seal it.

It made my head hurt to think about it sometimes.

"I'm Carlotta," she said, holding out her hand. I took it.

"You aren't going to zap me, are you?"

"Of course not."

Her hand was warm and friendly, and I relaxed.

"Tell me, is there anything you are burning to know about?"

SAVANNA SAMSON

Carlotta asked, leaning forward. Her hands pushed the cards toward me.

"Like what? My future?"

"It's always about the future. Anything that happens from this moment on is the future. By the time we finish reading the cards, it will be the future."

"So I guess tell me how the rest of the night will go."

"First, you must shuffle the cards."

My fingers trembled as I touched the cards. For a moment, I was certain a bolt of lightening would shoot down from the heavens and strike me dead. I can't say I'm old fashioned or even superstitious, but tarot cards have always unnerved me. Taking a deep breath, I picked up the cards. They felt normal. A regular deck of cards.

"What do I do now?" I asked.

"Shuffle them," she instructed. I flipped the cards around in my fingers until she told me to take out seven. I did as she said. I watched the cards and her face like I was following a ball in a tennis game as she interpreted the weird little pictures. I noticed there were a lot of giant stakes or clubs or something in the pictures. There was also a beautiful blond woman sitting on a pile of pillows.

"There she is," the gypsy smiled.

"There who is?" I asked.

"Savanna. There she is, waiting for you."

"Who is this Savanna?"

"She is your destiny."

The gypsy girl ran her hands along the cards.

49.

"You've had a rough road, Franco. It shows, here in the cards."

There was a card of a man sitting up in bed crying, with a bunch of swords hanging over his head.

"That doesn't look good," I said

"It means you have to learn to let things go, Franco. As much as events have hurt you, hurt you deeply in some cases, you can't dwell on the past. It will eat you up inside."

Tears sprung up in my eyes. The card moved me, and her words, though general, hit a nerve within me. Maybe I did dwell too much on the past. Analyzing and picking at the situations I was in until I sometimes nearly went mad from the process.

"Sleepless nights?" she asked.

"Yes."

"Alone and sad. Worrying about what should or could have been, worrying about if anything ever will be."

I nodded. Although I was somewhat aware of how I tend to dwell on the past, seeing it portrayed in a card I randomly picked pricked me. It was creepy.

"Does this mean that I'll always be this way?" I asked.

"No. The card is showing you a pattern of behavior. It is up to you to decide if you want to stop it or not."

"I can't stop it."

"Worrying is a habit. Just like anything, you have to teach yourself to not worry."

"I can't. It's like something always reminds me of something."

"So learn not to be reminded. Live in the moment. In the moment, there is no past, no future, there is just now."

"I like the sound of that," I said.

"Try it."

"How?"

"Close your eyes."

I closed my eyes.

"Think of nothing but the fact that you are sitting and you are warm and safe."

"But . . ."

"Shhh . . . no intrusive thoughts. No worrying where your friends have gone or if people will think you're stupid sitting here with your eyes shut. None of that matters when you are in your moment."

I tried to let my mind go blank. First I stared at the back of my eyelids and wondered about the black that I saw. Was it a color or was it the back of my eyelids, and weren't they red? I tried to listen to the frantic pounding of my heart. Then I listened to my rapid breathing. Why was I so nervous? What would happen to me if I thought about nothing?

The idea of thinking about nothing caused me to panic. Instead, I tried to imagine the gypsy girl naked. The thought pleased me greatly. My breath calmed down and my heart beat regularly again. Her breasts could be any size under that green shirt. Maybe they were large, maybe they were a mere handful.

"Are you relaxed?" she asked.

"Yes."

"Are you ready to listen to me?"

The idea of her perky nipples flashed in front of my eyes.

"Yes."

"Imagine that you live every day of your life in your moment. If you see something you like, you have it. If you make a mistake, you forgive yourself. Do you understand me?"

"Yes."

"You may open your eyes."

I looked at her and the room seemed off-kilter for a moment as my eyes adjusted. She was staring intently at me.

"So Franco, when you meet Savanna, you will remember that nothing matters but the moment you are in. Enjoy the pleasures she will show you."

"I don't even know this Savanna. I will meet her tonight?"

"Yes, tonight. In a few hours. First, you have a few adventures to taste. You need to be prepared to meet her."

"Prepared?"

"Yes."

She slipped her blouse from her shoulders and revealed nice perky breasts of a medium size. She took them in her hand and played with them, watching my face.

"Are you prepared to meet Savanna?"

"I don't know."

"Maybe I can help you."

She stood up and came over to me.

"Move your chair back," she said.

I edged my chair back and she straddled me. Her hands played with her breasts as she stared at me.

"What are you thinking about?" she asked.

"Your beautiful breasts, of course. What else would I think about?"

"No. Your eyes still have that lost look. Like you are thinking too much."

She rolled one of her boobs across my face. I tried to catch her nipple with my teeth but I wasn't fast enough.

"I'm not thinking about anything, really," I said. Although I have to admit, I was wondering about what she said about meeting this Savanna. Who was this woman and why was I meeting her?

"You are thinking again," she accused me.

"All right. So I'm thinking. Shoot me."

She lifted her breast and aimed it at me.

"Bang bang, you're dead." She joked. I grabbed that boob and suckled on the nipple. There is one thing I can't resist and that's a firm boob right in front of my face. She was such a tease, and loving it.

"You are thinking about Savanna, aren't you?" she asked as I greedily suckled.

I nodded my head, pulling her tit with it.

"Of course you are. You would be a fool not to. However, you need not worry over her. Everything will unfold as it is meant to be. All you have to do is live in the moment. Then everything will work out."

"No consequences?" I asked.

"No consequences in Paradise," she said. I released her tit and buried my face in her cleavage.

"You don't know how happy that makes me," I sighed.

"Oh, but I do," she said as her hand pressed against my hard-on.

"You are so beautiful," I sighed. "It is always a treat to be with a beautiful woman."

"A man like you must have many women."

"Not all so beautiful. After all, sometimes we adore a person for her mind as well. Sometimes the two don't marry very well."

"Yes, and sometimes they make a fine duet." She stood up. Her blouse slipped to the ground.

"Would you like to try out the theory of the moment? Fuck me and think of nothing but the delicious sensation of your swollen, hard cock ramming into my tight hole. Don't think about logistics and reputation. Relish the pleasure."

Her fingers worked on unbuttoning my leather pants. I lifted my hips to help her. I realized they were so tight that I was going to have to stand up. She unpeeled them from me like a banana. I wasn't wearing any underwear, so my cock sprung up to nearly full size as it greeted the air. She stared at it for a moment then greedily sucked it into her mouth. She worked on the end for a while, then slid her mouth down until I swear I could feel the back of her throat. She did that several times, moving a little faster with each stroke.

At first, I found my mind starting to wander away, toward Savanna, but then I focused my mind back on the delicious job the gypsy was doing on my dick. Her slurping was loud and enthusiastic. My hands reached out to her head and took fist-fuls of her tangled curly hair in my grip as I pumped her up and down on my dick. She gagged and I pulled her head off. She gasped and caught her wind, then returned to deep-throating my shaft. I pumped her hard against me and I felt like I could spray my load any moment. But I didn't want to come just yet. I wanted to fuck her sweet pussy as well.

"Think about the moment," she said as she took her mouth from my dick.

The cool air was intrusive to my hard-on and I worried I would lose it.

"Think about how good my mouth feels around your dick. My swirling tongue. The soft cushion of the back of my throat. Imagine shooting your load down my throat and gagging me with the immensity of your come."

My dick grew hard again at her words.

Oh, I could just imagine. My cock. Her throat. It sounded like heaven to me.

She resumed working on my cock.

First, she spit on it to slick that sucker up. Then, she swirled her tongue around her spit to even it out. My dick ached for her to swallow it again. She teased me a while longer, running her tongue up and down my shaft. I quivered with anticipation, my legs trembling.

"Think of the moment," she whispered as she took my length to the hilt. I leaned my head back with a moan. There is no way to describe the delicious sensations that she played along my cock, between her well-seasoned sucks and her dancing, tapping tongue.

I pulled her head toward my hips again, this time thinking of nothing but how great her mouth felt. I pumped a few more times before I shot my load down her throat. She sat up and sputtered for a moment and then swallowed. I leaned back in my chair, panting for breath. She wiped her mouth with the back of her hand.

"See how much better life can be if you live in the moment." She grinned.

"Oh, I see all right."

I sat looking at her. She reshuffled the cards and pulled one. The lovers. Even I could see that one.

"Is that us?" I asked.

"Do you want it to be?"

"I know that I wish I hadn't come down your throat because I'd really like to taste that sweet pussy of yours." I leered at her, licking my lips.

"I bet you could get your second wind if you gave me a lick."

She pulled her chair out and sat in it. She spread her legs and lifted her skirt. Playfully, she opened and closed the lips of her pussy.

"Come lick me." She coaxed me. I slipped off my shoes and my pants. My dick felt great. I felt great. I wondered if I would be able to get it up again.

"You are thinking again," she said. "Live in the moment. Taste my sweet pussy."

She spread her legs wider and held open her lips so that I could see her hole and her clit. She had a large clit that seemed to throb with expectation. I licked her slowly. She raised herself to me and I tapped her clit lightly with my tongue. She seemed to enjoy the rapid pulsing, so I kept at it for a while. My fingers slid into her pussy and moved in and out. She was slick already with anticipation.

My other hand played with my dick as I drank her sweet juices. I hoped I could get hard again. Then I remembered what Carlotta had told me. Think only of the moment. Think of how tasty her pussy is, how good my hand feels on my dick, how good my dick will feel inside her pussy. My hand stroked myself a little more rapidly and she squirmed beneath my dancing tongue.

Soon, her hands were pulling at my head. I continued to lick her while she moved my head in a fucking motion. Her clit was really hard now and I could tell by my fingers working her cunt that she was going to come any second. She shuddered and her pussy clamped against my fingers. She got even wetter as she shuddered and moaned.

"Oh yeah," she sighed. "Oh yeah."

She looked down at my dick.

"So, how are you doing? You gonna be able to drive that baby home?"

I stroked my cock a little more as I stared at her glistening pussy. God, it looked so delicious. All creamy and moist, ready for my big hard dick to slide right inside.

She positioned herself on the chair so that she could sit on her ass but with her legs in the air. I had to half crouch as I shoved my hard cock into her. She felt like she was coming again as I entered her. I fucked her quickly at first to keep myself hard, and then I slowed myself down. I savored the sensation of her flesh tugging against mine. I knew I was big for her and that position could be too deep so I was careful to only go as far as her g-spot. I hung around that area for a while, and soon her heavy breathing turned to moans of delight.

"Oh, yes," she said. "Right there. That's the magic spot."

She opened her eyes to look at me as I continued to pump at her pleasure zone.

"Oh my god, that is so good," she said, half delirious with pleasure. Although the position was awkward, I wanted to feel her come again. I wanted to feel her pussy clenching against my dick and her juices flowing down my shaft.

I continued to ram away at her g-spot. Her legs tightened around my shoulders, and I felt her pussy throbbing as she cried out. A gush of come came spilling out of her as well. It made for a slick ride as I continued to take on wave after wave of orgasm.

I pulled out, my cock bigger and harder than it had been when she gave me a blow job. I didn't think it was possible. She took a cloth from her tarot table and wiped up the come that soaked her legs and pussy. She watched me as she carefully wiped herself clean.

"Do you like my tight hot pussy? Do you want to fuck it some more?"

"Your pussy is the best pussy ever," I said. And in the moment, it was true.

She stood in front of the chair and leaned over it, holding onto the seat for support. I stared at her delicious ass and pussy hole. Her lips were stretched from my frantic pumping, swollen from coming so much yet wanting to come more. I stroked my dick and got it ready to take her for another drive.

I slid in easily, and her pussy instantly clamped around my dick as if it were being given a big warm hug. I stayed like that for a moment, and then slowly pushed my way in further. I could get nearly all of it into her. She moaned and I slid it out again. Back and forth we rocked, nice and slow as we waited for the well to fill back up.

Soon, she was trembling with anticipation again. I started to fuck her a little faster. She started to enjoy the fucking immensely and was bucking her hips against mine. I grabbed those luscious ass cheeks in my hands, loving how fleshy they felt between my fingers. It was heavenly.

I rammed into her harder, trying to prolong the sensation yet craving it at the same time.

It was with great strength and determination that I rode her like a messenger might ride into battle to deliver important news to the colonel. As I plowed into her, I thought about the moment. How well we were doing in this moment.

My cock released a load of come into her and she fell forward onto the chair.

"Oh my god," she gasped as she tried to draw air into her lungs. "You are so good. No one would guess all the hang-ups you have."

"I have no hang-ups."

"Nonsense. Everyone has hang-ups. Just ask around."

"Well, whatever you think my hang-ups are, you probably have them now. I fucked them out of myself." We chuckled.

"I'm glad to hear you say that. Then my job here is done." She became more businesslike as she pulled her clothes back on. Once she was dressed, she gathered up the tarot cards and sorted them into a neat little deck.

"So that's the tarot reading. A couple of cards and then a trip around the world."

Carlotta smiled.

"Not everyone gets the deluxe treatment," she said. "You are special and don't forget it."

"Me, special." I grinned as I pulled my own clothes together.

"Great changes are coming, Franco. Be prepared."

"I thought I was just getting prepared. Like a lamb to the slaughter."

"No need to get snide," she said.

I thought about how I was supposed to be getting prepared to meet Savanna. I guess all that mattered was knowing my dick was in proper working order.

"Is there anything else I need to know about my future? Besides that I'm destined to meet this Savanna person? What about my job? Will I ever marry?"

"Franco, your job is secure. In fact, your job is so secure that you could take time off and you would still have it upon your return. You are good at your job and valued highly by your boss and fellow employees. There will be some travel. A business trip and a romantic trip. Your money situation will thrive even more. You can have the pick of so many things in your life. Once you decide what you truly want, how you truly want to live your life."

"I'm glad to hear there's no job-hunting in my future," I said.

"No. You are a Golden Boy, that's for sure. Everything you touch is golden. You have to believe that completely."

SAVANNA SAMSON

"I know I'm good at what I do."

"You have moments when you know that. In fact, you have moments of extreme arrogance. Yet paradoxically, you have moments of extreme insecurity, too."

"Isn't that human?"

"Yes it is. Very human. You are human. You have to remember that, too. You are allowed to be upset, and you are even allowed to cry."

"Don't tell my buddies that," I kidded.

"You will marry one day. Not for a long time." She folded her hands.

"Who will I marry? Savanna?"

A big grin spread across Carlotta's face.

"I can't tell you that right now," she said.

"Aw, come on." I tried to pry it out of her, but she wasn't giving up any information.

"Well, then, what about kids?" I asked. "I'm sure you can tell me if I'm going to have any kids with this mystery woman."

"You will have children."

"How many?"

"Two. A boy and a girl."

"Really?" The thought made me very happy, and for a moment or two I believed her.

"But before you get married and have kids, there's a lot to do."

"Like what?"

"Life. Living life."

"I guess I have to go through some kind of trial by fire first, to appreciate what I have."

"Something like that."

"So what do I do?"

Carlotta shook her head.

"Don't you remember what this was all about?"

"What? Fucking you?"

"No. It was about learning to be in the moment. Not to worry about the past or the future. Just exist. Right here. Right now. That is all any of us can do."

"Right. The moment. And when I live in the moment, my life will turn out great?"

"It should. Your future looks bright. And you are a very handsome man. No question that things will go your way."

"I hope things go my way."

"But first, there is Savanna. She is your destiny." Her words followed me out of the tent.

"Right."

As I left the tent, my head was spinning. All this talk of Savanna, Savanna. What was the deal with Savanna? Did I even care if I met this Savanna?

I had already fucked my brains out. On a normal night, I would be more than ready to concede I'd had a great time. I would even have been happy to call it a night and return home to my clean, crisp apartment and my bottle of wine with Vivaldi on the stereo. But there was more to come. The gypsy had told me so. And my gut was telling me so.

I spied Mark over at a corner table, having his tea leaves being read by a woman with cropped red hair. I slid into the chair beside him.

"What's the scoop, Mark? You gonna win the lottery?"

"Yeah, sure. Aren't we all?"

His fortune-teller gave me a sideways glance.

"He will win the lottery, but not very much."

"Hell, I won the lottery the other day. Five bucks on a scratch ticket," I said.

"Exactly," the fortune-teller said, returning her glance to the tea leaves.

"What have you learned so far?" I asked.

"Apparently I am actually going to get married and even have three kids."

"Wow. When's this gonna happen?"

"Probably in the next five years," the fortune-teller said. She stared into the cup, turning it slowly. "You'll need a lot of strength to get through the next few weeks. There are going to be some shake-ups at work, and you may have to be creative to figure out an income for a while. In the end, you will land on your feet."

"Job change, eh, Mark?" I elbowed him. Mark had been complaining about his job for a while now. If there was going to be a reshuffling, it would be for the best.

"Maybe I should finally open my own company."

There was a tsking from the tealeaf reader. She shook her head.

"No. Don't start your own company. Not yet."

"Why not?"

"It won't work. Timing is wrong. Don't worry, you will land on your feet and be in a better place."

"In the end, that's all that matters to me. Having a job," Mark said.

"A job you enjoy," I reminded him.

"Yeah. Well, when I meet my future wife, I will be too busy making babies to worry about my sucky job," he said.

Over at another table, I saw Tony leaning over a crystal ball. I excused myself from Mark and the tea leaf lady to indulge my curiosity about what his fortune was saying.

Tony was peering into the ball.

"See anything?" I asked him. My words startled him briefly. He blushed and shook his head.

"I don't see a damn thing. I don't understand how these things work."

"That's why you go to a professional," I said. I looked at the crystal ball reader. She was dark-haired and staring intently into the ball with big blue eyes.

"He's going to do fine," she said. "There's money, and women. Lots of women."

"Will I get married and have kids?"

"Yes, you will have three children. Two boys and a girl."

Tony whooped and slapped my hand.

"Right on."

"Nice big house in the country. A summer place too."

"I can't even imagine a house in the country. How would that happen?"

"Your wife. She loves the country. She likes to paint. You have a stable with horses. Money won't be an issue for many years."

"Can I fast-forward to that life now?" Tony asked. The girl laughed.

"Sorry. All things in due time. First you have to make a few mistakes. Once you make your mistakes and study them and learn from them, then your path to abundance is waiting."

"It's that easy?" Tony asked.

"No, it won't be easy at all." The girl looked at him, her blue eyes glassy and penetrating. It was kind of creepy, actually, the way she was looking at him.

"You have to learn from your mistakes. That is hard for any human to do. You have to recognize and learn from your mistakes. Only then will you move forward."

"OK I hear you," Tony said, sliding out of his chair.

"Treat people with respect, and you will earn it for yourself," she said.

"Gotcha."

"As for you . . ." she pointed at me.

"Me?"

"Yes, you. As for you, your destiny is here tonight. What you learn from this night will be carried with you for a lifetime or more. Be wise."

"I hope I'm not going to catch any disease," I jested. She frowned.

"Don't taunt the forces. You will meet your destiny. How you choose to handle her is your choice, your free will."

"Her?"

"Savanna."

"Again with this Savanna. Are any of my friends meeting this Savanna?"

The crystal ball reader stared at me with a Cheshire-cat smile.

"Your destiny is different from that of your friends."

"OK."

Tony and I walked back to Mark. He had finished his fortune.

"I think I've just about had it with this place," Tony said.

"This club?" I asked, surprised.

"No, not the club. All this fortune-telling crap. It's getting on my nerves."

"Sounds to me like maybe the gypsy hit a nerve," I speculated.

Mark laughed.

"Well, I'm pretty happy that I'm going to have a good life one day."

"If any of this stuff is true, we're all going to land on our feet," I said. "Wouldn't that be sweet? Maybe we should compare notes in ten years and see how much came true."

"Yep. We'll do that," Tony said sarcastically.

We returned to the hallway and continued on with exploring the club.

# CHAPTER 4.

It was time to relax. My head spun with thoughts of what the gypsies had said. What did it matter what my future held? I was in a Halloween funhouse. The tales they told me had no bearing on the real world, on my real life.

Halloween was a time of make-believe, so that's what I figured the fortune-telling was all about. Make-believe. They were paid by the club to say things to the customers. We all would hear things both good and bad. That's part of fortune-telling. Sure, the tarot reader had stumbled upon some facts about me, yet then again, maybe it was a lucky guess. Or maybe she did possess some sort of knowledge about fate and love and life.

I would have to live out my life to discover the truth.

I had to remember what she told me and see how my life followed suit.

The next room we entered was a blue room. Well, that's what I called it anyway, because it was all in blue.

There was blue lighting throughout the room. Blue walls shimmered as if we were under water or in an aquarium. Electric blue was the dominant blue. Inset into the walls were several giant aquariums. The water was blue. Fish ranged from silvery blue to dark blue, and many other shades of blue. Even the twinkling strobe lights had a blue hue to them.

The people that worked the room wore blue wings and blue outfits. Their skin was a pale blue that looked positively creepy in the electric lights.

I sat down on an overstuffed circular couch that could hold about twenty people.

"I gotta take a load off," I said as I sank back into the soft cushions.

"What can we get you?" Tony asked as he and Mark prepared for the bar.

"Oh, anything is fine. Something blue might be interesting. Surprise me."

I sat staring ahead at the little dance floor. There were a few people dancing to the strange electro-techno beat. It was kind of like when music in the seventies tried to be science-fictiony and futuristic. Some people loved that techno stuff, but I was never a big fan of it. It got on my nerves after a while. Of course, if I'm on a hot date or something, I don't complain.

I'll endure the techno music and hope that the girl has better things to listen to than techno when she has her own personal moments to listen to music of her own choosing.

I hadn't thought about the girl that had been my techno friend in a very long time. I wondered what had happened to her. If she stopped coming out or moved or settled down.

My techno flashback took me to the late nineties. The years hadn't flipped over yet and I was barely of age. Life was pretty good to a young man such as myself. I could do the bare minimum to get by in life and still do well. I showed up for work and sleepwalked my way through my shifts. I studied and did my homework instead of trying to figure out a hundred ways to get into Freida McAlister's pants. Freida McAlister was one of those buxom cheerleader types that every freshman hoped to bang. I never did get her. Probably because I didn't want to share what everyone else had had a taste of. It wasn't really that challenging to bag a girl that half the football team had already banged.

My techno friend, Tori, was such a nice girl. She really was. I don't know why I was so mean to her except for the fact that she liked techno and we were both young and stupid back then. I also knew she had a crush on me, so I have to say, I used her and abused her as people are wont to do to nice people.

Tori inspired in me an urge to play out a certain kind of fantasy that I never dreamed to do with any other woman. The fantasy of myself as a jerk, I could say now, looking back on my younger, vanilla self. She fed the latent exhibitionism that I hadn't recognized or embraced yet in my life.

She was a tiny little thing. About five foot nothing to my six foot two. I'm not sure what she weighed but I bet it wasn't more then a hundred pounds. It was great fun to tease her because she had a fiery little temper. I felt strong and virile next to her.

The first time we met, she was dancing in a throng of people. I had admired her tiny lithe body and the way she could move it. I imagined it riding up and down my shaft in a glistening streak. I wondered how tight her little box would be as I slid into her with my well-endowed rod.

The craving to plow her was insatiable and that was mainly what drove me to meet her. We ended up fucking that very night, in a back alley. I realized that I had some sort of power over her. It might have been the way she stared at me and hung on my every word. Being young and arrogant, I misused my status and found every opportunity to humiliate the poor thing.

Yet she stayed, so she must have gotten something out of it, too.

The blue room reminded me of one night when we had been tripping on some fine wine and a little bit of pot. We were on our way out to a club. She wore an electric blue catsuit. It was wild. You could see her every inch of her tight little body. The nipples on her tiny tits were visible through the vinyl. The lips of her cunt moved as she walked or sat. The crack up her ass split her cheeks into two perfect mounds that ached to be spread and ravished.

That night, every eye was on her at the club. At first, I liked it. I liked being with a hot woman that everyone was watching. However, after a few drinks, I became possessive. I didn't want the other guys checking out my chick. Instead of taking her home, I was an asshole.

The rest of the night, I flirted outrageously with other women. I kissed a few, right in front of her. Her eyes welled up with tears as I fondled breasts and asses and made loud lewd comments for her to hear.

Even though every guy and girl in the place was watching her, she clearly only had eyes for me. But being young and a prick, I didn't see that. I didn't see that at all.

By the time we were ready to leave, she was struggling to hold back her tears.

I've never hit a woman or anything like that, but I'm sure how I treated her was far worse then any physical abuse.

I badgered her all the way home, accusing her of wearing the outfit for everyone but me. I don't even know how I thought it would even matter, since we weren't going steady. But I saw her weakness. I saw how she wanted me, could have loved me.

It was all about power.

Once we were inside my place, I made her sit in a chair in the kitchen. As I tied her to the chair with several belts, I accused her of being a slut, of wanting other men, of wanting women.

Seeing her sitting there, all tied up, excited me. She didn't try to struggle. In fact, she sat quite passively, her eyes down. We had never played S&M games together, so I had no idea if she even knew what they were or that this was one on my end, though I'm sure on her end, it was just an asshole abusing her.

Her outfit turned me on so much I could barely stand it. I took a bottle of olive oil from the cupboard and poured some into my hand. My hands glided over her vinyl outfit, and her oily slippery body turned me on even more. I rubbed it on her face, and through her hair.

"What do you think? Is this what you wanted?" I asked her. She didn't reply.

My hands rubbed her little breasts through the outfit, down her lean body and across her gleaming thighs. I was so turned on that I thought I would die.

"What do you want from me?" She finally asked.

"I want you to behave yourself."

"I did behave myself."

"No, you are a tease and a tormenter. Terrible things happen to girls that tease and torment."

She hung her head silently. Finally she spoke again, her voice trembling.

"I want you, Franco. I don't want anyone else but you."

"A likely story. You don't even know me. We have nothing in common." With that comment I shoved my dick in her mouth. She sucked on it, gagging and nearly throwing up on it as I pumped it into her mouth. It was exciting, looking at her shiny, oily body all tied up, her little puckered mouth working my dick. At last, I blew my load all over her face.

When I untied her, I expected her to cry or run to the bathroom or something. She did nothing but sit there. At last, I tired of her sitting there and ordered her to go home. I know she wanted me to fuck her. I could see it in her eyes. But my urge to be a powerful asshole was stronger then the urge to fuck her. I didn't have to ask her twice to leave. She gathered up her belongings and left, still slick with oil.

After the door was shut behind her, I masturbated again, thinking about fucking her tight little ass.

I really didn't think I'd see her again, but I did. Many more times. Each night ended in some form of humiliation for her. One time I fucked a girl I picked up in a bar, while she watched. Another time, I made her give me a blow job on the dance floor of a regular club, not a sex club. There was something in her that made me want to act aggressively toward her.

The last time we were together, we were at her house. She had on that weird techno music and she was dancing around me, shaking her tiny tits, trying to get me excited. I played with the rings in her tits for a while, and traced the lines of her tattoos with my fingers.

Something inside of me was tired of her. I had never really been engaged with her. Maybe it was that music. Maybe she just looked too freakish for me. I was dancing with her, and soon we were dancing out on the balcony. It wasn't the warmest of days, but there we were, necking on the balcony. My dick was hard and ready, I wanted to slam into her tight little hole.

"We should go inside," she said.

"Nonsense," I said. "Out here is good."

"But what if . . ."

"Shush." I spun her around so that she was looking off the balcony and before she could say another word, my cock rammed its way up her skirt and into her pussy. I clutched her naked tits and fucked her on the balcony. She clutched the railing with white-knuckled fingers.

"Afraid the neighbors will see?" I asked, breathing into her ear. She was lost in the pleasure of my dick but still concerned about being seen. She said nothing.

"What do you think they'll say about this?" I asked her as I withdrew my cock from her pussy and spread her ass cheeks. I pushed my cock into that tight, unrelenting hole.

"Oh, god . . . no. You can't." She protested but it was too late. My cock was slamming into that tight little asshole.

I rammed my fingers up her pussy, nearly getting my whole fist in as I fucked the shit out of her ass on that balcony. There were neighbors that saw us. This I know for a fact. But who's going to complain about watching people fuck on a balcony? By the time anyone could do anything, we'd be done.

Knowing people were watching us turned me on. Knowing that my dick in her asshole wasn't one of her most favorite things turned me on even more. I pushed her over, reaching into her pussy with my hand, pumping her good with my dick. She was excited; there was no doubt about that. As much as her head was telling her this was wrong and we had to stop, a fact she voiced many times, her body was as much into the ride as mine.

At last, I was coming into that dear, sweet asshole to the beat of some sort of electrocrap.

That day on the balcony was the last I ever saw of her.

Maybe she got evicted.

Tony and Mark returned with big blue drinks. We sat on

one of the big wraparound couches where several other people sat and watched the world go by for a while. Among the blue-room workers, there were many customers in assorted Halloween costumes and fetish gear.

Three people dressed as slaves, I guess, excused themselves to get past us and slumped down on the couch. The tall young man wore black leather pants that were laced up the sides and a slave collar. He had tousled shoulder-length brown hair and dark eyes. There were two women, one on either side of him. One had short black hair cut into a bob and the other was shaved bald. They both wore submissive outfits of leather criss-cross straps and collars. They sat together talking, toasting each other with blue drinks that were poured into giant martini glasses.

I watched them as they talked and soon came to realize that they worked for the club.

"Hey," I said to them. "I'm Franco." I reached over to shake their hands.

"Hey, Franco," the man said, "I'm Scorpio." He clasped my hand strong and hard. "How's it going?"

"Good. It's going good," I said. "Absolutely no complaints so far!"

Scorpio identified the bald girl as Star and the black-haired girl as Desmire.

"Tony, Mark . . ." I pointed to my friends. Everyone shook hands.

"We're just taking a break for now," Scorpio said as he took a sip from his drink.

VAMP

"From playing?"

"We work here. Of course, if you can call what we do work."
He laughed and the girls giggled.

"You work in this room?" I said looking around at all the
blue everywhere.

"Hell, no. We work in another part of the building. Thought
we'd take a break before the night gets too . . . intense." Scorpio
laughed again.

"What do you do? Do you scare people?" I asked.

"Only with my hideous looks," Scorpio said.

"Yeah, real successful . . ." I slapped him on the arm.
Scorpio was a nice-looking man, no need for him to put
himself down.

"Seriously, what kind of work do you do?"

"Well, in real life, this isn't what I do—I do have a real job
in the real world."

"Don't we all?"

"Anyone who wants to come here needs a real job," Mark
said. "The drink prices are outrageous."

"What can you do? You pay for a good time in the big city."
Scorpio shrugged.

"I am impressed so far with the layout of the place," I told
Scorpio.

"Yeah, I was one of the ones to help set it up. I built quite
a few of the sets and equipment."

"Good job. Course, I haven't been very far yet, but I'm
impressed so far."

"Glad you like it."

The waitress brought more blue drinks for my friends and me. We clicked glasses with Scorpio and the girls.

"Here's to a great night."

"Here's hoping you guys have a good time," Scorpio said.

"Cheers, boys," Star said.

"Back atcha," said Tony.

We drank and talked and watched the blue-room people. It was very relaxing despite the annoying techno music.

There was a stage show, as there were in most of the rooms of this club. It was nice to see the girls on the stage bending themselves into a variety of contortions in their blue leotards. The girls performed separately and together, creating large pretzel-type formations using their entire bodies. Their skin and hair were blue too, and in some of the formations you couldn't even tell where one person began and another ended. At the end of one intricate pyramid formation, the lights switched to some sort of intense black light. The dancers glowed eerily as they undulated and moved arms and legs. It was so freakish, watching those dancers. It was like being in some weird, primitive worshiping ritual where someone was bound to be sacrificed to a god of some sort at any moment.

The music switched from techno garbage to serpentine. The dancers rolled along the floor, as if they were tumbleweeds and then hitched up with a partner. They twisted together and apart, a dancing-mating ritual. Blue tongues darted at each other, hands ran along each other's smooth creaseless forms. They rolled and squirmed and climbed over each other until another image formed, which they held for a moment before collapsing into another one.

In a way, their dancing reminded me of the rolling sea. How the seaweed and sea creatures shift and change with each dance of the wave. How on the bottom of the ocean sand and shells are pulled back and forth. All the blue and their fluid, languid motions reminded me of water. Water and air and sea and freedom.

Beside me on the couch, Scorpio and his girls were finishing up their drinks.

"Nice to meet you, man," Scorpio said as he stood. He slapped my hand and then reached over to slap the hands of my friends.

"See you around the club," I said.

"Yes, you certainly will, Franco," Scorpio said as he winked at me.

I gave him a half smile.

I didn't really know what he meant by that wink. At the time, I hoped he didn't think that I was gay and even had a moment of panic about the idea. Hell, the closest I've ever been to another guy has been at an orgy where we're both working on the same girl. I've no interest whatsoever in getting down with a guy. He didn't look gay either, as he slung his arms around the two girls, who seemed tiny next to his immense height. So the wink must have meant something else.

Of course, by the end of the night, I knew exactly what his wink meant. It was the last wink of freedom. The last wink of tasting my life as normal and anticipatory instead of being captured in the chaos of my heart, where I am still held prisoner.

But then, the night was young; we had barely begun our adventures. Whatever had happened to me in the fortune-telling room was beginning to leave me. I felt calmer, after meeting Scorpio and the girls. Seeing real employees made me feel as though I could relax, that all this talk of Savanna was just a game for the Halloween festivities. At the time I didn't think anything of it, but later on, as I looked back on the events of the evening, I realized that Scorpio and the girls never once mentioned Savanna or my destiny to see her.

That was fine by me. I didn't know then that they knew far more then I would ever know.

The waitress returned and gathered up our empty blue martini glasses. She asked if we wanted more. I didn't. I felt as though I had already drank enough to sink a boat, and I wanted to make certain I was able to stay on top of situations, as it were, as they came up. The guys were thinking along the same lines so we all declined a drink for the moment.

We watched the dancers for a while longer. This time they were making a giant circle or wheel or something. It was like something right out of Cirque du Soleil, how they were flying and winding and wrapping around each other. It was the most beautiful and artistic spectacle I'd ever seen in my life.

I wondered how long it would take someone to actually train to do all those stunts. There were no prop wires. Nothing that I could detect. The dancers just kept on going, doing their bizarre contortions and ballet steps. I guess it was kind of like modern dancing but more extreme. Who knew anymore what kind of dance was what? Everything was so different. New rules being invented all the time. Hip-hop dance had only been around twenty years, if that, and had mutated out of street dance.

"What do you think of the night so far, Franco?" Tony asked me.

"I'm digging it."

"Are you glad we forced you outside to play?" Mark grinned.

I nodded. "Most definitely."

"Hey, you guys, we need to touch up our makeup. I've noticed that we're sweating all over the damn place," Tony said, as he peered at my face.

"Over by that wall there is just mirrors. Let's just do it there."

"Sure, god knows where there's a bathroom in this joint anyway. Have to walk another half hour to find one."

We wandered over to one of the large mirrors on the walls and Mark dug the makeup out of his tight pockets. We re-powdered our faces and touched up our lines and shadows. I put new rings around my eyes, and in the black light of the room, my pupils glowed strangely like an animal from another world. I looked over at Mark and Tony and saw their eyes glowing strangely too. It was cool, almost erotic, like watching each other's eyes glow in the blue light.

"Say, Tony," Mark said as he gathered up the makeup. "Whatever happened to that little dark-haired girl you were dating for a while there?"

"Sophie?" he asked

"I think that was her name. She had short dark hair and big eyes. She seemed like fun."

"Yeah, I think it was Sophie. She was fine. However it was the same old shit as it always is. Girls just don't know how to have a good time."

"What do you mean?" I asked. Tony was great at snaring women, but he grew bored with them after a while.

"She wanted commitments. Schedules, appointments, dates, commitments."

"An organized kind of gal, was she?" I asked, trying to imagine free-spirited Tony under some broad's iron fist.

"Yeah."

I knew that would never work for Tony. He didn't mind a bossy-boots girlfriend but he'd never keep one for long. He'd keep them around 'til he tired of their bitching and he'd lose interest in whatever features had attracted him in the first place. Tony was the true bachelor dude. Although as we all were pushing thirty, he did actually make murmurings about wanting to settle down.

"Too bad. She looked like fun," I said.

"She was fun. Who knows? It may not be over forever," Tony said.

"You know these commitment girls, though. They find the guy they need pretty quick. It's always the scatterbrains that are free for years," Mark said.

"Not necessarily."

"I wonder if Sophie would have liked it here," Tony said as he stared around, sinking into deep thoughts.

"Was she kinky?" Mark asked, punching him in the arm.

"I probably could have convinced her to come to a sex club. Not so sure she'd participate with anyone else, though."

"Yeah, some girls just can't think of sex as sex."

"I'm not so sure about that," I said as I motioned over to a couple going at it one couch over. "Think the girls here don't think of sex as sex?"

"He has a point," Tony said, half to himself.

"All the guys are fucking someone. And not all of them work here," I said, looking for more couplings to prove my point.

"So you think everyone has a kinky side, hidden away somewhere?" Tony asked me. I nodded.

"For sure. I'm just grateful I found mine while I'm still young enough to enjoy it."

We all high-fived each other. Mark turned to Tony, probing once more.

"So, no one else on the horizon?"

"No. Not right now. Relationships are too much work, man. I can't handle it."

On one hand, I agreed with what Tony said, yet on the other, I couldn't help but play devil's advocate.

"They aren't as much work as scrambling for a date every weekend and hoping to get laid. At least you know you're getting laid in a relationship."

"I suppose there's some truth to that. For some people. Of course then there are all those virgins who are saving themselves for marriage," Mark said sarcastically, watching the couple on the couch.

"Ha-ha. Yeah, right. Like that's going to happen," Tony said.

"Don't underestimate the virgins. There's a whole new movement going on these days. The new celibacy is like a new religion."

"So you can lose your virginity again and again."

"Apparently so. Even TV shows make fun of it," I said.

"Well, that's a good thing, I guess. Tell me, does the hymen grow back?" Tony said.

I shrugged. "Only if a doctor puts it back."

"Well, then it's all just talk, nothing to do with reality. If you've fucked, you've fucked. End of story and no big deal either," Tony decided.

"You know some people consider sex a big deal, a huge deal," I said.

"Well, it is. Especially if you haven't been getting it."

"Some people would think we're going to rot in hell just by being at this club tonight," Mark said.

"We're all going to rot in hell because we're celebrating Halloween. What's the difference? Bring it on!" I waved my hand in the air. As people looked at me, I realized I spoke too loudly. My adrenaline was racing.

"Man I'd love to sink my rod into some sweet virgin," Tony whispered as he leered at the couple fucking on the couch.

"Me too," Mark agreed, also mesmerized by the undulating bodies writhing in blue light.

"Maybe you'll be lucky enough to find one that's waiting for her wedding night."

"Hell, I didn't say I wanted to marry her," Tony said.

A low, long bell tone, or maybe it was a gong, resounded loudly in the room.

The dancers finished their pose and one by one left the stage.

My friends and I looked at each other. Was it a fire alarm or what was going on?

A woman wearing a long blue robe appeared on the stage.

"Welcome, to New Blue You," she said, raising her hands in welcome.

"Tonight, we have a special treat for you. We will be teaching you how to relax your mind and body. You need to learn how to send your body into an ultra-trance of stimulation and relaxation so that you can enjoy the evening better. Even though this sounds like a paradox, you will reap the rewards when we are done. Whatever experiences you've had so far tonight will pale in comparison to the exquisite awareness you will exhibit after the exercises are complete."

There was a light smattering of polite clapping.

"First, everyone needs to spread right out. Get as far away as possible from each other but still be able to see me. If you are here with friends, get away from them. Find new energy to share and build on."

Everyone in the room started to spread out. Those that weren't interested left the room or watched from the bar area. The woman on the stage commanded our attention.

"Our first exercise involves breathing. This sounds simple and trite I'm sure to some, yet others know the importance of breathing. We can choose to inhale calm, sweet thoughts or vindictive, hateful thoughts."

She breathed in and out a few times. Her breath caused people to settle down and take notice.

"Breathe in deeply, and consider how the air fills your lungs, your body. Feel it rush through your blood and down your legs, your arms, and out the top of your head."

She led us through several relaxation techniques. Soon we were sitting cross-legged on the ground, our fingers curling into Os. I was already feeling more relaxed and open to the possibilities of the evening. I had done yoga many times through the years, so none of the exercises were odd to me. What was odd was doing them in a nightclub where everything was blue.

We lay on our backs, breathing in the air, staring at blue all around us. It was easy to imagine a calm blue ocean and the tranquility it would bring.

"Everyone roll around on the floor until you form one great big circle."

It took a few moments but soon something resembling a circle sprawled across the room.

We were to reach out and touch the hand of the person next to us. My fingers touched the people on either side of me. There was a faint tingling as our energy connected. As the pulse within us grew steady and cohesive, I was growing aroused.

Our hands clasped. The girls on either side of me were sighing. I peeked a look at the girl on my right. She was darkhaired, wearing a cowboy outfit. Her shirt was tied at the waist and she wore jeans and chaps. The girl on the other side of me was dressed as some sort of fairytale character. Maybe she was Alice in Wonderland with her blue dress and white pinafore. Yes, she was Alice in Wonderland, because there was a white rabbit hanging out the pocket of her dress.

Her hair was blond and she wore a blue headband. I wondered how Alice was doing in all of this. Her white stockings were falling down, but it was of no consequence, since we were all lying on our backs. Our leader's gentle voice washed over us.

"Now reach out to the person beside you and place your hand between his or her legs. Cup his or her groin gently and feel the energy. The warmth."

I placed my hand in Alice's crotch as Cowgirl placed hers in mine. My dick was growing hard already and Cowgirl stroked it softly.

I couldn't feel Alice's crotch over her dress so I slid my hands up her little blue dress and touched her ruffled panties. The heat of her groin assailed me. I realized this was one horny girl. Although we were supposed to only be touching the person and grooving on their energy, I couldn't resist using my thumb to rub Alice's little nub. She spread her legs wider and I softly pressed down on it. I applied pressure and then released several times, while yoga lady talked us through a few more breathing exercises. Cowgirl's grip on my dick was getting stronger. She slid her hand up and down my leather pants and then she started tracing the rod through my pants in earnest.

I wanted to unzip my pants but I noticed that no one else was doing that. Instead, I moved my free hand over to Cowgirl's crotch. She was hot and moist through her little white shorts. She rubbed her groin against my hand.

"Breathe," the yoga lady told us. "In and out."

She started counting softly through the microphone, breathing in for a set number of counts and then breathing out again. Soon the whole room was breathing as one. Cowgirl was getting more excited by the moment. Alice was less enthusiastic. Alice didn't seem the least interested in grabbing my dick, but that was OK, since Cowgirl was doing a great job rubbing my meat. I turned my head to see if Alice was doing her partner.

Alice was lying beside a woman dressed in a Little Bo Peep shepherdess outfit. I had seen her earlier. Bo Peep's outfit was hiked up to her waist. Alice's fingers played in her pantied snatch with ease.

Ah, so that was it. Alice preferred ruffled panties to leather dicks. That was cool. I focused more on Cowgirl. Feeling brave, I slipped my fingers inside her shorts. They were so tiny that my fingers reached her hot little pussy with ease. I rubbed her moist little clit and than found her hole. I slipped my finger into her hole.

"Breathe," the teacher instructed.

We breathed and I relaxed more. My cock grew harder as I willed myself into a Zenlike state of relaxation. What wasn't there to be relaxed about? I had a pussy for each hand and my dick was being rubbed. I had died and gone to heaven.

Soon it seemed like the room itself was breathing. We didn't need the teacher anymore as we breathed in unison. Our breathing pace picked up as our hands continued to explore. I noticed on the far side of the room that a man and woman were spooning, still fondling the other partners. I believed the man was fucking the woman, yet the circle wasn't broken.

Leisurely, people turned to each other, spooned each other and started to fuck slowly. Cowgirl undid my pants and pulled out my dick. I slid my pants down my hips with my Cowgirl hand, not losing a beat on Alice. Cowgirl wrangled her shorts down her hips and stuck her ass toward me. I slipped my dick into her wet cunt with ease. Beside her, a man was fucking a woman as Cowgirl's other hand rubbed his butt. I could feel his movement, which was my movement. We all worked together in a delicious rhythm.

Strange music was playing and I closed my eyes. All I thought about was the sensation of my dick sliding into Cowgirl. It was sheer heaven. Alice's cunt was wet and Bo Peep had a finger up her hole. Alice squirmed with delight as we brought her to orgasm. On my dick, Cowgirl rocked and pushed against me until she came.

It didn't take me long to come inside Cowgirl. Around the room, people came in glorious unison, gasping and moaning.

The yoga teacher instructed us all to breathe again.

"Don't lose the pattern of your breath," she said. "Keep breathing and you will experience the most glorious of sights."

As I breathed deeply, I envisioned a world where people were kind to each other. Where you could do or be anything you wanted. You could walk down the street and if you saw a nice-looking girl, you could stop and fuck her in a corner. My dick was still inside Cowgirl as I thought my lascivious thoughts. I started to grow hard again.

"Keep breathing. Keep going," the teacher said, her voice soft over the microphone.

My mind wandered to a place that was blue. I was in a blue bubble, floating over the world. Looking down at my feet, there was a beautiful woman sucking my cock. Below her, I can see all the people from my past, walking around. I laugh at them. I am the one floating high above in my beautiful bubble while they wandered around the streets aimlessly.

A rush of knowledge flooded through me. I felt as if I suddenly understood things. Everything was crystal-clear now. My destiny awaited. In another bubble in the distance, I could barely make out a blond woman reaching out toward my bubble. She was calling to me but I couldn't hear her. I knew her, but I didn't know her. Her distant cries stirred an echo within me.

As quickly as the knowledge came, it dissipated. I clutched at it, but it slipped from my mind. I felt a sense of remorse, as if I had just lost a secret. It didn't matter anymore. My breathing was in rhythm with the room and my cock was sliding in and out of a beautiful woman.

Cowgirl moaned softly, her cunt wet and slick with the juices of many orgasms and my come from before. I relished the sensation, and picked up my pace.

It wasn't long before I was coming again. This time it was a long, slow shudder. I grasped Cowgirl by the hips and pulled her onto me as I throbbed deep inside of her. She cried again and I felt her pussy clench against my dick.

"Slowly finish what you are doing," the yoga teacher instructed.

She gave everyone a few minutes to complete coupling.

"Lie on your back, your hands at your side." I pulled my hand back from Alice and Cowgirl.

"Close your eyes. Breathe."

I breathed and was grateful for how good I felt. So much tension had been released. I felt like a new person, full of energy and excitement.

She led us through some more breathing and then had us sit up.

Next, we were to find someone else in the room to do more exercises with. I found myself paired with the woman I had seen earlier in a cavewoman outfit.

We sat facing each other as the yoga teacher led us through some more exercises. We had to mirror each other's movements and facial expressions, working as though we were one.

Our hands ended up on each other's bodies. My partner had large breasts with nipples like thumbs that protruded through her leopard-skin minidress. I pulled and tweaked on those lovely nipples. She pulled and tweaked on mine.

My hand reached down for her pussy. She reached down for my cock.

We rubbed each other between the legs for a moment, staring into each other's eyes.

The yoga teacher instructed everyone to get naked. We peeled off our clothes and costumes as quickly as possible. As soon as everyone was settled back into place staring at each other, she spoke again.

"This time in the exercise, close your eyes and run your hands over your partner. One person goes at a time. I'll tell you when to switch."

The Cavegirl went first.

She ran her hands along the top of my head and down my face. She lingered around my nipples enough to tease them to attention, slowly traced down my arms. She squeezed my biceps a little bit. If I had my eyes open I would see that she was probably smiling. Women love my biceps.

Her fingers clamped around my dick and gave me a tug. Then they reached down to my balls and stroked my scrotum. Her fingers traced along my ass as far as she could go with how I was sitting. She returned to my cock and stroked it again for a moment. Her hands continued their journey along my thighs, my knees, and my shins.

It was time to switch.

I ran my hands on her hair and around her face. Her shoulders were soft and her breasts large and heavy. I played with those large nipples for a moment, pulling on them and twisting them between my fingers. I made my way down to her beaver. I touched her lips. She was clean-shaven and smooth. Her little clit was hard beneath the folds. I moved my hands down her legs.

When I got to her feet, I pulled them out and massaged them. Her feet were soft and she sighed appreciatively.

"Now that you have explored your partners, I want you to stand up."

She had us stand as close as we could to each other, barely touching. Cavewoman's boobs were so huge that they prevented any other part of our bodies from touching.

"Move slowly toward each other, as if you are melting into each other."

We pressed our bodies together, wrapping our arms around each other. She was warm and soft. A curvy soft woman. She was a pleasure to hug and I could have held her body against mine all night long.

We stood that way a very long time.

By the time the yoga lady was speaking again, my nerves were trembling and my dick was aching. I didn't even know I had it in me to get hard yet again, but here I was. That night was incredibly magical when it came to how many times I fucked. I will never be able to repeat it. I can't imagine ever repeating it. It must have been a combination of spells and Halloween magic. No man could fuck like the three of us did that night.

I grabbed her meaty ass in my hands as my cock pressed against her pussy. Her breasts rubbed against my chest. We held and stroked each other as the yoga lady told us things. I didn't care anymore what the yoga lady had to say. I was enjoying the flesh of the woman I was holding. For the first time in ages, I felt connected. Not necessarily to the girl herself, but to the entire room. We were sharing some sort of strange energy. It made me dizzy when I stopped to really think about it. How could we all be reduced to a room of humming energy?

My nerves were so alive. I felt everyone's thoughts and lusts. It seemed like I could touch anyone in the room and they would accept me. The idea of a universal love appealed to me. I reached out to the couple beside us and drew them in. Cavewoman reached her arms out to them as well. Soon the four of us, two men and two women, were embraced flesh to flesh.

The women sank to their knees when the yoga teacher told them to. They took our dicks in their mouths and suckled. At first, I wasn't sure if Cavewoman even knew how to suck dick. She was having a hard time putting it in her mouth.

"You are so big," she finally whispered, her eyes wide.

"Am I?" I asked innocently. She resumed her efforts at taking me in her mouth. She tried to deep-throat me but it was too much for her. In the end, she licked and sucked my dick while using her hands to stroke me. The woman beside us was sucking her partner with great abandon, clearly familiar with his equipment and how to use it.

After they were permitted to suck our dicks for a while, they were ordered to stand up again. Next, it was our turn to bury our faces between our partner's legs. I suckled at Cavewoman's sweet honey-pot, tasting her juices as I licked her folds. She put her hands on my head, pushing her hips toward me. I lapped and sucked, teasing her clit and slipping my tongue up into her hole. She spread her legs further, clearly enjoying all I had to offer. Her legs started to tremble. She moaned and swayed above me, delirious with pleasure.

The sight of it turned me on and I licked her more thoroughly. Her cunt got a fantastic washing by the time we were told to stop.

For the next exercise, Cavewoman stood in front of me with her back to me. We were instructed to touch our partners all down the front with our eyes shut. We were to linger on any areas that we felt we needed to linger on. Before long my hands were cupping and squeezing her large breasts. The weight in my hand had me daydreaming about how good they would feel slapping against my face as she fucked me.

My cock was hard against her ass crack. I ran my hands down between her legs and stroked her pussy.

We were told to switch, so now I stood with my back against her and she ran her fingers down my chest, straight to my boner. She seemed to really enjoy playing with my balls. She kept cupping them and rolling them. It was like she had never played with balls before. I figured that maybe she hadn't. Maybe she wasn't used to much sexual activity or maybe she was just nervous fooling around with a stranger. Either way, it didn't bother me. It was just an observation, since I'm usually with people who have been around the block a few times. Enthusiasm always works out well in the end, and the girl certainly had a lot of enthusiasm.

Around me, people were starting to fuck again. I made Cavewoman bend over and slid my dick into her. She gasped and I felt her tighten up before I barely had the head in. The pressure just excited me more. I played with her tits as she started to relax and I slid into her a little more. I worked my cock in and out of her slowly, going a little deeper each time as she opened up to take me in. It was hard to get even half my dick into her, but I could tell she wasn't used to the angle. I wriggled around until I found her g-spot. I slowly pushed against it. Her breath hitched and a surprised "oh" came out of her mouth.

"Oh my. Right there," she sighed, putting her hands on her knees for balance.

"Oh my lord, I never knew that was there." She muttered and murmured as she lost herself in the anticipation of a mind-blowing orgasm. She started to buck back against me, squirming around so that my cock head hit her g-spot with every stroke. She shook her hips and quivered and reached one of her hands down between her legs. She played with herself as I pushed and kneaded her g-spot. I started to pick up the pace.

At first she was hesitant, I was slamming into her pretty fast and furious. But once she trusted I would slip on past that treasured g-spot she relaxed and the fun really began.

I held her hips and pounded her down against me, taking care not to lose sight of her pleasure zone. It took a lot of self-restraint to not just do what I wanted and I hoped that she would come soon.

My cock grew hard as I pumped her faster. Soon her shy little oh's were laced with full-fledged moaning. She sounded like she was crying as she suddenly spasmed and liquid poured down her legs. I pulled out my dick and more come gushed out. My dick and balls were soaked from her juices. I shoved my cock back into that hole before it could close up on me again.

This time, I thrust into her as deep as I cold go. She tried to push me back with her hands but I was lost in my quest for pleasure.

I rammed her hard and fast and deep. Even though she protested weakly, I knew that she loved it as much as I did. My dick slammed in and out and she nearly fell over a few times. I pumped frantically, as if I hadn't been laid in years instead of ten minutes ago.

With a yell, I was ready to shoot my final load. She quivered as I held my dick in her, spending my load and thinking about how weird life was as the last of my orgasm ebbed away.

After our intense experience, the yoga teacher gave us all a cool down. When the lights came up a little bit, she left the stage. There was polite clapping from around the room. I found Mark and Tony.

"What did you think?" I asked.

"That was the freakiest, weird-ass yoga shit I've ever done in my life," Tony said. "Wow."

"I liked it," Mark said.

"What's not to like?" Tony said.

"What's not to like, indeed?" I agreed.

# CHAPTER 5.

$\mathcal{W}$e wandered, delirious and hungry, through the winding halls of Paradise. People came and went, laughing and joking in their garish Halloween makeup. My body was alive with excitement. There was a sickly-sweet anticipation rushing through me like a young child feels Christmas morning, when the snow is crisp on the windowsill and the smell of the pine tree in the living room tickles your nose. My stomach growled. The walls thumped with music. There were so many people there that night. Throbbing bodies danced above me, below me, and through the walls beside me, celebrating the bittersweet time of year.

Halloween is a strange holiday for most people, I think. The idea of becoming something you're not for a while holds great appeal. It's almost like giving yourself permission to taste the things in life you normally repress. When you're a child on Halloween, you choose to become something you love or fear or both. It's a chance to see what life is like from another angle.

As a child, I remember being a superhero. Superman, it was. The blue tights were strange on my legs. Hugging them yet cold at the same time. The sensation made me vulnerable to what was happening around me. At the time, I contemplated whether Superman could perform his super powers better in tights because there was less of a barrier than jeans or leather pants might have, and he could be more in tune with his senses. Maybe that was why Spiderman wore tights as well. Keep those Spidey senses tingling.

We came to another room. Inside, it was all neon-bright and garish white. It was decorated like an old fifties diner.

"Right on," Mark said.

We walked in and sat at one of the red vinyl booths. Looking around, we saw that all of the waitresses looked like something out of an old TV show. The girls wore little white hats and had beehive hairdos. One of the girls wore roller skates. Their skirts were high cut, showing off long, shapely legs. A brunette with high hair and ringlets approached us with a sultry stare.

"Would you like a menu?" she asked, licking large, pouting lips. "Sure." Tony grinned. She smacked her gum twice and walked toward one of the bussing stations to scoop up a couple of menus. We watched her ass cheeks in appreciation. She had tiny white bikini underwear on. Her butt was a luscious mound peeping out of both sides of her underpants. She stood up, straightening her dress, as she slowly walked back to us.

She gave us our menus and pulled out her pen.

"Would you like something to drink to start?"

"Sure. A beer would be good."

"Make it three."

She left to get our beer. There were a few booths that had people in them. As well, there was a long, gleaming white bar where people ate and drank.

The roller-skating waitress whizzed by. Her legs were long and lanky, especially since she wore black fishnet thigh-highs. She held them in place with a black garter belt. Her uniform was black, with a white apron and hat. She looked almost like a French maid.

Our waitress returned with our beer. We glanced at the menus as she placed them down in front of us. Her breasts spilled through the open neck of her pink dress.

"Do you know what you want yet? Or do you need some more time?" She stood with her pencil poised on a notepad.

"Oh, I'm ready," I said. "I'll have a burger and fries."

Tony laughed.

"Yeah, why not? Suits the place."

"Make that three. With extra cheese," Mark said.

"Three burger specials, one with extra cheese. Gotcha."

As she walked away, Tony lifted his glass.

"To one fantastic Halloween!" He said.

"Cheers. To think, it's not really even Halloween yet."

"I think this is going to be the best Halloween ever."

We drank to that sentiment.

"I wonder what's next, or if we've seen everything yet?"

"Oh, I'm sure there's plenty more."

"Yeah, we've only just begun."

It didn't take long for the food to arrive. Hungry from our adventures, it didn't take long for us to make it disappear. The waitresses circled us, taking our plates and wiping our faces. It was great fun to be pampered.

The waitress on roller skates zipped by me a few times. She winked at me. At one point, when she zipped on by, she told me her name was Suzy.

While Mark and Tony reminisced about loves gone by and the strange readings in the fortune-telling room, I was watching Suzy. She was very efficient as she waited on people.

At one point, I went to use the bathroom. Upon my return, I heard my name being called.

Suzy waved at me from the meat locker. I hesitated at the door, remembering far too many horror movies. Her hand reached for mine and she pulled me in, pressing her lips against mine. She was taller than me, partly because of her roller skates. Her beehive towered above us both, nearly brushing along the ceiling.

It was a cold little room and a dull light glowed from the back as she swung the door shut. Long iron rails gleamed along the top. A small gasp escaped from my lips as my eyes grew accustomed to the dim light and saw three men swinging on meat hooks. I relaxed as one of them winked at me.

"What brings you here on a Halloween evening?" she asked, her lips tugging mine.

"Just thought I'd see what was going on," I said. Her breasts pressed against my chest.

"Where's your girlfriend?" she asked, nibbling on my ear.

"I don't have one at the moment," I said.

Her words were hot in my ear.

"You have a girlfriend. A man as handsome as you has a girlfriend."

Her hand slid down my leather pants and squeezed my balls firmly.

"Are you a bad boy?" she asked, this time pulling my lip with her teeth.

"No . . ." I tried to speak. She released her hold on my lip. Her fingers squeezed my balls even tighter.

"I can see that you are a very bad boy. A terrible boy leaving his sweet young girl at home all alone. You'd rather play with a real woman, wouldn't you?" Suzy took my hand and before I could register what she was doing, she had me handcuffed to the meat rack. I looked up at my hands as if I had just experienced the work of a great magician.

"Your hands are like an angel . . ." she said. "A broken angel with wilted wings." She laughed. I didn't understand what she was talking about. She stepped toward me and unbuttoned my pants.

"Let's see what you've got, you bad boy." She pulled my

semi-hard cock from my pants. "My oh my. You have a pretty dick for such a prick."

She yanked my pants the rest of the way down. Her mouth greedily wrapped around my dick. She worked it in between spewing venomous words.

"Does she suck cock like I do? Does she get right down to the root?" I closed my eyes and moaned while she worked wonders with that delicious mouth of hers.

She sucked and licked my cock noisily. I moaned with delight, relishing her practiced tongue despite the strange accusations she shot at me.

Suzy stood up and turned around. She slapped her own ass cheeks several times with her firm, flat hand. Her fingers clutched and kneaded her ass, pulling her cheeks open and shut, flaunting her lusciousness at me. She pressed her hips back and the warmth of her legs wrapped around my shaft. I ached to feel her warm, moist pussy. She teased me, wiggling her delicious ass.

"You want to fuck this, baby?" she asked, turning her head and batting her eyelashes.

"You know I do," I said.

"You're just going to have to wait." She walked around behind me and ran her hands up and down my back. Her breath was hot on my back as she kissed my shoulder blades.

"You are so strong. Do you work out?"

"A couple of times a week."

Her hands crept under my shirt and toyed with my nipples. She squeezed and twirled them. The air was chilly but her warm body pressed against mine was warming me up.

She kissed my neck, nuzzling her face into my hair. My cock still stood straight out like a divining rod.

Suzy roller-skated around to the front of me again. She gripped my cock firmly.

"My big strong stud, are you ready?" she asked. She skated back for a moment and lifted her skirt. Her fingers toyed with her pussy. She spread her lips so that I could see her perky little clit. I licked my lips.

"You look delicious," I said.

"I am delicious." She returned to me and spun around. Her hips leaned back toward mine and this time, I slid home. Her pussy gripped me tightly and she put her hands on her knees for balance. We moved awkwardly, she on roller skates, me with my hands tied up. However strange it was, we found a rhythm and were soon moving in a fluid motion. She grew wetter with each thrust of my cock. I slipped in and out of her several more times before she disengaged herself.

Suzy went over to one of the men hanging on the meat hooks. She ran her hands up and down his body. She lifted one of her roller-skated feet and then shoved his dick into her. She fucked him for a few strokes and then slipped off to the next guy. After she had tasted all three men, she returned to me.

Her hands slid up and down my arms.

"I love a man with muscular arms." Suzy sighed. She reached up and unhooked the handcuffs. I rubbed my wrists, wriggling my fingers. She unbuttoned her blouse.

"Take my tits into your big strong hands, you bad, bad boy," she said, releasing her breasts from a push-up bra. Her nipples were large and hard as I teased them with my fingers. I lowered my head, flicking them with my tongue. She held them up into my face, squishing them into my cheeks. I suckled on those lovely nipples for a while and then lowered my head.

I kissed my way down her flat, taut stomach. As I reached between her legs, I lifted her skirt. I pushed my face between her thighs. She glided back and forth along my tongue, pushing herself gently with her skates. Her little clit was hot and firm as it quivered between my teeth.

She sat back on one of the shelves and spread her legs.

"Come and get me, big boy," she cooed.

She propped her skates up on another shelf. I stood between her legs and drove my hard shaft home. She gasped as I deeply entered her.

"Fuck me, you dirty boy," she whispered. "Fuck me hard."

I drove into her with a mighty thrust, impaling her again and again. She reached up to grab on to my shoulders. Her pussy trembled around my large throbbing love-pole. Her juices were dripping around my shaft and the sounds of me fucking her were loud in the little room. Behind me, I saw that the three men were watching us.

"They wish they could fuck me hard like you can. But they can only dream about it. Their dicks aren't big enough."

She laughed at them as I thrust into her again and again.

"They wish their dicks were as big and hard as yours. They are pathetic."

The shelves were shaking as I fucked her. I was certain the whole room would collapse.

"More," she cried. "Fuck me hard and deep. Let those men see how a real stud fucks."

"The room is going to crumble," I said, "Here, let's find somewhere else."

I led her over to another shelf and pushed her over it so that her ass was facing me.

"No," she said.

"I want to see you." She turned around. "Lie down."

I stared with dismay at the floor.

"It's pretty cold in here. And those are just wooden planks."

"Are you arguing with me?" she asked, waving the hand-cuffs at me.

"No, I'm just saying it looks pretty cold and hard down there."

"Not as cold and hard as you're going to be if you don't lie down this minute."

She skated over to the first man still hanging on the hook.

"Roger here would be happy to lie on the floor for me, wouldn't you, Roger?" She pulled Roger's long curly hair back so that his head jerked up.

"Yes, my mistress. I am aching to lie on the floor so that you can punish me some more."

She laughed and let go of Roger's hair. He sighed as his head lowered once more.

"So you see . . . if you want to fuck me, it's down on the floor with you."

"Maybe we could go back into the diner . . ." I suggested.

"Not a hope in a hell. I like it in here. It complements my outlook on life."

I nodded and studied the planked floor again. There were large spaces between the planks. I guess it was for things that dripped that no one wanted to think about. It looked cold and dirty. I imagined all the people walking in here with crap on their shoes, getting things from the freezer. I think this walk-in freezer was always here at the club, so there could have been years and years of gunk on that floor.

I looked at her face. Her large dark eyes were flashing. She clearly desired me, and quite frankly I desired her too. I wasn't averse to playing a few games tonight.

In fact, Halloween was all about becoming something you are not. Live in the moment, I told myself. Would I die if I got dirty? If I were cold?

Surely the warmth of her cunt would be worth whatever dirt got on my back. So I peeled off what remained of my clothing and lay flat on that cold wooden floor. My body started shuddering instantly and I knew it wouldn't be long before my penis followed suit. I closed my eyes as I felt her warm hands sliding up and down my penis. It was soothing and refreshing, and for a moment I just wanted to drift away to sleep.

In an instant, I was jerked awake by a new sensation. I opened my eyes to see a skate firmly planted on my chest. She stepped on me gleefully.

"You are a bad boy, leaving your girlfriend at home like that. Halloween night, even. It's such a shame."

"I keep telling you that I don't have a girlfriend," I cried out. The pressure on my chest was suffocating me. My senses were tingling, crying out in ways they hadn't before. It was strange, feeling the rolling balls of her skates along my chest. I wasn't sure why I wasn't crushed to death. I guess it's not much different then high-heeled boots. In fact, as I lay there, feeling her rolling along my chest, I realized it was better. Much better. More soothing, like a firm massage. She jumped off.

"Are you ready to pay the price?" she asked, staring at me as she slid her mouth down my cock. She warmed it up nicely as I assured her that I would pay any price she desired.

"Good."

She crouched over my dick and slid herself on it. Her mouth formed a pouty circle as she oohed and ahhed. Long white manicured nails touched her hairless pussy, bouncing along her clit as she rode herself on me. Her thighs were firm and toned, as if she went to the gym nearly as much as I did. She moved her hips back and forth like a stripper, clearly enjoying the session.

After a while, I forgot that I was on the cold wooden floor. All my thoughts were on my cock and how wonderful she felt riding it. Her hands clutched my stomach as she squatted up and down, her powerful leg muscles giving her a rapid rhythm that I had never experienced. Within seconds, I could have shot my load into that warm vibrating pleasure zone, but luckily she chose that moment to change position. She lowered herself, brushing her breasts against my chest. Her legs were tucked up like she was a little monkey clinging to me. The position felt fantastic on my cock and I started to move my hips eagerly to thrust as deeply into her as I could.

"Wait," she whispered.

"What?" I asked.

"I want you to last a long time." She held perfectly still. She was trembling.

"Me? You want me to last? Maybe it's you who wants to last?" I said.

"Nonsense. I can come fifty times an hour should I so desire. I could fuck forty men and still hunger for more."

"I'd like to see that," I said.

She turned to me and licked her lips.

"So would I!"

She started to move her hips again. The angle was different and still felt great. She knew what she was doing as she gyrated her hips first one way and then another. I barely had to move. She rode me like a prize stallion. Every move she made enticed me toward the finish line. I remembered that she wanted to come first, that she wanted to come many times, so I thrust myself up into her, hard, and held it. She bucked wildly for a moment and then quivered. Her moans filled my ears. She gasped for breath for a moment and her hips started to roll once more. I lowered my pelvis and let her ride me for a while longer. My hands played with her breasts as they brushed against my face. I squeezed them together along my cheeks, imagining being smothered to death by large beautiful bosoms. There were worse ways to go. She was getting ready to come again and I grabbed her hips and plowed into her. She moaned and jittered as I pumped hard and fast. Her breasts flopped as she held herself up with her hands on either side of my head. She gasped for air as I continued to pound her. I nearly came, but I held back. I stopped thrusting and she collapsed over me for a moment.

She picked herself and looked at me. She laughed.

"You sure know how to please a girl. Now get yourself up so that you can pump my pussy a little longer."

The men watched as I led her over to the shelves again. I saw that all three of them were firmly erect. She saw me looking at them.

"A filthy bunch of perverts, you are!" she said. "Eyes down."

The men lowered their eyes. She skated away from me and over to each one of them.

"I will deal with each and every one of you later." She slapped each one on the penis and then returned to me. She bent over one of the shelves, and reached her hands back. She spread her pussy lips wide so that I could see the come dripping out of her pink sweet hole.

"You gonna make me all wet?" she asked. "I know you can make me wetter."

She laid her chest on the shelf, continuing to hold open her legs and pussy. I stood admiring the view for a moment, stroking my long, hard shaft. Her asshole was a tiny round button. I wondered how she would react if I jammed my cock into that instead of her pussy. I could just imagine the tight warmth of her struggling against me as I pummeled her.

"Fuck me." Her tone was nearly a whine.

"Impatient, are we?" I asked.

"Not impatient. Just waiting far too long to be serviced properly."

"As you wish." I thrust my cock into her pussy, angling it so that I could feel her g-spot. I rubbed her with my cock head, and felt the telltale squirm. She groaned and moaned, cramming herself against me.

"Oh there, baby. Right there . . ."

I continued to pump her until I felt warm liquid dripping down our legs. She sprayed us again as she cried out.

"Oh my god, that's so good." She pushed herself against me rapidly and caused yet another gush of warm liquid. I heard one of the men behind me moan. My cock was slick with her juices and slid sloppily all around. I pulled out as more of her come gushed out around our feet.

On one of the higher shelves there were stacks of clean white towels. I took one and wiped juice from my legs. I turned her around.

"Suck your pussy juice off my dick." I pushed my dick at her. She blinked at me with large brown eyes.

"Not before you lick up every drop of juice from my cunt." She sat up on the shelf and spread her legs. I stared at the glistening pussy juice dripping down. My cock was so hard I thought it would burst. I slowly ran my tongue up her leg, along her inner thigh. My tongue trailed along, lapping at her sweet juices.

At last I reached the folds of her pussy. I took each fold in my mouth, and sucked and tugged. She put her hands on my head and pressed her cunt further into my mouth. My tongue found her clit and tapped on her little button. She squirmed beneath me, pressing my head still harder against her. She pushed my head down lower, until I was sucking on her dripping hole. Liquid still leaked out of it. I reached my tongue into her and stuck it up inside. Her velvety softness was like cotton candy. I lapped with long strong strokes, drawing her come into my mouth. She tasted sweet and I sucked on her until there was no more juice to suck. She rubbed her pussy against my face as I ate her.

"Clean me up good," she cooed. "That's a good boy. Lick that cunt clean."

I stood up and faced her again.

She kneeled down before me and took my sticky dick into her mouth. She sucked it to the hilt. She held it in one hand and gnawed on the end. She lapped every side of it, sliding her tongue slowly and carefully along the shaft.

"Let me come in your mouth," I begged as she teased me. I wanted her to deep-throat my cock, take it down to the hilt so I could fill her belly with my come.

"No, no, Franco. You bad boy. You're not allowed to come." She licked my cock from bottom to top and flicked the end with my tongue.

"You need to save some of your strength for later."

"Later?"

"There are so many rooms for you to travel before you reach the end. Save yourself. You will need your strength."

"You just want to torment me as you have the others." I pointed to the three men hanging with hard-ons.

"No. You are special, Franco. Believe me, I would love to have you stay here with me all night. It's not many men that can hit my g-spot like you. And there are very few men that can make me ejaculate as you have tonight. You are doing very well."

"Oh, am I being graded on this now?"

She laughed.

"It will all be clear at the end. You'll see."

She helped me get dressed. She buttoned my shirt and brushed the dirt off my pant legs.

"Don't you want to come again?" I asked her as I slid my hand up her pussy. She slapped it away.

"I can't come with you again tonight, Franco. There is much work for you to do. Now go, find your friends and be off."

# Chapter 6.

*W*e entered a room that was dimly lit. As our eyes grew adjusted to the darkness, we saw many cages. The walls were dank concrete, with water streaks running down the sides. There was a bar at the far end of the room where a few customers milled around and talked. Some tea lights were scattered on several little tables by the bar. There weren't very many people at the tables; most were standing around with drinks, watching the scenes.

There were cages of many sizes. A giant one was in the middle of the room and I could make out a large naked black man clutching the bars.

The cage beside us was about my height and slightly wider than me. A man in a torn shirt and ripped pants reached out at us.

"She is here. Beware . . . she is here."

He clutched at my shirt as I passed him by. I shook him off and kept going.

Mark and Tony kept pace. We walked past a couple of smaller cages. Inside each one of them was a woman, curled up in a ball. Beside her was a bowl of water. It was reminiscent of the humane society or some kind of animal shelter, only there were humans instead of cats and dogs.

Further on, we got to the big cage with the large black man. He was large in every aspect of the imagination. I couldn't help but stare at his massive cock. I didn't think I'd ever seen anything that huge outside of a porn site. Certainly I'd never had occasion to see one up close until now.

He wore a submissive's collar and his glistening chest was scarred with whip marks. There were shackles on his hands and feet. He stared at us as we stared at him.

"Wonder what he's in for?" Mark laughed.

"He's not in jail, you idiot," Tony said. "It's his fetish. To be locked up and chained."

"Some people are weird," Mark said. "I don't like the whole being-locked-in-a-cage idea."

"How do you know?" Tony said. "Have you ever tried it?

"No. You?"

"No. But some people seem to get off on it, that's for sure."

The black man startled us as he began to speak.

"The witch is near."

"What witch?"

"There are lots of witches near," Tony said, waving his hand around the room at several vampiric-looking women.

"The true witch. The one who seeks desire."

"What does it have to do with us?" Mark asked.

"Not all of you. One of you," the man said. "The chosen one."

"Who's chosen?"

"Franco."

"Hey, how do you know my name?"

"She told me. She told me to tell you she is near, and waiting for you. Her hunger grows."

"Well, where is it I'm supposed to meet this witch?" I said. "Lord knows I've had enough guessing games tonight."

"The time will be right when it is right."

"Of course," I said flippantly. "It's always right when it's right."

"Don't mock me. I speak the truth."

"Whatever," I said. "Let's go." I walked on quickly toward the bar. Once there, I ordered beer for all of us. We sipped on it and looked around the room.

"What is with this witch shit, Franco? How does he know your name?"

"I don't know. Probably hidden cameras or microphones all around this joint."

"That would make sense," Mark said and took a swig of beer. "It's creepy, no matter how you slice it."

"Yeah. Watch your credit card, man. This might be some big scam for you to get hosed."

"Wouldn't be the first time," I laughed. I thought of many nights of putting bills into lap dancers' g-strings, believing they would date me, believing they found me interesting in some way. Whatever this witch, this Savanna, had in store for me I could handle. After enough times of standing in the lobby of a closed club waiting for a date that never came, I knew better then to spend my money foolishly.

There was a pole fastened into the ground over by the bar. A young woman was standing at it, her wrists tied together and hitched up near the top of the post. We watched as a new scene began to unfold.

An older man, brandishing a small whip, approached her. He looked at the bucket beside her and kicked it. It fell over with a loud enough clang that people turned to stare before resuming their business.

"You've been a bad girl," he said. "A nasty bad girl. You should have learned from your last punishment, but apparently you didn't. Now you have to pay."

"Oh, please don't punish me, master," the girl said. The man replied with the stroke of his whip.

"Silence."

The girl was quiet.

A tall woman wearing a vinyl bodysuit on her lean torso walked quickly past us, her long legs accented by thigh-high stiletto boots. In her hand was a leather leash, affixed to the chain-link collar of a beautiful, naked, black-haired girl. The black-haired girl crawled on her hands and knees like a dog. Her naked ass was round and pleasant, with several crisscross patches of recent welts. Her ass must have been tingling and throbbing as she crawled along the cold concrete. Her knees were scuffed and no doubt bleeding.

"Heel." The woman jerked on the leash. The black-haired girl sat at attention, staring at me.

"Do you want to sniff him, Blackie?" the dominatrix asked the girl. Clearly her name was "Blackie." She sat back on her hind legs and raised her arms like paws. She barked, her tongue hanging out as she panted.

"You don't mind if she sniffs you?" The Dom approached me, not giving me time to answer. Blackie started sniffing around my ankles, taking in great whiffs of my evening. Her beautiful butt waggled back and forth. She sniffed up my legs and into my crotch for a moment. She went around behind me and sniffed me up and down again. She rammed her face into the ass of my pants, gnawing at me.

"Enough, Blackie. Down." The dom yanked her back. Blackie whimpered as she skulked away. The Dom walked on without a word, Blackie scampering beside her, gazing back at me once or twice with wide hungry eyes.

We walked down another row of cages. Inside one was a woman shackled spread-eagle to the wall. A man kneeled below her and was eating her pussy. A female Dom stood over them, giving orders and snapping her riding crop.

In another cage, there were several men gathered around one woman. She was hunched over a bench of some sort with a dick crammed in her mouth. Several men stood around her, stroking their dicks and saying nasty things they wanted to do to her.

One of the men spread her legs roughly while another one shoved his dick into her. She cried out, nearly spitting out the dick. She was soon filled with a cock in her cunt and one in her mouth. The men had their way with her as we walked on.

Where we were going, I didn't know. However, I was curious to see what was in each and every cage.

Some of the cages lay empty. Presumably they wouldn't be empty for long as more people joined in the play.

In a way, the place reminded me of a kennel even though a lot of the people were more into bondage than into being puppies or ponies. There wasn't any music in there, so it was interesting to hear all the different noises in the air.

Between grunts and groans of fucking, there were slaps and screams and commands. The energy was thick with a flurry of activity. Just hearing the cacophony in my ears filled me with a sense of anticipation and excitement.

A tall, orange-haired drag queen approached me. She was festively decked out in orange and black ruffles and frills. She carried a feather fan, trimmed with black lace.

"Where do you think you're going?" she asked me.

"I'm just walking around," I said.

"She's waiting for you. Why are you dallying?"

"Who is waiting for me?"

"Why, Savanna, of course. Haven't you been told this all night, honey?"

"Yes, I have. Everyone tells me she's near, she's around, but they don't tell me where she is. I've never even met the woman. I've never even seen a picture of her, so how will I recognize her?"

"Now, now, my dear Franco. Don't fret. You will find her soon enough. Have your experiences, put your mind at ease. Once Savanna enters yours, you will never be free again."

"I highly doubt it," I said.

I didn't much like the look she gave me. It creeped me out. She turned her attention away from me and toward my friends.

"Would any of you boys like to spank a naughty girl?" the drag queen asked. Mark said he'd give it shot. They went off down the aisles somewhere to find a good place for a spanking. Meanwhile, Tony and I looked around at the cages and people between the cages.

In a way, it seemed like a little community within a community. One tiny little room to house all the concerns of thirty or so people. It was so strange, almost like a tribe, in a way. I considered myself part of the alternative-lifestyle tribe when I went to places like this. But for the most part, I stayed with my work tribe or my childhood friends' tribe. Not too many tribes called my name.

Tony saw a girl with her ass stuck back to the cage bars. Through the bars, you could just see the gaping hole of her ass. It looked a bit stretched, as if it had been used lately.

He reached his hand through and touched the golden globe. She wriggled it teasingly.

I continued walking on.

The black man was being led over to a post. He was tied up, his hands in the air. A beautiful girl in a riding outfit was examining her whips. She wanted to be certain to use the proper one on her errant submissive. She held them out to him and let him decide. Once the choice was made, she set to work using the chosen whip on his flesh. His cries of pleasure and pain followed me as I continued on.

The doms all worked very well together in this dungeon. There was an easy ebb and flow to the atmosphere as well as an air of erotic mystery. It made me wonder where people were the rest of the time in their lives, and wasn't I lucky to be here in this one favorite moment?

Another cage held a chair, designed much like a birthing chair. It had a high steel back, winding steel arms, and pedestal legs. There was a hole in the center of it. A woman was strapped into it, naked save for the leather straps around her arms and legs. Her long, dark hair was tousled, as if she had been wrestling the straps for hours. Her face was tear-streaked and sweaty. She stared over at me for a moment and there was a sly little glimmer of joy in her eyes. The paradox of the moment wasn't lost on me. In great heights of pain there is pleasure to be found just from the mere fact you experienced the sensation. Pain or pleasure made one feel alive. There is no greater primitive feeling then the elation of all your nerve endings singing in unison. The mind, body, and soul connection was a powerful thing. Placing body, mind, and soul as one into a moment of extreme sensation could result in the most exquisite of ecstasy.

Was it possible?

As I pondered over my epiphany, I watched through the wires for a little while as the woman had a variety of things poured over her.

One by one, people came by and dumped a pail of some sort

of debris on her. I realized that her sweat wasn't sweat at all, but buckets of sludgy stuff. One person threw a wad of paper at her. It landed in her hair for a moment before it fell into the puddle of filth at her feet.

The woman amused me for a while as I tried to understand why someone would choose such a messy way to live out fantasies of degradation. My mind was filled with thoughts of the shower room at the end of the night as she washed away chunks of litter from her hair.

My attention was caught by a new sight. I wandered over to sneak a peak. There was a delicious girl wearing a prison uniform. She ran to her bars as I walked by.

"Oh please kind sir? Will you help me get out of here? I will do anything you desire."

She opened her shirt and revealed two large smooth breasts. I considered them for a moment before slipping my hands through the bars to touch those beautiful round orbs. I pushed and pulled them in my fingers. They were fake and I could feel the bags inside, but it didn't matter to me. They were both a miracle and wonderment, and I was pleased to have the opportunity to stroke their magnificence.

"Can you get me out of here?" she whispered urgently.

"What are you in for?" I asked

"It doesn't matter. Just let me out. Let me out and I'll give you a blow job."

I laughed.

"You want out that badly, I'll just let you out."

I tried to pull on a latch, but there wasn't any. I rattled the cage but the door wouldn't budge. There really was no way for her to get out, since I couldn't get in.

"You have to get the key from the bitch. The big asshole, come-sucking bee-yotch. I won't rest until I'm out of here."

"Now, which asshole, come-sucking bee-yotch should I be looking for?" I asked her.

"One that has the keys. Any keys. Maybe she hangs them up somewhere?"

"I don't know. I don't know how to find out."

"You're a handsome man, you can figure out anything your heart desires."

I started listening to the noises of the night. The air was thickening. You could almost feel the sweat, the heat from pulsing, wet bodies being tied up and flogged and fucked. All the bodies around me writhing in the darkness fed my deepest fantasies.

Prison Girl grabbed at the crotch of my pants, as if my dick was going anywhere. She held it firmly.

"Fuck this pussy. Fuck this little hot puss with all your manly skills."

I slipped my cock out of my pants and held it out. She grabbed at it and pulled it between the bars. Her mouth hungrily started to suck on it.

"That's so good. That's one big fucking cock," she said gleefully as she shoved it down her mouth greedily and pursed her lips down so far they nearly touched my balls.

"You're impressive," I said as I admired the depths my dick plunged down her throat. She let it go with a pop.

"You want more, big boy?" she asked, stroking my hardening dick.

"Go nuts, baby," I said, shoving her head back down. "Suck that cock nice and hard so that I can fuck the shit out of your sorry little ass."

She mumbled appreciatively and continued to slurp and suck. My fingers clutched the bars for support as pleasure coursed through me. She stopped sucking and stepped back, wiping her mouth.

"Let me see that pussy of yours," I said, kneeling down.

"You're going to get the key, right?" she asked.

"Sure, I'll get it. Right after I suck on your clit for a while."

"I think you should . . ." Her words trailed off as my tongue started to lick her clit. She held her pussy open as I tongued her good. I slid my tongue into her juicy honey pot, tasting the sweetness that lay within. My tongue flickered along her cunt, and she quivered every now and again, as if she were savoring every last minute of this fuck and didn't want the moment to ever end.

I stood up and grabbed her hair. I pulled her around so that her back was to me and I gripped her tightly by the hair and shoulder. My other hand positioned my cock so that I could enter her. I slammed my cock into that delicious tight pussy hole and gave her everything I had. It was weird fucking through bars. My adrenaline was racing as I fucked her over and over. The bars shook as I pumped. It may or may not have been enough because we had the barrier; I just know that she was howling as I slammed into her. As I had watched others all night, I realized that now, people were sneaking peaks at me. The thought of it turned me on.

"You want a big cock, you filthy prison whore. You'll get a big cock. You'll wish you never saw this cock," I shouted as I fucked her.

I pulled out.

"I want to fuck that dirty little asshole of yours," I said.

She bent over and held her ass cheeks open. I slipped my cock into her tight hot asshole.

It was a welcome massage. She cried out as I pushed in further.

"Oh God . . ." I couldn't tell if the cry was pleasure or pain. I didn't care. The images of all that I had seen tonight were racing through my mind. I thought of the gypsy girl and the diner girl. I thought of Alice and the Cowgirl. All these beautiful women dancing on the end of my dick all night long.

I shot my load into Prison Girl's asshole.

As I pulled out, I watched as strips of come gurgled out of her.

"Thanks, bitch," I said, zipping up my pants and finishing the scene.

"What about my key?" she pouted.

"Get the next guy to get it. I'm going to clean up."

"You guys . . . you are all alike."

"I know." I grinned as I started to walk off.

"I don't know what Savanna sees in you anyway," she pouted. I stopped and turned around.

"What do you know of Savanna?" I asked, stepping back toward her.

"Give me the key and I'll tell you."

I thought about it.

"Naw. I don't care what you know. See ya later." I walked off.

"Asshole," she screamed at me. I laughed. I knew she loved it. It was her fetish, to be used and tossed aside. She was a prisoner to her own fantasies.

In the bathroom, I was able to wash myself up a bit. Luckily I still had some eyeliner in my pocket, so I was able to fix up my runny smeared eyes. I was looking more ghoulish as the night went on. The man in the mirror looked as decadent as I felt.

I ran into my buddies who had come into the washroom to freshen up. We compared notes on our antics and played with our hair for a while.

"Zombies," Mark grinned.

"Fucking zombies." Tony laughed.

"Yeah!" I said.

"God, I feel great," Tony said.

"I've never had so much pussy."

"You know there'll be more, too. That's what's even better."

"They must pump oxygen in here or something for us to be able to fuck all night like this."

"I wish I could fuck like this every day. I'd never leave the house."

"Maybe it's a Halloween spell," I said.

"Ooooo . . . scary boys and girls." Tony lifted his arms in a bad imitation of a vampire.

Mark was staring at the stalls beside us. We heard the banging and then saw the signs.

We watched the feet under the stall of someone fucking

someone. I wondered why they bothered hiding. Maybe that was their fetish, to feel dirty in a bathroom stall.

There was something magical about forbidden sex. About catching a minute or two to do it somewhere weird and exciting.

I thought back to one time when I was a lot younger. I was dating a nymphomaniac exhibitionist. In some ways, it rocked. In others, I was one tired boy. Too bad we didn't get along outside of the weird and wonderful sex life we enjoyed.

One time we were at a club and she was rubbing against me on the dance floor. I was humping her right then and there and she slid her panties aside to let me slip in.

The only problem was, it wasn't a sex club, it was an ordinary dance floor.

I realized we couldn't do that for long or we'd get caught so we decided to head into the women's bathroom. We found an empty stall. She faced me, planting her lips against mine, rubbing her cunt against me as she raised one leg against the wall. I slipped into her again and began pumping in earnest.

In moments, we realized that the position was futile for getting off fast so we switched around. She leaned over the toilet and put her hands against the far wall while I hammered her sweet pussy. It didn't take long for me to come. I was afraid of getting caught, yet it was so wonderfully exhilarating.

Exhibitionist sex is addictive. I guess that's why I liked coming to these sex clubs. I could see by their feet that they had realized that standing doggy was the only way to go. It sounded like they were getting ready for the home stretch.

We left the bathroom and returned outside.

We saw a woman walking a man on a leash. He crawled on his hands and knees as she slapped him with a riding crop. He yelped now and again as her blows hit him. Yet he would try to hump any lady they walked past. The mistress would pull his leash tight to correct him, which he'd usually ignore. That would cost him another lash of the crop on his naked ass. She led him to a bowl and forced him to drink from it.

Hungrily he lapped at the water while she kicked at his butt. He kept lapping at the water, rebalancing himself as she kept trying to knock him over. As he was finishing up his drink, she walked around in front of him.

She spread her pussy lips wide open so we could all see her wet pink pussy. She brought the crop down to her side.

"Come."

He edged closer.

"Kneel." She hit the floor again with the crop.

He kneeled in front of her and buried his face between her legs. His tongue danced magically on her clit. She rolled her hips into his face, in rhythmic fucking motions. He gasped for air as she pounded into his face. His long tongue continued lapping at her cunt.

She changed her grip to grab his ears. She slammed him into her over and over. He started to whimper and bark.

"Quiet, you bad puppy."

He would be shushed for a while and then bark again. It must have been the vibration of his deep barks that set her off. She pulled him right into her and cried out as she came.

The man whimpered until she knelt down to pet him.

"Good dog." She patted his head. He panted happily and licked her face.

"Enough," she said as she picked up his leash. She led the man further until she found the Dom with the lady dog.

The Doms pulled the doggie couple together. The man sniffed at the woman's ass. The woman sniffed at the man's ass. They circled each other, sniffing and barking. For a moment I got so caught up in their antics that I forgot they were human. They rolled themselves into a sixty-nine, alternately sniffing and licking each other.

First, the woman climbed on top, and she pushed her pussy into the man's face. She took his dick into her mouth and nibbled on the end of it. Then the man was on top, his dick slipping in and out of the woman's mouth. His mouth was buried between her legs.

The man then got off the female and turned her over. She stayed on her hands and knees. He mounted her from behind, grabbing her breasts in his hands. He started off slowly, carefully pushing and pulling his dick into her. Before long, his pace started to pick up as impatience overcame him. He thrust into her, over and over again, howling as he did so.

She moaned and howled as his dick slammed into her. He fucked her hard and fast. She howled as he fucked her furiously. Their braying caught the attention of everyone in the room.

At last, he pulled out and sprayed her back with his come. He howled one last time as he shook the last of it off.

His dom patted his head and led him away.

We went on to discover what else there was to see in this strange room. Another cage before us held two beautiful women dressed in jungle outfits. Their antics were mimicking wild women by pulling at the bars of the cage and yelling in a strange tongue at us. We were going to ignore them at first, but then we stopped. There was something strangely appealing about their savagery.

As the women shrieked and screamed, the cage door was opened. The big black guy was pushed into the cage with the women. They all stood and stared at each other, as if they were wild animals, frozen with checking each other out. The women circled him, admiring his height and muscles. They ran their hands along his chest, his thighs, feeling his strength.

One of the women sank to her knees and took his huge dick into her mouth. Or at least, she tried to wrap her mouth around it. The other woman was rubbing him, getting off on his smooth gleaming skin.

We didn't stay to see what happened next. It was time to move on to the next room.

# CHAPTER 7.

After passing through steel double doors, we entered a makeshift forest. Old, blackened trees twisted from the floor to ceiling. The decoration in this room was very impressive. The illusion that this was a forest in the middle of the outdoors somewhere was executed in intricate detail. On the ceiling was a twinkling night sky, complete with the odd shooting star whizzing by. Thousands of tiny stars glittered and twinkled. Subtle streaks of lights indicated meteors and shooting stars.

A wish was perched on the edge of my lips. If only the stars were real. If only my wishes could come true. Wishes were meaningless in real life. If you wanted something, you went after it. Otherwise, there was no point. Wishes were the result of inspiration and perspiration.

My wish was real, though. My wish was desire and truth.

The problem with wishes is that even if they do come true, there is always a twist, a catch. Just like in those horror movies, even the most innocuous of wishes can be detrimental.

To wish for something is to covet it. And nothing good ever comes of coveting something or someone.

In my musing, it came to my attention that there was no music here except the soft, eerie fluttering of a flute. The sound was breathy and elusive, painting the picture of a moth dancing in starlight. Only there were no moths. There was no starlight either. This was a massive room, decorated like the others. The stars would bring me no wishes, and so it didn't matter.

The beginning part of the forest wasn't very big, and within a few feet we found ourselves standing in a clearing. Before us were three hunched figures peering into a large bubbling cauldron. There were trees in many directions and I knew we weren't alone in the room.

From behind a few trees, we could hear moaning and the sounds of flesh slapping against flesh. It seemed surreal as the flute continued to play.

A fire crackled beneath the cauldron, spitting and sparking. It seemed to me that it must be some sort of fire hazard to have a fire in a club—it added an interesting dynamic to the scene. Dry ice drifted into puffs of smoke, rising from the boiling contents of the cauldron and disintegrating into the air. The woods, the bubbling cauldron, and the three figures leering into the cauldron all made me feel deliciously creepy in a Halloween kind of way.

In the cauldron, there was some sort of reddish-brown liquid bubbling. It smelled of apples and cinnamon and something musky. The musky smell was like tree trunks or cedar or moldy old books. It was hard to describe. I tried to see what was floating in the cauldron but in the dim light and dry ice it was impossible to make out.

One of the figures looked up at me. I gasped as I stared at her hideous face. Her nose was long and gnarled, her chin nearly as dreadful. Great slats of wrinkles were set deep into her face, her dark eyes barely visible through the folds. Her hair, like that of the other two, was wild and wiry. There was gray in it with streaks of flaming red. Firelight danced in the shadows of her crevices. The woman beside her looked up at me as well. Her hair was curlier, with gold streaks running through it. She raised a hand to me, beckoning with a long, bony finger.

"Come closer, beautiful man. Let my sisters and me see you better."

The third hag looked up at the sound of her sister's voice.

"Look, Esmeralda. A beautiful prince has come to lay claim to his kingdom."

"And who does he bring with him?"

Esmeralda put down her giant spoon and walked around the cauldron. Mark and Tony edged closer to me.

"Don't be afraid, young men. We don't bite . . . much."
Esmeralda took Tony's hand and led him over to the cauldron.

"Aren't you curious about what we are doing?" Esmeralda
asked. Her voice was high and crackly. It sounded like static.

"Well, yes." Tony nodded as he sniffed gingerly at the smell
coming from the cauldron. "I must say that I am curious. Very
curious about what you are cooking up."

The witches all laughed. The sound was shrill.

They huddled together on the other side of the room, whispering to each other. Behind us, somewhere in the trees, the
couple was still going at it, enthusiastic howling echoing
around the room like rutting wolves. It all befit the scene in a
magnificent way. These three witches disturbed me even
though I knew we were just in a haunted house.

Something brushed against my leg. Looking down, my
heart skipped a beat as I jumped away from a giant spider.
The witches turned and looked at me as I clutched my chest.
The spider jerkily roamed away. As it turned, I saw a wind up
key on its side. It lurched along for a moment and then came
to a stop.

Mark wandered over to the cauldron, chuckling at the
sight of me jumping a foot in the air. I noticed he looked
back at the toy, as if expecting it to come scuttling after him.
I chuckled too.

Mark peered into the cauldron.

"What is it?" Mark asked.

"Put a finger in and taste it," the witch with the red flecks
in her hair dared.

"I'm not tasting any spook-house shit." Mark laughed. "Dry ice can't be good for you anyway."

"How badly do you want to know what is in it?" Esmeralda asked. She stepped beside me and ran her gangly finger along my face. The sensation was rather gross and I didn't want to encourage her.

"Why should we even care what is in it?" I asked.

"You know you want to know. Everyone wants to know," she teased.

"Maybe I'm one of the few who doesn't really care."

Esmeralda shrugged and returned to stirring the brew. My flippant response had clearly agitated her. She looked up at me once before returning her attention down to her gruel.

"You shouldn't have upset her," the witch with gold flecks in her hair warned. "She was only trying to play with you."

"Maybe I don't feel like playing." I started to walk away.

"Don't bother with him, Suspiria. He doesn't know what he's talking about," Esmeralda said. Her voice had a haughty twinge to it.

"Very well. But we have work to do. Halloween approaches and we need the energy of the cycles," said Suspiria. "Don't you agree, Aurora?"

Aurora was the witch with red flecks in her wild hair. She nodded solemnly.

The witches ignored us and returned to the cauldron, where they started to sing. At first, the song was wordless. A haunting tone fell from their lips. They whispered and sang and hummed. I was ready to walk out the door but the song started to lure me. I realized that they were no longer singing nonsense, but slowly real words were popping into their song.

The flute played louder and soon a soft tapping drum was heard. The fornicating couple must have finished, as there was only the sound of heavy breathing coming from the trees.

The witches stirred and sang and I felt a strange sorrow flooding through my loins.

> Sing the song of Savanna
> Her spirit lives on the wind
> Her mind is wide open
> She wants to let you in.
> Oh, moonlight bright
> Beyond the stars
> Her true love wanders
> Near and far.
> Clutching a torch
> He searches
> Searches
> Searches the midnight skies
> Hoping to see desire in her eyes
> Once more.
> When they meet
> The world will slip away
> They will become as one
> Together they will stay.

They started to sing the song again. I heard that word again. That name. The name of the girl. The top dom I guess it was.

"Who is Savanna?" I asked.

The witches stopped singing. All three of them raised their hands toward me.

"Savanna is everything. She is around us and in us," Esmeralda said.

"Savanna is everywhere. In the stars and in the moon." Suspiria sighed.

"Is this her special night?" I asked.

"Yes, this is her special night. The time of year when she can be anything she wants. She is a powerful sorceress. But she doesn't use her powers foolishly," Esmeralda said.

"Is Savanna married?" I asked.

"No. Not yet. She is searching for her lover," Suspiria said.

"She lost her lover," Esmeralda said.

"Oh. She had a lover. What kind of lover?" I asked.

"It was a lifetime ago. Literally," Suspiria said.

"She has been spending her life looking for him. Hoping to lure him back. But she can't seem to find him," Esmeralda sighed.

"What does he look like?" Tony asked.

"She doesn't know. She hopes he looks the same as he did before, but she isn't certain at all what to expect."

"She is hoping he will be here tonight."

"That is why we are making the special potion." The witch with the red streaks in her hair, Aurora, returned to the cauldron and lifted the ladle.

"What's the deal with the potion?" I asked.

"Does everyone take it?" Mark looked into the cauldron and shuddered.

"No. Once it is prepared, Savanna will take it and give it to a select person or two," Esmeralda said. She lifted the ladle and let the smoky potion drip from it. The spicy scent filled my nose.

"By the looks of that thing, she could do the whole club," Mark said.

"What happens when someone drinks the potion?" I asked. "Is it like a Jekyll-and-Hyde thing?"

Tony laughed and did a spastic imitation of a man drinking the potion and turning into a monster. Mark laughed. The witches watched, not saying a word. Finally, Suspiria spoke.

"The man will adore Savanna as she adored him in the life before. Then they can finally be together as they should have been."

"That sounds romantic and all, but what happens if a man who isn't the man drinks the potion?"

The witches all turned to each other and shrugged.

"Nothing," Esmeralda said.

"It's not going to backfire or anything?"

"Naww . . . not likely," Aurora said.

The way the witches looked at each other didn't convince me very much. I wondered if they even knew the answer. We'd all find out together, I figured.

"What's in it?"

"Apples, cinnamon, orange peel, lemon rind, rose petals, and some other things I really can't tell you," Esmeralda said.

"Come on, you can tell me."

"'Fraid not, young man. The cauldron has its secrets. That's what gives the spell its power."

"So I guess you stand here all night showing people your brew and babbling on about Savanna?" I asked.

"I do that, and many other things." Esmeralda reached for my crotch with those long gnarly fingers. I pushed her away, expecting her to be frail. She was stronger then I thought and held her grip.

"What's the matter, Prince? You want your ladies to be young and hot?"

"I'm not looking for any ladies. I just came here to have some fun on Halloween."

"What do you consider fun, Prince? Would staring at my tits help ease some of the pressure?"

Esmeralda lifted her shirt high above her head. I squeezed my eyes shut, expecting some sort of latex-induced monstrosity. Instead, as I slowly opened my eyes, I saw two of the largest breasts I'd seen off a strip-club stage. She stood in front of me, waggling her helium-filled balloons.

"Wow," I said, staring at their immensity.

"You want to touch them?" Esmeralda asked. I stared into that withered crone's face and then down at the size-bazillion silicone jobs bobbing near my mouth. Her nipples jutted forth, big enough to be a full breast for some women. I couldn't resist poking my tongue out at one of them. She pressed her breast closer. I circled that large hard nipple slowly, then flicked it gently. I made the mistake of glancing up at her face and all was lost once more.

"I think we'd better go, guys," I said.

"Don't you want to see us finish the spell?" Esmeralda asked

"Why? What needs to be done next?"

They started to sing again in the weird annoying rasp. It was like a dying wind heaving in and out of a bagpipe. The three witches returned to their posts around the cauldron. The blue-haired one turned the ladle between her hands. The golden-haired one watched expectantly as she peered in. The third witch had reached over to the little table behind her and threw a handful of some sort of herb into the cauldron. They laughed as the herbs swirled around the ladle. Esmeralda stirred the herb into the liquid with circular movement. More dry ice rose into the air. Suspiria threw something else into the cauldron. A shower of sparks rose up.

When darkness sprawls across the land
And the moon hangs heavy in the sky
Savanna raises her forceful hand
Across the world you'll hear her cry.
She searches for her lover true
A man who carries her heart.
And when at last they meet again
They'll never be torn apart.

The witches sang the song three times, hovering over the steaming cauldron, randomly throwing more pinches of this and that into the pot.

"Who will be the first to try?" Esmeralda pulled the ladle from the cauldron and dripped the contents back down into it.

The smell of burning apples and stale cinnamon filled my nose. That the potion went from a warm-smelling elixir to a foul-smelling stew so quickly was rather amazing. There must have been something quite fetid in that last handful of whatever it was she threw into the brew.

A few people came raucously into the room. A short stubby man wearing a loincloth led two women in leopard-print skirts by ropes. They had no tops and their breasts bobbed as they walked. Their laughter stopped when they saw the witches before them.

"Hey . . . where are the beautiful people?" the short stubby man shouted. "I paid good money to see beautiful people." He yanked the rope of the girls and they nodded in mock agreement.

"All I see is some old hags," one of the girls returned.

"Whatcha gonna do to us, hags? Cast a spell on us?" the other girl taunted.

"My eyes! They are burning out my eyes with their wretched ugliness. I demand a refund." Stubby Man wavered in mock pain.

The witches stopped stirring their potion and turned to stare menacingly at the man and women.

"I am paid good money to entice beautiful people. You don't belong here," Suspiria said, pointing at Stubby Man.

"Hey, I resemble that remark," Stubby Man said as his voice fell. He hung his head. "Sheesh."

He walked away, muttering about the witches. Mark and Tony laughed.

"He thinks he's Tarzan or something."

"Must have paid those Janes to come with him. No way girls that hot would hang out with a toad like him. But what do we have? Each other?"

"Don't know about you losers, but I've had pussy-breath all night long," Tony said.

"Yeah, but you know what? We still go home alone. We came alone and we'll be going home alone. And it will be the same day after day for who knows how long," I said.

"Jeez, man, you're bumming me out," Mark said.

"Naw, we're better then that old geezer. No way they're with him for real."

I sighed. He had a point. Any one of us could have made a call or two and had enough hot girls to join us to have a gang bang. Being young and handsome carried certain perks. Although it wasn't all fun and games, and often you ended up sitting home alone on a Saturday night.

It's not egotistical to say I'm handsome. I know I am. I was born that way. It's not vanity speaking, it's just a fact. Same as the fact that my hair is brown and I'm a man. I was blessed with a handsome, if flawed, face.

Even I could see in the baby pictures that this was no ordinary child. Many people have told me throughout my life that I should have been a model. I have to admit, I toyed with the idea. I thought about it a lot when I was a teenager. People stopped me on the street all the time when I was a kid, telling me what a nice-looking boy I was.

Looking back, you'd think I would have had a lot of confidence. But I didn't, really. That was why I always went back to Rosa.

Sure, I'd experiment here and there. I remember one time the captain of the cheerleading squad let me squeeze her tits under the bleachers. It was a scene right out of a movie, only instead of the handsome football stud it was me, Franco, the shy bookworm.

She had giggled as I felt her tits and it made my dick feel as if it were ten feet long. She was so young and firm and ripe. I can still feel those big delicious tits as if it just happened. Her nipples were so hard you could feel them right through the fabric of her uniform.

I was so nervous and so excited. She probably would have let me fuck her right then and there, now that I look back on it. But at the time, I couldn't believe she was even letting me touch her. I felt her for a few minutes, than mumbled something about how I had to go.

She never talked to me again after that.

At the time I thought she was horrified at the thought of me touching her. Now I know she probably wanted to get laid. She probably thought I found something lacking in her when it was just the opposite. I didn't feel worthy. And she probably felt rejected. Hindsight is certainly twenty-twenty when you get to a certain age.

Poor Stubby Man would never feel worthy, no matter how many girls he had on his arm. This was exemplified by the fact that he spared no expense at shooting a few more foul remarks at the witches before he left with his harem.

"That was not Savanna's bidding," Esmeralda said softly.

"What does it matter? He deserves to have fun like anyone else," I said.

"No one cares what you look like, especially here. It's what's in your heart that counts," Aurora said.

"That's a bunch of New Age tripe if I ever heard it," Tony said.

"There's something to be said for beauty." Mark nodded.

"Do you desire beauty?" Suspiria asked me.

"Not at all," I said. "I desire desire."

"Wonderful." Suspiria took me by the hand and led me over to one of the trees. She peeled off her robe to reveal a killer body. I was stunned by the paradox of a gorgeous body and hideous face.

"How do I know you would be worthy of Savanna, should you choose to try the potion?"

"I'm not trying any potion. Especially one that smells as foul as that."

Suspiria laughed.

"It isn't your choice. If Savanna decides you are to drink the potion, then drink the potion you will."

"No. I don't have to drink any strange concoctions that I don't want."

"I'm not going to belabor the point. Be aware that life as you know it is coming to a close. Soon you will eat, drink, and sleep for your mistress. Your body will crave no other."

"Not much of a chance of that happening. I've never been known to fall in love."

"A cruel man too. A cold, cruel man. You need to have the frozen heart of suspicion melted away."

SAVANNA SAMSON

Suspiria walked back over to the table by the cauldron. I
watched her beautiful ass walk away from me and lovely large
bobbing breasts walk back toward me again. She held in her
hand a large stick with a pointed crystal on the end. She raised
it in the air.

"You need to be healed, oh suspicious one. Remove your
clothing."

"I don't think so . . ."

Her voice was cold and firm.

"You will remove your clothing now."

It wasn't really my first choice, but something compelled me
to remove my clothes. Maybe it was the commanding tone of her
voice. Or maybe it was just her gigantic tits so near to my touch.

"Dear Franco," she began, "how you hide behind your clothes.
Why can't you just relax and enjoy the person you are inside
your skin?"

"I do enjoy the person I am inside my skin. I enjoy myself
quite a bit actually."

"You are such a liar, dear Franco. Stand over here and close
your eyes."

I went over to where she pointed. I closed my eyes. She
walked around me, humming. I felt her presence as she ran her
hands along my body, slowly. Her touch was oddly soothing
and it was like a layer of skin was being sloughed from me.

No, not skin. It was as if worry or agitation were slipping away.

"Open your mind," she instructed. "Open your mind to the
world of possibilities."

"How? How is it that I open my mind?"

·145·

Suspiria stood behind me and placed her rubbery fingers over my eyes.

"Look into the blackness. See the light beyond. There in that light is the world of possibilities."

Her breasts brushed against my back.

It was hard but I strained my eyes to see the light in the darkness. At last, it was coming to me. Very faintly, but there it was. Glimmering in the distance.

The world of possibilities.

"I see it," I said. "I see it."

Suspiria released her hands.

"Good. Now you may open your eyes."

I opened my eyes and the room had turned from an angry orange to a soft pink. The fire below the cauldron didn't spit and sputter so angrily. It crackled warmly, as if it were brewing hot chocolate for a close family gathering.

Esmeralda walked around in front of me. She had removed her mask, and standing before me was a lovely young lady with blue hair and a soft pretty face.

"Do you believe in the world of possibilities?" Esmeralda asked.

"I'm starting to."

She lifted the wand she held in her hand and pointed it at me.

The rest of the night
Will be fun and light
No more worries or sadness
Your heart fills with gladness.

I laughed and reached for the wand.

"No," Esmeralda said firmly and walked away from me. She replaced the wand on the table. She turned to look at the other two witches. Suspiria was straddling Tony, trying to pull his shirt off. Aurora was talking to Mark while she stirred the bubbling cauldron.

"What do you want?" Esmeralda asked, walking toward me.

"What do I want from life, or from you?"

"What do you want in this minute? In the world of possibilities."

"I want to touch those big beautiful breasts of yours," I said, as I reached out. I took them in my hands. They felt delicious as I rubbed them. I kneaded them together and lowered my face to them. I licked first one giant orb and then the other. I started at the top and worked my way around and around her breast until I ended up suckling on her sweet nipples. I sucked on the puckered nipples, drawing strength from her calm soothing touch on my head.

My hands held her hips as I ran my tongue down between her breasts and into her flat navel. She didn't have much of a belly. I nuzzled the inside of her thighs. My lips licked and tasted her in little love bites. She spread her legs. My tongue flickered at her clit, hidden so prettily in her labia. I took one of her labia lips in my teeth and gently pulled on it. She moaned softly. I did the same to the other lip. My tongue returned to her treasure and I lapped at it, softly at first and then harder.

Slowly my hands ran from her hips to her pussy. I spread her lips and licked even harder at her clit. She wriggled in delight above me.

"More," she sighed. I lovingly lapped at her. I slipped my tongue inside where she was growing wetter by the second. My tongue was a hard little penis as I darted in and out of her hole. I returned to lapping at her clit. I took it in my teeth and flicked my tongue against it. She pushed her hips into me, as if she were fucking me.

"Oh, yes, Handsome Prince. Suck on my clit."

I sucked it hard, enjoying her writhing beneath my touch. I looked up at her face and saw her head was back as she enjoyed the dance of my tongue on her cunt. She was trembling and I knew it wouldn't be long before she came. I slipped one of my fingers into her hole and moved it gently in and out.

"Oh yes, like that," she sighed. Her clit throbbed in my mouth, growing harder as she grew more excited. Her legs were spreading wider apart and she held my head as if she wanted to ram it right up her cunt.

Esmeralda pulled on my head spastically, shivering as she suddenly cried out. Her juices poured into my mouth. I lapped at them hungrily, keeping my tongue dancing on her clit. I shoved three fingers into her and could touch her g-spot. I rubbed on it while sucking on her clit. She held my hand with her hand, working it into herself against her g-spot. It was hard to keep my mouth on her clit, she was moving so rapidly. But I hung in there and she gushed into my mouth as she cried out with another orgasm. I licked the juices streaming down her legs. First one side and then the other.

Mark had one of the witches, Aurora, lying on the ground while he ate her out. Her hips bucked against his face, her hands clawing at the earth. Behind him, Tony was bending Suspiria over the prop table. He had his big hard dick in his hand and was aiming it right for her juicy hole. His face changed into total pleasure as he sank deeply into her. She moaned as she felt his length entering her. He held himself in her for a moment as if to savor the moment. Then, as if he could control himself no longer, he started thrusting quickly into her. His hands were gripped on her ass as he slammed her. The prop table rocked precariously and she moaned with delight at his hard fucking.

Mark had slid his fingers into the witch. From where I was, I could see two fingers up her twat and two up her ass. He moved them in and out slowly as Aurora twitched with glee.

My witch, Esmeralda, had caught her breath. She motioned to the tree stump over by a clump of trees.

"Sit on that," she instructed. I sat down and she knelt before me. She took my cock into her mouth. It was already half hard but the minute she wrapped those warm lips around it, I was good to go. She gobbled it down, lustily slurping and sucking on it. She ran her tongue up the side and swirled around the head for a moment. She ran her tongue down the other side. She raised herself up higher so she cold get a good angle as she deep-throated me again. It took all my composure to keep from shooting into her mouth. Thinking about her in the ugly witch mask helped shift gears for a moment.

Esmeralda suckled me as if she hadn't sucked a cock in weeks. Her skill was admirable as she tried to coax the come from my rod. But I wouldn't come. There was so much more to do.

Slowly, I reached over to her and drew her to me. I sat her down so that her pussy enveloped my cock. We faced each other and her tits rubbed against my chest. I held her by her firm round ass, hoping she wouldn't fall off. My years of working out at the gym paid off as I lifted her up and down on my rod. It felt amazing. Her breasts hit me in the face as she jiggled up and down, up and down. She tried her best to add traction, but I held her like a pretzel, slamming that delicious cunt down on my dick over and over again. She was so tight, so hot. It was as if I had found my home. My cock throbbed; it ached as I tried to decide whether I wanted to come yet. It would feel so good to just let loose inside that dark hole, but there was still more. The night was young and I needed to feel more abandonment. Tasting the night had awakened parts of me that had lain dormant far too long.

For so many nights I haunted the bars or the fetish clubs, knowing I could have any woman I desired. My dark-eyed stare rendered most women speechless until they got to know me. My presence was commanding, after years of practicing posture and facial expressions in the mirror. But so seldom could I taste pleasures of the flesh without paying a price. Whether it was in the dance of coercion or in the extricating of oneself the next morning, there was always some work involved in getting to go to the school of carnal knowledge.

Tonight the samples were free.

Tonight I was letting loose in the spirit of Halloween. My dark side was out once more and it felt great. Charming, daring Franco could do whatever he wanted as long as he kept his looks.

I looked into the eyes of the witch and she smiled as she bounced breathlessly.

"You are amazing," she gasped.

"So are you and your tight little cunt," I said, fixing her with my killer stare. She blinked and looked away, her face growing red. When she looked back, her blue eyes were large and fearful.

"You will fuck me all night?" she asked.

"I will fuck you 'til you come again and again."

"You mustn't forget what you came for."

"I came to meet people like you." I slowed my pace as I tried to catch my breath. She stopped moving and slid off.

"You have more to do. You have to go on your journey."

"But I'm not finished with you yet," I said. She leaned over to kiss me and pulled my cock in her hand.

"You want to come? Finally?" she asked.

"I want to come all over your pretty little ass," I said. I leaned her over the stump and kissed her neck. I nuzzled my chin into her, and she wriggled in anticipation. My breath was hot on her neck and I moaned a little. My hand was on my cock as I pulled on it thinking about how good it was going to feel rammed up to the hilt in her hot little cunt. I stood back and looked at her. Her ass in the air, ready and waiting for me. Her pussy already gaping from my big dick slamming into her earlier. My cock throbbed at the thought of how good it would feel to be back inside of her.

I moved toward her and rubbed my shaft against her butt.

"Fuck me, Franco. Fuck me so that I scream."

I teased her some more, rubbing my cock along her gaping hole. I played with her lips, touching our warm flesh together. At last, I had to be inside of her. I plunged my cock into her, feeling her parting to let me in. It was as if I were tunneling through a warm slick of mud. I pulled my cock back and forth, widening her with one hand while my fingers reached around and patted her clit.

"Fuck me, Franco. Don't tease me so . . ."

My own urgency was setting the pace and my hips began to thrust into her. Tony was still fucking his witch, but now they were leaning against a tree. She held on to lower branches for support, leaning against the trunk. Tony held her by the hips with one hand, slamming her cunt onto his cock. The other was propping up her leg. I thought about how deep he must be inside of her. The idea of the sensations he was feeling compelled me to slam into my witch even harder.

Mark was doing a sixty-nine with his witch. She crouched over him and he eagerly lapped at her twat while she sucked on his huge dick. She spit on it and rubbed the spit around with her hands. She cupped his balls and tugged on them. She twisted herself around so that she could take his balls into her mouth.

I fucked Esmeralda even harder. Her moans were turning to cries, and through my frantic thrusting I could feel her clenching against me as she came. Her pulsing nearly caused me to come but I held back.

Mark thrust his cock into Aurora's mouth, and she pulled on his balls again. She turned around so that she could sit on his big hard dick. She looked over at me as she lowered herself down onto him. Her eyes rolled back as she sighed. She impaled herself on him, enjoying the sensation for a moment. She lifted herself again and started to work fucking him in earnest.

Over at the tree, Tony was into his final thrusts. He waited a moment and then slammed himself into Suspiria with a groan. She put her arms around his shoulder, her hips moving as she squeezed the last of his come from his dick.

Mark was fucking his witch hard as she crouched above him. His cock moved in and out so rapidly that he was like a machine. Aurora shuddered and cried above him. She rode wave after wave of orgasm, liquid rushing down her leg. Mark bucked one more time and he cried out as he came.

I could last no longer myself and I pulled out, spraying my load all over the back of the witch with a gasp.

The six of us lay quietly for a while, catching our breath. The soft flute music started up again. Soon, more people were entering into the room. The witches began to pull their costumes back on.

Tony, Mark, and I dressed as the witches sang. Their haunting song followed us out of the room.

When darkness sprawls across the land
And the moon hangs heavy in the sky
Savanna raises her forceful hand

Across the world you'll hear her cry
She searches for her lover true
A man who carries her heart
And when at last they meet again
They'll never be torn apart.

# CHAPTER 8.

The room looked like a laboratory right out of a horror movie. Wires and cables snaked along the ceiling. A big metal machine with flashing buttons and dials blinked in the middle of the room. Rods projected high above the machine crackled with blue streams of static electricity dancing between the poles. There was a giant plastic vat of some sort of liquid in which a body appeared to be floating. In front of us was a long operating table with shackles. Several smaller tables surrounded it, filled with shiny instruments and leather straps.

At the top of the machine, a man stood, looking down on us. He wore a white lab coat and black-rimmed glasses. His shoulder-length hair was in disarray. He laughed as he paced above us. He spun giant wheels that looked like ship steering wheels. More lights blinked and the greenish glow flickered.

"Max," the man in the lab coat leaned over the railing on the top of the machine and shouted down. Underneath the platform, a petite woman wearing a lab coat came out holding a clipboard. She had short red hair and cat's-eye glasses.

"Yes, doctor?" she called up.

"Turn it on."

"Yes, doctor."

She went over to a large panel of buttons and knobs. She pushed a few buttons and pulled a switch. The electricity surged again and the crackling grew louder. The machine hummed and sputtered. It sounded like a rusty door trying to open.

"Christ, that's loud," Tony said, holding his ears.

"You're not kidding." The machine groaned and moaned. It reluctantly coughed and spurred until the vat of water started to bubble. The doctor ran over to the platform above the bubbling vat.

"What does the gauge say?" he asked.

"I think it's ready, doctor," Max said, peering at a few dials and marking down the numbers in her book.

Mark laughed. "I love this Frankenstein shit."

"It's like it's right out of the movies," I said. I noticed that the body in the water was twitching. The wires attached to the torso jerked along the top, shaking the cables and wires above it.

The doctor wrung his hands together as he ran along the platform. His assistant read numbers off the dials and continued to write them down. His footsteps echoed along the metal staircase as he hurried down toward us.

"You should see . . . you would not believe it." He stopped in front of us.

"Sorry. Allow me to introduce myself. I'm Dr. Frankenstein." He took each of our hands and shook it furiously.

"Dr. Frankenstein. You may have heard of me?"

"Yes," I said as he shook my hand. "You make ugly monsters out of corpses, right?"

Tony and Mark chuckled as he clutched my hand tightly.

"Not so . . . not so at all. You've heard rumors, not the truth. What you will see will amaze you."

"The doctor knows of what he speaks," Max said.

"So what do you have then, doc?"

"Max, come here . . . come here now." The doctor waved Max over. "This is Max, my lovely assistant."

As I shook Max's hand I was aware of how tiny she was. She was petite, like a little doll. Her feet were so tiny I thought they could fit in the palm of my hand. She wore pumps but even the little bit of height didn't add much. Max was stern and firm and obviously in awe of the doctor. Her voice had a strange European accent.

She shook hands with Mark and Tony, then turned back to me.

The doctor stood over the vat and trailed his hand in the water.

"Warm . . . warm like the liquid of the womb."

"You are creating life."

"Yes, life."

"Max, prepare my creation for resurrection."

Max started to unhook the wires and strap large belts to the shackles around the creature's wrists and ankles. The body still quivered and twitched. The water was too murky to make out any features. It grew apparent when a hand flipped up into the air that the creature was wrapped in bandages.

There was much splashing and strapping and fiddling with the monster. At last, it seemed like they were finished whatever it was they had been trying to accomplish.

Dr. Frankenstein laughed maniacally as he pulled on the ropes. A complicated mass of ropes and pulleys hoisted the creation out of the water. The creature lurched into the air. One of the straps on the wrists wasn't fastened correctly and it tugged open. The wrist flopped down, splashing into the water.

"Dammit!" Dr. Frankenstein shouted.

He lowered the ropes and the pulleys dropped the creature back down into the tank. He turned to Max.

"What is this? What kind of sloppy work is this?" Max lowered her eyes.

"I'm sorry. I guess I didn't tighten it enough."

"You must be punished." Dr. Frankenstein's eyes flashed furiously.

"Please . . . I can fix it. Let's just get her out of there."

"No. First, you need to learn that sloppy work is not permitted or acceptable. Once you learn your lesson, then we can proceed."

"But the coordinates. . ."

"Forget the coordinates. Bring me your tools."

Max slowly walked over to one of the tables and returned with handcuffs, a ball gag, and a leather strap.

Dr. Frankenstein handcuffed her to one of the large poles that ran up the side of the machine. She stood with her back to him.

"Bend over."

She did as she was told. We admired the view of her bottom that peaked out from beneath her short little lab coat. She didn't appear to be wearing any underwear, which was an added treat.

He stood around the front of her and fastened the ball gag around her mouth. He played with her short hair, running his fingers through it until he pulled tightly.

"Remember, what we learned? Check and double check." She nodded, her eyes wide. He let go of her hair and went behind her holding the leather strap in his hand. He spanked her ass and legs with it several times.

"Franco, you must help teach this wayward child a lesson." Dr. Frankenstein handed the strap to me.

"If you insist."

I raised the strap and lowered it several times on her little butt. She wiggled and squirmed.

"Will you remember what you are supposed to do, next time?" I asked.

She gurgled through her ball gag.

"What was that?" I hit her harder, this time on the back.

"Yesth!" she managed to scream out at me.

"Good. Mistakes are costly. Time is money. Money is time."
I handed the strap back to the doctor. He nodded at Tony.

"You need to punish her as well."

"Right on." Tony snatched the strap from the doctor and
waved it in the air a bit, feeling the weight of it and how it
hung in his hand. When the strap met flesh, it hit with a
loud smack. She quivered as a long line appeared on her butt
cheeks. Tony brought the strap down again and again. At last
he stopped and handed the strap to Mark.

Mark lightly slapped her back, crisscrossing his strokes. His
tapping gradually grew harder until he was striking her with a
force similar to the rest of us. Mark focused mainly on her
little shapely legs. When he was done, Max had a series of
stripes from head to toe.

The doctor regarded her with a smile. He unhitched her
from the post and removed her ball gag. She spit and drooled
for a moment, then wiped her mouth.

Max took a moment to adjust her clothes and demeanor.
Within minutes, she was back to being the efficient assistant.

Max reached into the tank and fixed the bracelet on the
creature's wrist. She double checked all the restraints, chains,
and pulleys. Once she was satisfied that everything was in
order, she raised her thumb to signal OK.

Once more the creature was hoisted into the air. Through a
series of pulleys and ropes, the body was swung from its
watery resting place and over to the long metal table.

The body was shackled firmly by the arms, legs, and across
the torso.

We watched with interest as wires were added to the extremities of the creature. Wires ran into her fingers and toes, into her bandaged breasts, and into the top of her head. We couldn't see her face or her flesh, as she was tightly wrapped. Max tugged and fiddled with all the wires while Dr. Frankenstein ran back up to the top of the giant machine with all the big wheels.

"Is she ready?" the doctor called down.

"Yes," Max said.

The doctor flipped a giant switch. There was static and a blue flash. Smoke puffed out of a few wires. Sparks flew, the machine started to whirr and buzz and then fell silent.

"What is it now?" the doctor cried out in frustration.

"I don't know."

"Find it. Fix it," he barked. Max searched through the wiring as the doctor came barreling down the stairs. He grabbed her by the arm and dragged her over to a chair. With a flip of his strong hands, he flung her over his knee and raised her skirt.

"You are too careless today. Too sloppy. You need to fix my creation."

He spanked her several times on her ass. She kicked her little legs in the air as his hand met her ass.

"Yes, doctor. I will be more careful."

"Next time, you are in deep trouble. Very deep trouble."

"Yes, doctor."

Our focus returned to the body on the table. It was a woman. There was no doubt about it. The bandages clung to her torso, her breasts jutting through in one spot where the bandages were coming loose. There was no way to tell if she was beautiful or hideous. There was no sign of blood or anything. Max slipped off Dr. Frankenstein's lap and returned to work fiddling with the wiring.

At last she nodded.

"It is ready, doctor," she said.

The doctor went back up the stairs. He looked down one more time, as if to make sure everything was all right. He flipped a couple of switches and turned one of the mighty wheels. The machine was engaged. The lights flickered wildly with a kaleidoscope of colors. The room was like a strobe-lit dance floor. The machine moaned and groaned even more loudly then before. Electricity sparked and poofed, creating little blue surges of dancing light between wires. I could hear the static in the air. It made my hair stand on end. I didn't know if my hair was really standing on end, but my scalp and arms felt creepy-crawly goosebumpy.

Near the ceiling, the tall rods were a dazzling display of electricity dancing back and forth. This was definitely something out of some old science-fiction movie.

The doctor ran down the stairs in excitement, anxious to see his creation. He searched around for his tools. Max led him over to the creature and calmly placed a pair of scissors into his hands.

The doctor cut through the bandages around the creature's nose and mouth. As the bandages were carefully peeled away by Max, the creature gasped and shuddered. Water leaked from her mouth and nose. She snorted and snuffled.

The doctor cut around her face, pulling away the sticky,

soggy bandages. The creature squinted at the light. She tried to put her hands up to her face but they were tied to the table. She pulled against her restraints, grunting.

"Relax, Agatha. It will be over soon enough," Dr. Franken-stein said soothingly to his creature. Agatha stopped flailing for a while as her large dark eyes watched him cut away the bandages.

"Max, give me a hand," he commanded. Max helped unpeel the bandages.

Slowly the fabric was shucked away from her like a cocoon. The creature that lay before us was stunning.

"This is fantastic," Dr. Frankenstein muttered. "Absolutely fantastic."

He pressed a button and the table rose up just like in the movies, until the creature was in an upright position. The doctor shone a flashlight into Agatha's eyes. She turned her head away, wincing from the light. The doctor examined her from head to toe. His poking and pawing were agitating her. She struggled against her bindings. From where I was standing, there wasn't a mark on her except around her neck and wrists. No other indications where she was sewn together were apparent and even the neck and wrist scars were minimal. She was nothing but beautiful perfection.

Her legs were long and firm. She had a beautiful pussy. Max squirted shaving cream on Agatha's pussy. Agatha squirmed.

"Be calm, Agatha," Max said firmly as she shaved Agatha's pussy.

Tony watched Max and Agatha intensely.

"Do you need help with that?" he asked Max.

Max shook her head.

"This is a job for professionals," she said in her businesslike manner.

Max spread Agatha's pussy lips delicately, pulling the razor very carefully. The creature's clit was swollen. It took all my self-control not to lick it.

The doctor was brushing the creature's long, black hair. He gazed at her with adoring eyes.

"My beautiful creature. You are mine . . ." he sighed.

Max looked sharply at him and cleared her throat. The doctor blushed and hurriedly changed his statement.

"Well, you are my creation." His voice was plaintive, nearly whining. "But you belong to Savanna." He stood up and stared over at the tank sadly.

"Savanna?" I asked.

"Savanna wants a playmate. Savanna is very lonely," Dr. Frankenstein said, folding up the used bandages and throwing them in the garbage.

"I heard that Savanna was hoping that tonight would be the night her lost lover returns to her," I said.

"Yes, she pines for her lover," the doctor said. "Yet she is insatiable. While she waits, she needs to have many. She thirsts for excitement. It is never enough. Each year, I make her a new creation and it's never enough."

He threw his hands up in despair.

"This creation would be enough for anyone," Mark said, running his hands along Agatha's legs.

"There is always a problem," Dr. Frankenstein said. "Always."

"She's gorgeous. What problem could there be this time?"

The doctor muttered and mumbled as he crossed the room and went to his desk. He flipped through notes, checking and double-checking facts and figures. He made a few calculations. At last, he seemed satisfied. He pushed his glasses back up to his nose.

"She will be perfect for Savanna. Look. We can test her ourselves to be certain."

Dr. Frankenstein went over to one of the tables. He returned with a leather strap thong and a big dildo. He stood over the creature. Max was still primping her.

"Savanna can have her any way she wants. Look, I'll show you. Out of the way, Max."

He fixed the leather straps around the creature's hips and ass. He attached the dildo. It stood straight up from the creature's freshly shaved pussy.

"Imagine beautiful Savanna enjoying herself on that perfection. This dildo is Savanna's favorite."

"I've never seen Savanna so I'm not sure what to imagine."

"You will see her soon enough. Of this, I'm sure."

He took the dildo off again.

"In the meantime, we have to make sure that the creature works. That she can withstand regular wear and tear."

"How do you do that?" I asked.

"Why, I'm going to fuck her, of course. I have to make sure that all her nerves are wired up properly."

"Sounds weird and gross," I said.

"Does she look weird and gross? I don't think so. I think that it won't be long before your own dick is itching to plow through my creation."

I looked at Agatha. Her pussy was smooth and she was already in a state of arousal.

"She certainly has a nice clit," I said, appreciatively.

"Yes, she does, doesn't she?

"Do you want to touch it?" Dr. Frankenstein looked right at me, as if he had an x-ray into my mind.

"Why don't you taste her? Tell me if she meets your standards?"

I leaned over and eagerly explored that beautiful area between Agatha's legs. I lapped at her pussy, still smelling the faint scent of shaving cream. She pressed her pelvis into my face as I licked her a little bit harder and faster. It was fun, watching the creature react to my practiced tongue. She grunted and pulled at the restraints.

The doctor pushed me away.

"Enough. I get to try her first. But of course you boys are welcome to stay around and play with her when I'm done."

The doctor lowered the table back until she was lying down again. He unlashed the many buckles and restraints.

Agatha sat up. Bewildered, she rubbed her wrists and ankles as she stared around the room.

"Do you know where you are?" the doctor asked. The creature stared at him with a blank look.

"Good. She can't talk. Hopefully she can't think either. She is just a toy for Savanna."

"I wish she was my toy," Tony said wistfully. We all nodded in agreement. Agatha was pure beauty, pure joy. Her skin was pale and flawless except for marks on her neck and hands where she had been sewn together. Her eyes were dark and large. Her mouth was big and pouty, perfect for sucking dicks. The doctor had done on a marvelous job on her proportions. Her breasts were large and her hips voluptuous.

Dr. Frankenstein held his hand out so that she could slip off the table.

"Easy now. Careful. We don't want you to get damaged."

Agatha gingerly stepped onto the floor. It must have been cold on her bare feet. She looked down as the coldness ran through her body.

"Walk," Dr. Frankenstein commanded.

Agatha walked a few steps and turned to look back at us. She was perfection. Her breasts were high and huge. Her waist was tiny, her stomach flat. She had a nice round ass. She could have been made for me. She looked like the elusive trophy-wife image I had been carrying around in my head for years. Her tentative baby steps turned into confident walking. Soon she was strutting around the room, her ass swinging like Marilyn Monroe.

Agatha returned to Dr. Frankenstein, watching him expectantly.

"Let me take a good look at you," he said.

He peered into her eyes, her nose, her mouth. He worked his way down her body, feeling and pulling at her skin. When he got to her clit, he touched it, wiggling his finger against it.

"We already know that works, I guess." He laughed, nudging me.

"I guess so." I still could taste her on my lips.

"Max, come here." Dr. Frankenstein waved Max back over to us.

Max stood in front of the doctor.

"Go on the floor, on your hands and knees."

She did as she was told.

"Now you, my creature, my Agatha, sit on her back."

We all watched as the beautiful creature sat on Max like a chair. It was strangely erotic, seeing that taut firm body sitting on the tiny little body of the assistant.

Dr. Frankenstein couldn't keep his hands from Agatha's perfect tits another moment. He pulled on them, fondling and caressing their plump full shape. Agatha patiently sat, watching him with those large dark eyes.

The doctor led Agatha over to the table and instructed her to lie down. She did as she was told. Within minutes, the doctor had straddled the table and was fucking Agatha. She moaned, as a woman would moan when a man is giving her pleasure. Her moans and sighs excited the doctor, and he plunged into her with great abandon. It wasn't long before he came.

He pulled his dick out of her.

"Suck my come from my cock, Agatha," he ordered. She lapped at his wet dick, slurping back his come like she had been doing it for years.

As Agatha licked the last drops of come from the head of his cock, he turned to look at us.

"Would you like to try her?" he asked.

Mark walked over to the creature and took one of her luscious tits into his hands. He squeezed it, rolling it around until her nipple was straight up in the air. He danced his tongue along her nipple, giving it little butterfly flicks. Tony was rubbing her legs.

His hands massaged up her calves and thighs. He planted his hands firmly on her butt cheeks. He spread them wide, staring at her pretty little ass.

"I'd like to fuck that sweet ass," he said.

"Be my guest," the doctor said.

While Tony fucked her ass, Mark shoved his dick into her mouth.

"Oh, that's so sweet," Tony said as he slid in and out of her. "You did a fantastic job, doctor."

"I know. I think Savanna will be pleased with this one. And when she's not using it, the rest of us can have fun with her. She's capable of fucking for days at a time without the need for rest."

"Wouldn't that be a wonder?" I sighed. "Imagine, doing nothing but fucking for a week. And having the stamina for it!"

"Let's change things around a bit," Tony suggested as he pulled out of Agatha.

Tony lay back on the table. They lay the creature on top of him so that his dick slid into her ass. Her pussy was wide open and gleaming. Mark rammed his dick into her mouth.

"C'mon, Franco. Use your love pole on that hot, juicy cunt."

I stared with wonderment at that delicious pink meat. My hand pulled on my cock, stroking it so that it would get harder. Watching her squirm up and down Tony's cock, and knowing how good it must feel in that hot little ass, made me mad with desire. I approached her and slid my cock in to the hilt. The sensation of us both fucking her was fantastic. Sometimes our strokes matched thrust for thrust. Sometimes I used fast quick staccato strokes while he massaged her ass-hole slowly. Her cunt clenched around my pole in a throbbing intensity. She groaned and I sought out her special spots. She cried and shuddered, her arms and legs flying all over the place.

Max crouched on the end of the table, sucking the doctor's dick. Mark turned around and slammed his dick into her little cunt. She squealed with delight.

For a while, we must have looked like some strange fucking machine out of Dr. Frankenstein's lab. We were a flurry of mouths and holes and pounding pleasure. We moved as one and we moved independently.

One by one, we blew our loads.

By the time it was all over, the only one not gasping for air was Agatha.

# CHAPTER 9

*T*he auditorium was mammoth in both height and width. A magnificent rendering of an old Paris opera house, with several rows of crushed red velvet seats that led to a stage, it boasted of elegance and drama. Inset into the walls were several small balcony boxes. The top ones were ornately decorated with cherubs gilded in gold. There were curtains across the back of the boxes. A few of the boxes held audience members who were watching the show intently. There was a large crystal chandelier in the center of the room, with hundreds of lights creating a dazzling star. We stood at the back of the auditorium, as we watched the play already in progress.

Several other party people were scattered in seats. Most watched the stage with rapt attention.

The stage itself was a spectacle. The scene was like something out of Wagner, with billowing pillars of fire emanating from torches in the floor. It was as if we were in a mountain or cave. Someplace secret and forbidden. In addition to the cave-like atmosphere, there were hundreds of candles. In the center of the stage, there was a large piano.

The music coming from the piano was lush and rich. In front of the stage, in the orchestra pit, I could see the top of the conductor's head as he led the orchestra through a chilling barrage of melody. On the stage, a woman was singing.

The singer looked exactly like something out of a Paris opera house way back in the day. She had on a long white gown with a lace-up bodice. Her long brown curly hair hung down to her waist. She had some sort of weave with flowers in her hair. She sang high, beautiful music while the pianist played. The orchestra swelled as she reached a fever-pitch. Her voice warbled and as an opera lover, I was pleased with the tone and clarity she possessed. I motioned to a row of seats about halfway down into the auditorium.

As we sat under that magnificent chandelier, I beheld the marvels of the room. Every inch of the house, from floor to ceiling, was celebrated with an interesting color or pattern. There were paintings on the ceiling, mostly of angels and other heavenly creatures peering down from the clouds. Mounted into the lower scalloped boxes were angels and gargoyles, staring down from the stage. Their long bodies with winding limbs and tails curved under the box and down the wall.

The curtains on the stage were pinned back in thick ripples of burgundy velvet. The edges were trimmed with silk and long golden cords held to either side of the stage. The crystals in the chandelier cast rippling reflections along the ceiling and walls and occasionally glinted off of a set piece.

The girl sang her heart out, pining for someone somewhere. Her singing echoed the hollow ache that cropped up in the pit of my stomach now and again. She wanted someone to love, to hold her, to protect her from the darkness. The idea was as old as humans, I supposed. We all want to be loved and love, to be held, to be comforted. We all want to know there is someone there beside us in the darkness to protect us from the horrors of the night.

How special would that person have to be? To share the ride of the roller coaster of life on a daily basis. I had never lived with anyone. I had intense relationships where we might as well have been living together, but I always had my own place to go back to when I was finished. I was always finished at some point.

The haunting song picked up into a catchy little number.

I supposed that at some point you either give up or settle for what you can get, or you spend your life wandering alone, knowing that love could happen at any minute. This could be the moment, the night. It happens to everyone at some point, so it was just a matter of time. So why settle. Why should anyone settle? The façade is found out in the end.

The song comforted me in a strange way as I thought about how I should be glad I never settled. My heart was wounded, but I continued on. And now I had a mystery to solve as well. I was to meet my destiny.

I laughed to myself. Like that's going to happen. My buddies turned to look at me and I realized that I must look half crazy, laughing at myself. I put my hand up to indicate that my revelation would be too hard to explain. They returned to watching the show.

As the girl stepped away from the piano, something above my head caught my attention. I looked up in time to see a cloaked figure swing down a rope pulley contraption and land on the stage. He was tall, menacing because he wore a half mask on his face. I had watched enough horror movies to know this was the Phantom of the Opera.

"Cool," whispered Mark.

The Phantom grabbed the girl, who by now I surmised was Christine. The orchestra stopped playing.

"Go on . . . play," the Phantom urged the conductor. Christine was stricken with fear yet stared at the Phantom as he started to sing the song she was just singing. They sang a duet as his hands roamed across her breasts.

As the song ended, a young man with a blond ponytail stood up in one of the boxes.

"Let her go."

The Phantom laughed.

"Never."

The man was smartly dressed for the period. He obviously

came from wealth of some sort. Common sense told me it was the guy who had the hots for Christine. His name was Raoul or Ralph or something. We had arrived in time for the show. I wondered how many times they would have to perform this show this evening. Or was it one long continuous scene, played out in real time?

"I'm coming down," Raoul said. He slid his way over the gargoyle head and crawled along the mammoth body until he was even with the stage. He leaped down as the Phantom laughed.

"Nice fancy footwork," the Phantom said. "What are you going to do now?"

Raoul stood to the side, watching as the Phantom pulled one of Christine's breasts out of her dress. Christine had gone into some kind of faint or reverie after seeing Raoul jump down to the stage. The Phantom twisted and tweaked her nipple while his other hand held her firmly. He cradled her so that her head was resting in the crook of his elbow.

Raoul seemed to be hypnotized by the sight. The Phantom smiled.

"Come closer and see. See the delights Christine has to show you."

"I can't. I'm a gentleman."

"A true gentleman knows how to please the ladies. Isn't that right, Christine?"

Christine opened her eyes and nodded slowly.

"Pleasure is the true music."

Raoul kneeled down and took her breast in his mouth. He suckled and fondled it as the Phantom held it.

"That's right, Raoul, roll it between your teeth. The ladies love it rolled and flicked and suckled." The Phantom's tone, slow and deep, was made even more exotic by his French accent. The way Christine limply lay there while Raoul suckled her tit was a turn-on. I was hoping that the show would continue along this vein.

"You want to please the young lady?" the Phantom asked.

"I always please my lady," Raoul said, hesitantly.

"Have you ever fucked your young lady?" the Phantom leered at him.

"Why, of course not. I wouldn't do that until we were married. She is a treasure that needs to be delicately unwrapped."

"But of course, Raoul. All women are virgins when they marry," the Phantom sneered sarcastically.

"Allow me my illusions, kind sir," Raoul spat.

The Phantom stroked Christine's hair and nuzzled his face into her curls.

"Come closer, Raoul. Smell the sweetness of our fair maiden."

Raoul took a section of her tousled curls into his hand and raised it to his nose. He took a deep breath.

"She smells of roses in springtime after an afternoon shower." Christine stirred.

"She awakens, Raoul. Tell her of your desire."

Raoul looked at Christine, his face a cross between desire and trepidation. She fluttered her lashes and looked over to Raoul.

"Save me, Raoul. Save me from the ravages of my dear, sweet demon."

Raoul took her hand.

"I will save you. I will give myself fully to you."

Christine pulled his hand to her cheek and cupped it so that her hand was over his.

"I will do anything for you, Raoul."

The Phantom breathed into her ear.

"And me. What will you do for your master?"

"I have served my master well. It is time to release me."

The Phantom pushed her away.

"Never."

Raoul grabbed Christine and held her close.

"Leave her alone. Can't you see she doesn't want you?"

The Phantom raised his hands dramatically.

"Who gave you your voice? The voice of an angel. And the music to enhance it? Who was your teacher? Your friend? Your lover?"

Christine buried her head into Raoul's chest.

"Don't torment me so with your words. I won't listen to you."

"You will do as I say. You will do as your master compels you to do."

The Phantom threw a fireball. A flame shot up and when the smoke cleared, he was gone.

Raoul and Christine exited the stage. A giant mirror and a bed were pushed onto the stage.

Christine entered from a door on the side and went over to the mirror. She stared at herself. Slowly she ran her hands across her chest, as the Phantom had done. She closed her eyes and tilted her head to the side in a reverie.

"I long for his touch again. Yet he is such a monster."

Christine pulled her breasts from her blouse and played with the nipples. She tweaked them and pinched them, watching herself in the mirror.

"His hands are rough, yet they entice me with images of places I long to visit."

Her hands cupped her breasts and she raised them. She pushed them together and stood sideways, admiring her cleavage. She let them drop and went over to the bed.

Facing the mirror so that those in the audience could see her, she lifted the many skirts of her dress. She lay back on the pillows and spread her legs. Her pussy was hairy, but we could still make out her plump lips as she held them apart. Her fingers danced on her clit for a moment. She wriggled her hips. Her fingers slid up into her cunt. She pumped herself, the wetness of her juices slicking up her hand. She bucked her hips, fucking her hand frantically. She stopped and pulled her hand away to play with her breasts again. When her hands returned to her pussy, she was calmer. She writhed like a snake, sliding her fingers in and out of her hole. My cock was growing harder as I watched her. The orchestra played an Egyptian type of music and she moved her hips as though she were belly dancing. Her breath was growing heavier and her hand picked up the pace again. This time, she let herself fall over the edge and laughed as she came.

She lay back on the bed for a moment, and then sat up. She looked at herself in the mirror and grinned. She stood up and rearranged the many layers of her dress. As she turned to leave, there was a dark form in the mirror. She gasped.

"Come with me," the voice beckoned.

"I can't," Christine said

"You will come with me. Come, it is time for your lesson."

Christine stepped closer to the mirror and a black-gloved hand reached out, grabbing her by the wrist.

"You will come with me now. Come. Don't be afraid. I've never hurt you, have I?"

"Yes, master." Christine followed him into the mirror. The stagehands turned the mirror around and the light shifted so that the stage was dark and gloomy and festooned with many candles again.

The Phantom took Christine by the hand. He led her over to a section of the cave that held a steel chair, many rolls of chain, a wall with shackles, and a set of large standing candelabras. Many of the candelabras had three prongs, some had four. The weird thing about it all was that no matter how the settings changed, the piano and pianist remained constant. He continued to play as did the orchestra. Sometimes the music swelled loudly, other times, it was a soft ripple in the background. Right now the music was fast and frantic, giving a sense of suspense and adventure to the action occurring on the stage.

The Phantom sat Christine down at the chair. He went over to the piano and moved the pianist out of the way. The pianist stood to the side. The Phantom began playing one of his own compositions. Christine stared at him.

"Sing," he commanded. "Sing for your master."

She began to sing, softly at first. The thrilling sound of her voice eventually grew so that it filled the room.

"That's it, Christine. Sing for me!"

The Phantom played as Christine sang. Suddenly he stopped.

"You must sing now, the new song. The song for Savanna."

"Yes, master."

The Phantom started to play again. Christine began to sing.

"There's that Savanna business again," Tony said.

"Yeah. What's with all this 'Savanna this,' 'Savanna that?' She must own the place or something," Mark said.

"Who knows?" I shrugged.

As Christine sang, I became aware of a movement behind her on the stage. It was Raoul, sneaking up on the Phantom with a piece of rope in his hands. He crept along until he was behind the Phantom. As he tired to lower the rope around the Phantom's neck, the Phantom stood up and spun around. He grabbed the rope and Raoul's hands.

As he marched Raoul over to Christine, the pianist resumed his spot and started to play again.

The Phantom tied Raoul's hand to one of the hooks.

"Do you think you can really sneak up on me after all I've been through? I have senses like a cat."

"Can you just let Christine go and we'll be off?"

"Maybe I'm not ready to let her go just yet. She needs to learn more."

"I've heard her sing. Your job is done. She is perfection."

"Her singing is perfection, but alas, her flesh needs training. She is still young and so naive."

"If anyone is to train her flesh, it should be me," Raoul said.

"Alas, young man, you too need to be trained."

"You insult me, sir."

"You can be insulted or you can learn everything you'll ever need to know about the art of pleasing a woman."

Raoul scowled.

"Do I not write the most beautiful music to ever grace your ear?"

"I have to admit that you do."

"My music is the song of my loins. As expressive as my melodies are to your ear, my flesh knows how to pleasure flesh even more."

"He's right," Christine blurted out. Raoul looked at her in shocked amazement.

"You've tasted his flesh?" he asked, his voice sounding hurt.

"Not in the most carnal way, Raoul, but I can feel the passion that pulses beneath the surface. I want to taste it. I want you to know what it's like."

"I have passion for you, Christine. More then he could ever have for you."

"It's not a matter of who is a better lover. I am here to serve Christine. It is her time," the Phantom said as he walked over to Raoul. With his gloved fingers, he lifted Raoul's head by the chin so that they stared at each other eye to eye.

"Are you going to learn tonight, my pupil? Or do you want to be tied up?"

Raoul looked at the rope that was tied to the hook in the wall and then at Christine.

"I want to learn from you, master," he said.

"Very well."

The Phantom took Christine by the waist. He held her chin tilted up until their lips met. They touched several times. The Phantom softly nuzzled her along her cheek, down to her neck with the side that wasn't covered by the mask. From where we sat, it was freakish, how we could see the mask side of the man seducing the woman.

Christine grew limp as he breathed from her neck down her heaving cleavage and nestled his face in her bosom. The Phantom cradled her head and kissed her long and passionately on the lips. She fainted.

Carrying Christine, the Phantom returned to Raoul. The Phantom unhooked him from the wall.

"Very well then. Your first lesson will be to undress the girl. These clothes are difficult and cumbersome."

Raoul set to work unfastening her complicated dress. The Phantom held her while Raoul pulled and struggled with her clothes. It was strangely arousing watching the length of time it took to take an unconscious woman out of her period clothes and boots. The men both worked on her as she lay limp.

Raoul finished removing her dress while the Phantom tore a curtain from one of the set pieces. He came back and lay it on the ground in a grand flourish.

"Only the best for my angel." He sighed. He returned to Christine.

At long last, they lay her on the ground where they had spread out the curtain. She lay with her eyes shut, breathing quietly.

Once she was on the ground, Raoul pulled his sword from its sheath.

"How dare you touch her? You will pay, you monster."

"How am I the monster? I just held her out as an offering. You were the one that chose to taste. Not me. I was only trying to encourage you."

"Don't torment me with your double talk. The sooner you die, the better."

The sword zigzagged in the air before coming near the Phantom. The Phantom didn't seem surprised. In fact, his voice had an incredulous twinge to it.

"Why would you pass up a chance, a glorious chance that doesn't happen very often? Trust me, she's warm and soft inside."

"It isn't right. It just isn't right. I often wonder, how you can live with yourself?"

"A lot of us wondered that, I think."

The Phantom neatly jogged Raoul's attempts at a serious sword fight. He swooped and ducked, deftly skipping over Christine. He picked up a candelabra to ward off Raoul's attacks. Pieces of candle fell to the ground as the sword sliced through them.

The Phantom tossed the candelabra aside. As Raoul foolishly watched, his guard came down for the merest split hair of a second. In that time, the Phantom was able to take his sword and place it at Raoul's neck. He held Raoul tightly, his voice menacing.

"Not a man of your word, are you?"

"I am fighting for the lady's virtue."

"The lady has no virtue. The lady wants to enjoy all the sweet vibrations of life."

The Phantom shackled Raoul to the chains on the floor. He stared down at the trembling man. Although Raoul was young and virile, the Phantom clearly boasted remarkable strength and cunning.

The Phantom flipped back his cape and unbuckled his trousers. He knelt down on the curtain with Christine. He pulled Christine's legs up over his shoulders and, without any fanfare, shoved his erection into her.

"No!" shouted Raoul. "No, you can't."

The Phantom laughed long and low as he slowly shoved his cock in and out of the unconcious girl. The orchestra played on, the music turning staccato.

The Phantom pulled her hips savagely into his. She moaned, her eyes still shut.

"Raoul . . ." she whispered. "Raoul."

The Phantom stopped fucking her.

"So it's Raoul you want, Raoul you shall get."

He angrily stormed over to Raoul and undid the boy's pants. He roughly pulled the pants down to Raoul's knees, exposing a large, erect penis.

He grabbed Christine by the hair.

"Here is your precious Raoul. Go to him now."

He forced her face toward Raoul's cock.

"Suck it."

"I can't."

"Suck it, I command you."

Christine took Raoul's dick into her mouth and started to suck. Raoul protested but then fell silent as her ministrations caused his dick to swell larger.

"Harder. Faster," the Phantom commanded.

Christine obliged. When the Phantom thought that Christine had sucked enough, he pulled her back.

The Phantom lifted her up and planted her on Raoul's erect dick.

"Fuck him."

She sobbed.

"I can't . . ."

"Now," the Phantom commanded.

He moved her hips up and down until she found the rhythm. She squatted over Raoul, leaning forward on her hands that clutched Raoul's knees.

"He's so big," she protested.

"Fuck him. You wanted him. Now fuck him."

The Phantom lifted her off and turned her around so that she was facing Raoul's face. The two lovers stared at each other, embarrassed in their compromising position, yet delighting in expressing what they had always suppressed.

"Ride him! Ride him like a stallion!" the Phantom championed.

Christine got into the swing of the experience. She probably found her g-spot or something. Suddenly, she pumped herself furiously on Raoul. An orgasm shuddered through her and she cried out.

Raoul fucked her as best as he could. His cock slid in and out of her.

"Great show, huh?" Tony said.

"Sure is."

We sat in appreciation as the Phantom pulled Christine off

of Raoul and dragged her over to the piano bench. He pushed away the stunned pianist and threw her over the bench so that her ass was in the air. He slid his pants down and rubbed his cock, chortling in glee at her gaping pussy. The Phantom was good-sized as well and Christine gasped as he plunged into her a few times. He stopped and looked out into the audience. He laughed, loud and long and sinister.

The Phantom tied Christine to the piano leg and came down into the audience.

"Who will fuck Christine? We need a volunteer, or two, or three, to service my lovely student."

The Phantom approached my buddies and me.

"What fine young men wouldn't love to plunge their dicks into the lovely Christine?"

We didn't have to be asked twice. After spending all night fucking nearly anything that moved, we had no qualms about joining the Phantom and Christine on stage.

We went up to the front. My dick was throbbing in anticipation. Under the Phantom's guidance, we had our way with Christine. Raoul watched helplessly from the sidelines.

First, I shoved my dick into her mouth. Mark played with her tits while Tony slammed his cock into her pussy for a while, as she held on to the piano for support.

Tony then pulled out and led her over to the curtain on the floor. He lay down on the floor, eager for more pussy. Christine sank onto his hard dick. She leaned forward, perching herself on her hands. I took the opportunity to plunge my dick back into her mouth. Mark squatted behind her and worked his cock into her tight little asshole. Once he was in snugly, he started to move very slowly. I could feel the vibrations of her moans around my cock. It was bliss. I stared over at the phantom, who watched while stroking his cock.

"Fuck her harder. Don't be afraid. She loves it up the ass."

Mark thrust into her harder.

She gasped at the size of him, allowing me to fill her throat another inch or so. I slid in and out, savoring the warm wetness of her mouth.

Tony was pumping his hips in the air, trying to find a good rhythm.

Mark fucked that ass even harder as the Phantom urged him on.

At last, he shot his load into her hot little ass. The thought of it excited me so much that I came into her mouth. She coughed and sputtered, which sent Tony into his own orgasm. We all cried out as well as her, as we savored the pleasure. It was sweet exquisite music.

Slowly, we got ourselves back together. The Phantom had disappeared, but we could hear his laughter echoing throughout the theater. The orchestra played a dark, sweeping refrain. Christine got dressed and started to sing as she refastened her dress. She went over to Raoul and untied him.

When Raoul was nearly free, the three of us found the exit.

# CHAPTER 10.

*W*e entered a room of rocks and waterfalls. It was like entering a little lagoon in paradise. The joyful sound of water running and burbling and trickling was interrupted now and again by splashing. There were several hot tubs sunken in among rocks and cliffs. There were little trees and long hanging vines all over the place, creating pockets of privacy. Inviting wafts of steam floated above the bubbling waters. The air was thick with mist. The atmosphere was peaceful and mysterious. It was reminiscent of a serene tropical beach resort for the wealthy.

People were in a few of the hot tubs. Some of the hot tubs

were small, others were long and large. They seemed to flow into one another, creating the illusion of a natural hideaway.

One hot tub was high on top of the waterfall. The heads of a man and two women were just visible. They laughed and giggled and clinked champagne glasses. Their conversation sounded lively although they were far enough away that I didn't know what they were saying. Over by a few trees, nestled into the mock rocky hillside was a larger hot tub. Branches of trees partially obscured what was going on, but I caught a glimpse of several heads bobbing up and down. There was splashing and giggling coming from that tub as well.

Closer to us were a few little hot tubs and one long tub. In the middle of the one tub lounged three beautiful women in mermaid costumes. They sang as they combed their long hair. Their voices were high and warbling. They sounded like birds or some exotic creature. After a while, I could make out the words they sang.

> She beckons you with pale white fingers
> Summoning you with wanting eyes
> Her bidding is what you desire
> Her lust will hear your cries
> She will take you in her arms
> And speak of cities golden and bright
> Her lips will dance upon your body
> As she rides you through the night.

Their song echoed throughout the room. They sang it again as a round, combing their long beautiful hair and laughing.

One of the girls splashed her multicolored tail playfully in the water. Another picked up a little mirror to admire her hair.

"I love mermaids," Mark said.

"I love these mermaids, that's for sure," Tony said as he looked at the one nearest to him. She had long blond curly hair and wore seashells on her large breasts. She felt Tony's appreciative glance and looked over at him and giggled. She flapped her tail at him.

"I think she likes you," Mark said.

"I like her."

"Go to her."

We watched as Tony approached the mermaid. He sat down beside her.

"What's your name?" he asked.

"Shauna," she replied.

"Why, hello, Shauna," he said. "I'm Tony."

"Hello, Tony. Who are your friends?"

"This is Franco and Mark."

Mark and I waved at Shauna.

"Hi, Shauna," I said.

The whole deal felt like a scene out of a fairytale or maybe Peter Pan. I remembered mermaids in a lagoon somewhere in Never Neverland. The best part about this lagoon was that it was full of naked people enjoying hot tubs. I had always enjoyed sitting in hot tubs.

"May we join you?" I asked.

Shauna looked at the other two girls. They giggled and smiled.

"Of course."

I stripped off my leather pants and shirt. Shauna pointed over to the side of the lagoon.

"You should take your makeup off at the waterfall."

We looked at each other and laughed. Our makeup was smeared from all our cavorting. It made sense to wash, though. No one wanted to be in a hot tub full of other people's makeup.

The three of us walked over to the showers where there were towels and soap. We quickly washed off our face paint. When we were done, we returned to the girls.

"Is that better?" I asked.

"Much."

I walked into the water. It was warm and bubbling. I sat down near the girls. It felt so good to be sitting in a hot tub. I closed my eyes for moment as I let the bubbles wash across me.

I thought about the evening's events so far. It had been a strange and interesting ride. There were so many great rooms and exciting people. It was liberating to be around so many people who were so excited about Halloween. Self-expression was a great by-product of our modern times.

My body was totally relaxed as I drifted in and out of consciousness. There was a splash in my face and I jerked awake from my reverie.

"Hey, Franco. Are you going to play with us?" one of the girls asked.

"Play? What do you want to play?"

"We can play hide-and-seek."

"OK."

"Marla, you be it first. Everyone else has to hide. That spot over there by the rock is home free."

Marla hid her eyes. The other two girls dived into the water and swam away. The color of their costumes matched the foliage that draped all over the hot tubs. Even though I watched them hide, I could barely tell where they were. Mark and Tony climbed out of the Jacuzzi and hid over by the waterfall. I swam quietly to the other side and hid myself among the branches like the other mermaids.

"Ready or not, here I come," Marla finally said. My heart pounded excitedly as if I were a little kid again. I remember long, lazy summer evenings of playing hide-and-seek at my cousin's house with the neighborhood kids. We would spend hours running along the neighbors lawns and hiding in the bushes. I'm sure our parents didn't mind, since it kept so many of us busy for so many hours at a time. Sometimes I longed for the innocence of those days. It seemed as though in those days, I could hardly wait to grow up. Being grown up was such an exciting concept. I wanted to be independent and make something of my life.

I smiled as I realized that I was doing OK. I was independent. At least I was that night. That night, it seemed to me that everything was crystal clear. That I could do no wrong. That everything was bright and new. The pleasures of the evening had awakened senses in me that had lain dormant for so long. I was thrilled with the great lengths the club had gone to in order to be certain that everyone had a good time, that all ideas were entertained and everyone felt welcome. For the first time in a very long time, I felt like I was part of something special. That I kept hearing about this mystical Savanna excited me too. It seemed as if there was some great plot that was unlocking. A story to be told that I was a part of. It made me tremble with anticipation, for I could feel it in my bones; my Savanna was not far from me now.

Savanna.

She was waiting for me.

I had been told this all night. How I was the one she waited for. No one had said it to Mark or Tony. I hadn't heard anyone say it to anyone else.

Could I be the long lost lover? Could I be the one she was craving? The one for whom she had created the potion to bring back?

In that moment I wished it were so. I longed for adventure, for companionship. I never said anything to Tony or Mark, but in recent months, I had felt the ache of loneliness.

There had never really been anyone special for me. I've loved and lost a couple of times. But I figured, too, that in the loss, then something wasn't right to begin with. Something hadn't clicked in a way that it should have, or I would still be with of those girls right now.

There was something more for me. Something special that lurked around the corner, waiting for me.

Watching Marla hunt for us set my adrenaline flowing. She swam up and down the hot tub, looking up on the little hills, trying to see if anyone was hiding among the trees.

"I know you are there," she sang. "I know where you are hiding."

She swam over to the waterfall and reached behind it. Tony's feet appeared as he stepped out.

"No fair . . ."

"Why not?"

"I don't know. I just don't want to be first out." He grinned. He went over to the ledge we had sat on before and watched as she searched for the rest of us. Mark was just as easily found. His pale feet were visible by a plant just behind the waterfall. She slipped up out of the water, and tapped his toes.

"No way," he pouted. He went over to sit with Tony.

Marla swam over toward the side where me and the other two mermaids were hiding. She ducked her head under the water and swam quickly up and down. When she emerged, she swam over to Shauna.

"Gotcha!" she called out. Shauna laughed.

"Yep. You sure did."

The two mermaids laughed and swished around, flapping their tails. They kissed each other. They locked lips, and then pulled back, their tongues flicking playfully at each other.

Together, they pulled out Sophia. The three of them hugged and kissed while Tony and Mark clapped.

"More!" Mark cried out as they pulled away.

"Not just yet. We still have one more bad boy to find."

They started swimming toward my hiding spot. I took a deep breath and submerged myself. I swam as fast as I could toward the free zone. They were right behind me, I could feel them. I gasped for hair as I touched home free just as Marla grabbed my leg.

"Didn't get me." I laughed.

"Damn," she said. "That sucks."

"Now you have to suck." Sophia said.

Marla looked at me and batted her eyelashes.

"That's right. Now I have to suck." She ran her fingers along my thighs until she found my cock. She pulled on it a little bit. The sensation of the underwater tugging was marvelous.

She took a deep breath and ducked her head. Under the water, her mouth found my cock. She slid her lips along it and took it into her mouth. It felt weird but good at the same time. She serviced me until she ran out of breath.

"Hey, I thought you were a mermaid," I said.

"I am."

"Then why do you have to come up for air?"

"Don't you want me to do a good job?"

I laughed.

"Of course, take all the breath you want."

She smiled as she sank back down. I looked over to see that Mark and Tony were having their dicks sucked as well.

It wasn't long before my dick went from her mouth to the opening in her costume. Her cunt was warm and tight. She held on to the edge of the Jacuzzi while I fucked her. The water was the perfect temperature. I hadn't fucked in the water or in a Jacuzzi very often, so it was doubly thrilling to be fucking a mermaid, even if she wasn't real.

The girls were great about staying in costume. Tony had his girl flung over a rock, and he was cramming his big dick into her from a strange angle. Judging by the moaning and groaning of both him and his mermaid, they were thoroughly enjoying themselves.

Holding Marla's tits while I fucked that sweet pussy was a great and wonderful experience. I fingered her nipples and sucked on her neck. My cock slid in and out of the warmth of her pussy to the warmth of the pool and back again. It was like fucking in a dream.

At last, I wanted some real traction, so we ended up on one of the lounging rocks. I entered her from behind, since mermaids had no legs to spread. She flapped her giant glimmering tail as I fucked her. It was an amazing turn on, holding on to those scaly hips.

We fucked for quite some time, watching our friends fuck, and they were watching us fuck, too.

Fucking a mermaid was one of the highlights of my night.

When we were finished, we lazily lay on the rocks, as if we were sunning ourselves.

"What do you think of this lagoon?" she asked.

"I love it," I said.

"Would you like to stay here?"

"I would."

"Forever?"

"No, not forever."

"Oh, but you know you'd love to stay forever."

"I don't know about that. As a matter of fact . . ."

"You feel her, don't you?"

"Who?"

"Savanna."

"Again with Savanna."

"She is waiting for you."

"She is probably waiting for every man in this bar."

"No, she has a chosen one. She knows who she wants."

"How does she know it's me? We've never even met."

"She saw you. In a vision. It is you."

"I don't believe you. How much are my buddies paying you to creep me out?"

"Nobody is paying anyone for anything. Not a dime."

"Then why are you saying all this?"

"Because it's true."

"How do you know it's true? Was there a staff meeting where everyone sat around and decided to freak out a guy named Franco?"

"No. There was no meeting. We know. We all know."

"How? How do you know? I don't have any special tattoos or marks or anything."

"It doesn't matter. What matters is you have to decide. Will you stay here in the lagoon with us or will you continue your journey?"

"I think I should continue my journey. You probably have other things to do . . ."

"It doesn't matter what I want. I'm here to play and have fun. I would love to play and have fun with you. Again."

I looked at Marla. It was all so weird. I knew I was in a fantasy palace yet at the same time I was becoming disturbed by this talk of Savanna. Who was this Savanna? Was she a witch?

Was she some kind of psychopath? Out of all the customers in the club, why were they picking on me?

At the time, I figured it was a game they were playing with many of the men. It was a way of adding spice to the evening. Foolishly I even considered the fact that there was no Savanna at all. How naive I was in that moment. It was a game, all right. A game nearly as dangerous as any dance macabre. For one last magical night, I was free to choose whom and what I wanted. If I had known then what I know now, I would have chosen to stay with the mermaids.

However, the night beckoned me. A song nearly as haunting as the mermaids' siren song was invading my senses. It danced through me, stirring my blood. I felt compelled to follow it.

I looked around the steamy lagoon at the languid lovers lying among the bushes. People laughed and thrashed in the water. All around me, people tasted the delights of the flesh in the water. With masks off, costumes off, this was the true Halloween room.

Freedom of the flesh. Strangers playing with strangers. They flirted and fondled, whispering secrets through the bubbles.

My friends were relaxing in the arms of their lovers. They had succumbed to the sirens and seemed to be dozing. I chose the moment to take my leave.

# CHAPTER 11.

*I* knew she was near. I had been through so many rooms, my journey felt as though it would never end. It occurred to me that there was no Savanna, that she was just a myth. I opened door after door, finding rooms I had already explored; but I knew there had to be another room. With each curve of the hallway I told myself, just one more door. Just one more door.

Exploring the hallway yet again, I happened upon a small hallway I hadn't noticed on my first pass. There was a set of narrow stairs that wound long and long, up and up several levels. I followed them, my heart thumping.

My nerves twitched and my heart filled with an ache. I felt her in my bones. She was real. She was waiting.

Maybe what the witches had said was true. Maybe I was a long lost lover from another lifetime. How would I know? Would I ever know?

My nerves were shot when I reached the top of the stairs. I stopped to take a breath, wondering what I would say if I did finally see Savanna.

I opened the door and stepped into a cavernous room. It was lit with candles that were fastened into the wall with old-fashioned sconces. Shadowy faces of gargoyles flickered. Some of the gargoyles were comical, others looked fierce.

My boots echoed boldly through the hall. I walked further until I reached what appeared to be a room of some importance. Pomp and circumstance screamed from the walls. The domed ceiling was painted with an intricate mural of demons and gargoyles. At the end of the room was a mammoth throne. It was carved from some sort of rich dark wood and reached straight up to the ceiling. One either side of the throne were large flickering torches.

Seated on the throne was a beautiful blond woman wearing black leather bondage gear. Her breasts were exposed from the crisscrossing top. Her nipples and belly had rings in them.

"Come closer, Franco," the woman said.

I approached her.

"So you've come at last," she said.

"Are you—are you Savanna?" I asked

She laughed. It wasn't a mean laugh but one of surprise.

"Yes. Of course I am."

I gazed upon her beauty for a while. Although she had a stern countenance, there was a girlish playfulness in her face. She had dark eyes that stared at me with a faint recognition.

"What brings you here tonight, Franco?"

"Truth be told, Savanna, my friends brought me here, thinking it would cheer me up."

Savanna stared at me thoughtfully.

"What do you need to be cheered up about?" She leaned forward, as if trying to read inside my mind.

"I suffer a sadness . . . a melancholy." I stared down at my hands.

"What makes you so sad, Franco?"

I looked back up at her. All my life experiences flashed before my eyes. The times I wanted something that taunted me elusively, the pursuits and conquests that rendered my heart hollow. The idea that a beautiful face meant a beautiful life. All the nights of loneliness. Wondering why I was so different. Why couldn't I fall into step with the rest of the human race?

In that moment, I realized where my fate lay.

All of it made sense as I stepped toward Savanna.

"I've been looking for something." I didn't even know what I was saying as the words spilled from my lips.

"Something or someone?" she asked, cocking her head. She narrowed her eyes and I realized that she was trying to see me better. Perhaps she was trying to see inside me.

"I don't know. There's emptiness. A void that needs to be

filled. I thought my career could do it, but so far, I don't feel the elation a man my age should be feeling."

"You've suffered a heartache."

I nodded.

"Sure I have. Who hasn't? I mean, really, if you get to my age and you haven't risked your heart at least once or twice, then there's something wrong."

"Why do you think we keep risking our hearts, knowing they will be broken?"

"Because we're stupid humans."

Savanna laughed.

"No, of course not. There are pulls toward people. People we owe a karmic debt to. Some debts are bigger then others."

"I bet you say that to all the boys that wander in here," I joked. Savanna started to stand, but then sat down again. Slowly she crossed and uncrossed her legs, much like Sharon Stone famously did in that old movie.

"I don't joke about such things."

She sat staring at me. It was a direct and penetrating gaze. Again I had the sense she was trying to read my mind. I grew uncomfortable and shifted from foot to foot. Her eyes were blazing in the candlelight. Her blond hair fell past her shoulders. Her very posture commanded strict obedience. I wondered if I should have dressed better for the occasion. I was glad that my Halloween makeup was gone, though I supposed that my costume looked pretty lame without it.

"I can leave now, if you like," I said, and I turned toward the exit. My heart fluttered, yet there was a huge knot in my stomach—I heard her speak my name softly.

"Franco. Franco, come closer. Sit near me."

I turned back to face her. I didn't know where I was supposed to sit.

"Here at my feet." She patted the floor by her feet.

Her throne was on a step-up platform, so there was plenty of room for me to sit by her feet. I rested my own feet on one of the three steps. She wore long boots and she stretched her legs out.

"Undo my boots, Franco. My feet are tired and they need to breathe."

I set to work unfastening the many buckles that ran the length of her thigh-high boots. Why she didn't wear the zippered ones was a mystery to me? I guess she liked having men undo them for her and taking her sweet time watching them. She ran her hand lazily along my shoulder as I worked.

"Nice broad shoulders. You have to admire that in a man. It's a sign of strength."

"Thanks."

"Not obvious strength, for lifting. Even an ox has strength for carrying. I mean strength of mind, of character."

My fingers were getting sore from the endless undoing of buckles. I focused on the musky scent of her perfume, mixed in with the incense that permeated the club. When I looked up at her, she was staring at me contentedly.

"Are you done already?" she asked.

"Hardly. That was just the first one." I opened up all the

buckles and slid the boot slowly off her leg and foot. When the boot was placed carefully on the floor, she stretched out her foot and wiggled her toes.

"Much better," she sighed. Her foot tapped impatiently.

"The other one, please."

I set to work on the second boot. This one went much faster. Before I knew it, all the buckles were undone and she was wriggling her toes in relief.

"A foot rub would be really nice about now," she said. I obliged. I carefully rubbed the bottom of each foot. As I rubbed, she began to speak again.

"Tell me more about your melancholy, Franco. Does it haunt you every waking hour?"

"Sometimes . . ." I thought it over for a moment. That strange sensation of never being complete or good enough or whatever it was. "Sometimes it seems like it does. But surely that's not possible. I must have moments I forget about the sorrow that burdens my thoughts."

"I don't know, Franco. I know the melancholy you feel. It's like the ballet. So beautiful, yet sad at the same time."

"Yes. Music is how I feel. Like a vibration that isn't in key."

"Do you think you will ever be rid of your melancholy, Franco?"

"I imagine when I figure out what I'm missing, I'll be able to get a handle on it a little more."

"Maybe you are missing a lover. Someone you loved and lost."

"There's been no one who could fill this void. I've had it since I was a child. It's like a chronic wound."

I lowered my head to suckle on her toes. They smelled sweet and fragrant. She wiggled around in her chair as I sucked them.

"You do that very well, Franco," she said.

"Thank you."

Each toe was worked on one at a time. Slowly, lovingly. Each part of her flesh sang to me. The mystical siren song that had compelled me to come here was now singing in full chorus. Whatever my destiny was, whatever I had been waiting for or lured to, it was now. As I massaged and sucked on her pretty feet, I was ready to embrace whatever fate had in store for me.

"I need to get some other shoes." She picked up a little bell that was on the arm of her throne. Within seconds a pretty little slave girl scurried out.

"Fetch me my black stilettos." The girl bowed deeply and left.

"You may stand now." Savanna returned her attention to me. I stood back in place in front of her.

"Should I leave now?" I asked. Again I eyed the exit, hoping for a reprieve from this strange woman and her new hold upon me. Every moment I spent in Savanna's presence, I felt the void being filled up. It was like a well having rainwater added a bit at a time. It would come and then it would stop. I hoped that it would never stop.

Maybe I should have stopped the ride right then and there. Here I was, faced with the woman I was destined to meet all night, simply by the matter that many other people would no doubt stumble across this little alcove. I chose to live in the moment and faced her, my shoulders back, my head held high.

Savanna picked up a scepter that was longer then I was tall. She pounded on the ground with it a few times.

"No. You will not leave now."

Several people in slave gear ran in.

They all sank to their knees before her and touched their foreheads to the ground. One by one they stood up again, standing at attention. I recognized Scorpio, Desmire, and Star from the Blue Room.

"What do you desire, my queen?" A blond man stepped forward. He was naked except for the slave collar around his neck. On his feet were lace-up boots. I stretched my fingers and cracked my knuckles. Savanna gave me a look of haughty disdain.

"I need to examine this man, this Franco, a little better and I need your help, Leo."

Leo stepped back into place with the other slaves.

"What shall we do?"

"Prepare him."

Within minutes, the slaves surrounded me. Before I could think about what was going on, there was one for each arm and leg, gripping me tightly.

"What is it you need to see, Queen Savanna?" Scorpio asked, his dark eyes gleaming with the idea of adventure. Savanna looked me over and nodded.

"I need to see just how strong a man he is. His shoulders may be broad but how strong is his spirit?"

She stood up. For the first time, I saw her body. It wasn't hard to see since her outfit was comprised of black leather pieces strategically placed here and there. She was lean yet curvaceous. Her beauty captivated me. Hypnotized, I stared stupidly at her, forgetting for a while where I was.

"Undress him."

A tiny-waisted, pigtailed girl knelt down to undo my shoes. I hoped she would rub my feet but somehow I knew that wasn't going to be happening. Savanna was studying me again, her eyes half closed as if she could see things in the room the rest of us couldn't. And who was to say she couldn't.

It was October, when the universe is magic. The bridgeway between worlds was creaking open much like a rusty old door letting in an autumn breeze with whatever was caught on the wind. It wasn't like me to put much stock in the idea of witches and potions and other lives. My beliefs still were tied up in traditionalism where you lived this life and then you died. Where you went after you died depended on how lucky your ticket to heaven was and if you bought the right one.

However, there was something in the air that night. A thick static electricity, like a pungent burning texture that was invisible yet tactile. It was too hard to put my finger on.

I can call it magic.

The magic of Halloween was casting its spell on me. All the wonderful sights I'd seen and tasted made me not feel melancholy one little bit. This was a grand adventure and now the weirdo twist was beginning. After all, nothing can be good for too long, or it just isn't life.

The bald slave girl, Star, removed my shirt while two slave boys unbuttoned my pants and slid them off. When Scorpio saw the glint of recognition in my face, he averted his eyes and continued the task at hand. Briskly, he helped to strip me down. When the boys were done, they gathered up my clothes and stood back.

I stood naked before Savanna.

"What do you want to see?" I asked. "How well I can fuck?"

She smirked at me.

"Oh, I know you can fuck."

She turned her gaze up to the ceiling. Hidden among the gaudy faux arches and sconces, were nestled many television sets. Each room of the club had at least three cameras in it. She pointed to the dance floor room, the first room I had been in that night.

"Most people don't even go further than that room all night. Sure, they may wander to the dungeon for a few minutes or go outside to have a smoke. But they just want to dance and have a good time."

"So you've been watching me all night?" I asked, finding the idea of it rather creepy yet erotic at the same time.

"I know who you are. You are the Golden Boy. The boy to whom nothing bad can happen." Savanna smiled.

"I'm not too golden if I have dark hair, now am I?

"You are golden in your heart and mind and you know it."

As I stood there naked, I wondered how I measured up. A woman that beautiful surely had the choice of any man in the club. For all I knew, she already had every man in the club. Who knew how many people she would have caught in her little den of deceit and lies?

"Stand tall for me, Golden Boy," she commanded.

I took up straight. I'd play her little game for now. Something about her filled me with a great joy I hadn't felt in a long time.

Desmire buckled a thick leather collar around my neck.

"Let me see my Golden Boy," Savanna said.

The slaves paraded me around in front of Savanna, taking great delight in pulling me along by a leash affixed to a slave collar around my neck. Somehow I became the slave of the slaves.

One of the slaves bent me over. Two other slaves played with me. One them, Star, squeezed one of my ass cheeks in her hand. The other slave, Desmire, held open my other check. My asshole was exposed for the world to see. It bothered me a bit. I wasn't a prude by any stretch of the imagination, but having my ass spread open in a room full of strangers was intimidating.

Humiliating.

I knew my humiliation was what Savanna wanted.

Savanna stood up and carefully walked down her tiny staircase in those tall black stilettos and looked me over. Star held my leash tightly. Savanna ran her hands along my ass and up inside my crack. Her touch was strange but not unwelcome.

"What other attributes does my fine young stallion possess?" she asked, running her hand up my back. She put both hands on my shoulders and leaned herself into my back. The slaves released their hold on my ass cheeks. Her leather-clad body brushed against mine. It was almost as though we had once been joined and now were cut free.

The notion popped into my head a few times as the night crept along. A growing sense of peace flickered among all this urgency and strange stuff.

Her breath was hot on my neck as she whispered to me.

"Franco, is it you?"

I didn't reply because I didn't know what she was trying to say. In a way I was tempted to play her game. Tempted to throw myself at her as her soul mate.

But I kept my mouth shut. I let her whisper and sigh, stroking my back.

She disengaged herself and continued her inspection.

"Tell me about him. How are his feet, his legs, even his toes?"

The slaves surrounded me, poking and prodding every inch of my body. More then ever, I was proud of my hard work at the gym. I flexed my biceps, my legs. I even tightened up my ass cheeks for them. The girls ran their hands along my rippled abdomen, touching the bones and muscles of my chest.

"He looks great," the slave girl at my feet said. She looked up at me and winked. I winked back.

Savanna was now in front of me.

"Flex again." Savanna placed her hand along my bicep as I flexed my muscles for her.

She ran her hands along my chest, my legs. She pulled and stroked at my muscles. Her breath was hot on my neck.

"Wash him," she instructed as she returned to her throne.

The slave girls ran their tongues along me. They licked my arms and legs. They licked my balls and ass. Even my toes were carefully licked and inspected.

SAVANNA SAMSON

A basin of water was carried in by Scorpio. Leo carried towels of various sizes. The slave girls took the tiny towels and sponged me off. It felt so good and soothing. Savanna watched it all from her throne, her thighs pressed nervously together. My cock was growing hard at the thought of her watching me. I saw her eagerly watch every move, hanging on to every touch that met my flesh.

Pretty girls continued to bathe and scrub me, although there wasn't much work for them to do since I'd been playing in the lagoon earlier.

"Make sure he's nice and clean. I need my Golden Boy to be perfect."

When the slaves were done, Leo and Scorpio carried away the towels and basin. I stood strong in front of Savanna, as Star held my leash.

Savanna stood up from her throne. She carefully stepped down the tiny stairs, her mouth partly open as she approached me. Silently admiring her newly washed toy, she ran her hands along my gleaming, freshly scrubbed flesh.

She touched her fingers to my chest, tracing circles around my ribcage and then my nipples.

"What is your darkest desire?" she asked.

"I don't know, I haven't thought about it," I answered truthfully. I didn't have a clue what darkest desire I wanted that I hadn't tried. Although I had a lot of hang-ups in my life, experimenting was never a problem for me. If I wanted something, I could eventually find someone who could give it to me.

Savanna's fingers toyed with my nipples. She tweaked them and pinched them. Nipples were one of my dark weaknesses. There was something that really excited me about having my nipples tweaked and tugged. The sensation was exquisite; there was no doubt about that. The idea of a woman doing it to me throbbed in some primal-instinct voice. It was like a hang-over from primitive times.

She continued to toy with my nipples.

"Do you like that?" she asked, pinching my nipple. The sensation was pleasurable. She tightened her fingers.

"How about that?" It was started to hurt and dull throbbing ebbed through me. As I registered it as pain, my groin was aching with its own pain. Somehow the pain was connecting to my pleasure zone.

"More," I said, wondering how far the experience would take me.

Savanna twisted hard. A sharp pain surging through me caused me to gasp. She released her grip. Desmire was standing near her and Savanna plucked a set of nipple clamps from the girl's many chains and belts. She dangled them in the air, right at my eye level.

"You want more, I'll give you more, Golden Boy." She placed one of the clamps around my nipple. Slowly she tightened the little screw that pressed the clips together. When the sensation was teetering on the threshold of pain, I told her to stop. With the nipple rings on, she tugged on the chain. My nipples were stretched out a bit and it sent a jolt through me. She released the chain.

"Nipples are one of the treasures of the universe. They are beautiful to look at, beautiful to hold, and feel fantastic when stimulated properly."

As she spoke, she drew her hands to her breasts and toyed with her own nipple rings. She tugged them gently and drew in a sharp breath of air.

"Yes. The nipples. For so many of us, they are the key to our heart." Her mood changed from soft and dreamy to firm and authoritative.

She turned to Star.

"Prepare my whip."

The bald girl returned with a flogger. Savanna took it and slapped it in the air a few times.

The slave boys tied rope around my hands while the girls tied my feet. Four people held me by the rope. Savanna started to flog me.

She ruffled the whip along my back and then slapped me with a stinging slap.

I winced.

It was a sharp sensation. Not quite painful but not quite soothing, either.

My nerves danced as she flogged me again and again.

My buttocks quivered.

She whipped me along my back, my ass, and my shoulders.

"You are a strong man with your big broad shoulders. How strong are you now?" she asked as she bore the whip down again and again.

"I am strong for you, Queen Savanna!" I cried out.

She whipped me again.

At last, she grew weary of flogging me. She collapsed on her throne, the whip hanging loosely from her hand.

"Prepare the candles."

As slave girls bustled around, Scorpio and Leo unsnapped the intricate leather outfit that Savanna wore. Savanna was relieved of every stitch of clothing. She was naked save for her body jewelry.

The slave girls set to work setting up rows of candles. One by one, carefully and lovingly, white candles were prepared with oils and herbs. The girls hummed as they sang, stroking the candles like dicks. As each candle was prepared, Desmire lit the candles one by one with wooden matches. When the candles were fully dressed and lit, they formed a circle around the bed and me. My heart pounded as I remembered Halloween. Above me, there was a flutter that I barely caught out of the corner of my eye. When I turned to look up over the canopy of the bed, it was gone.

Savanna watched the girls with great interest. She leaned forward, her eyes glinting strangely in the candlelight. Savanna the Queen had become Savanna the Goddess.

Savanna stood at the edge of the little stairs and surveyed the final scene. The slaves that held my bindings had loosened their grip. There was no need for them to worry about me trying to escape. My soul was captivated by her essence, my flesh craved her flesh.

She was stunning in the flickering light of the candles. What tortures she had in store for me next meant nothing as I gazed at her beauty. The stinging throbs from the wounds where she had flogged me were forgotten as she started to sing.

It wasn't a regular song. The song had an odd Celtic feel to it. The slaves stood in various places around the circle and hummed softly. Scorpio pulled out a little drum that he tapped lightly.

Dance with me in the moonlight
Spend your life with me
By the dawning of the day
Your love will set me free.

She sang for many verses, her voice hushed and earnest. As she sang, she danced around the circle. Her movements were reminiscent of a belly dancer, the rings on her nipples and in her belly glinting as she twirled. When she reached the halfway point of the circle, Star and Moonbeam helped her don a black-hooded bathrobe. The robe was sheer and shimmered in the candles. She continued around the circle, resuming her belly dance. Her robe slipped haughtily down her shoulder as she rolled it toward me.

I was mesmerized. She turned to look at me, a strange half smile on her face.

"Do I please you, Franco?" she asked.

"Yes. You please me, Queen Savanna."

"How can I please you more?"

"I don't know . . ." But I did know. I wanted to share her mind, her body, her flesh. The flesh within her flesh. I wanted to sink my hardness deep into her depths and watch her cry for more. I wanted to hear her voice in my ear as I thrust into her time and again. I wanted to wake with her and fall asleep in her. I knew what my deepest darkest desire was.

"I want you," I said. "There it is. Plain and simple. I want you."

"I want you too, Franco. But now is not the time. There is more to do. You have more tests to take. I have to be sure."

Scorpio and Star returned with more candles. They set them down around me. Savanna stepped into the circle.

"You will watch as I fuck Star." Before I could say or do anything, Moonbeam and Leo were tying me standing up, at the foot of the bed so that I was facing the bed.

She positioned herself and Star in front of me along the bed so that I could see them. Scorpio returned with a strap-on dildo. He fastened it around Savanna's waist. She looked incredibly sexy with that big fleshy cock jutting out from between her legs.

She teased Star from behind, playing with her breasts and nipples while rubbing her fake cock against Star's ass. Star wiggled against it in glee.

She made Star lean over the bed, her head on the mattress turned to the side. Savanna spread Star's legs. Savanna's tongue reached out and licked the folds of Star's pussy. Star wiggled her ass again.

Another slave girl appeared and rubbed lube all over Savanna's dick until it glistened.

Savanna plunged the dildo into Star deeply, holding her around the front as she did so. Star cried out.

"Do you like that, Star? Do you like to feel my big hard cock jammed up your cunt?"

She plunged the dildo in and out several times very slowly. Star moaned. She pushed it into the hilt once more.

"How's that, Star? How do you like that big hard cock?"

"Fuck me, Savanna," Star cried. "Oh, please, fuck me hard."

Savanna took Star by the hips and plunged the cock in and out of her rapidly. Star's head jostled on the bed as her moans of delight came out in shaky warbling.

"Fuck me, mistress. Oh, fuck me good."

Star reached her hands between her legs.

"That's right, Star. Play with your pussy. Come on, tweak on your little twat and spray your juices all down my dick."

Star rubbed herself hard as Savanna continued to ram her. Savanna was a beautiful tigress, her blond hair shaking as she pumped the bald girl. Savanna tossed her hair around like a proud stallion, bucking into his favorite mare.

Star cried out, shaking so hard that I could feel the vibration from where I was. Star moaned and groaned, then collapsed.

"Don't think you get off that easy, my dear," Savanna said, grabbing the girl's hips and hoisting them up so that her butt was in the air. Savanna positioned the tip of the cock at Star's asshole. Star tried to relax as Savanna pushed the dildo in a little way.

"Oh my god . . ." the slave cried out.

Savanna turned to the slaves that stood by watching.

"You, Moonbeam . . . bring me some more lube."

Moonbeam quickly found the lube and brought it back. In the meantime, Savanna had donned latex gloves.

"Gotta grease up the little Star, do we?" she asked. She unscrewed the lid of the lube and squeezed some onto her first two fingers.

"Give the girl some lube," Savanna sighed, as she wiggled her two fingers into Star's ass. She moved them very slowly in a circular motion as if to widen the hole.

"Relax, Star," Savanna said. "Think of something nice and relaxing like the beach. Think about getting fucked up the ass on a beautiful beach."

"Yes, Savanna," Star said, and rested her head on her hands. Savanna worked her fingers into Star's ass. She moved them in and out a few times.

Star squealed with delight.

"Oh, you know me so well, Mistress Savanna. You know how to make a girl's asshole feel fantastic."

"All the better to fuck you with."

Savanna slipped three and then four fingers into Star's ass. She slowly worked her fingers around, perhaps savoring the sense of power and the heady rush of giving pleasure.

Savanna worked Star's asshole in a primo way. I couldn't believe the view.

At last Savanna tired of working Star with her fingers. She stood behind her and stroked her fake penis as if it were real.

"I can hardly wait to feel your hot tight pussy clamped around my dick."

"Fuck my tight ass now, Mistress Savanna. Fuck me, please."

Savanna stroked the back of Star's thighs with one of her hands, running her fingers nails along her sensitive flesh.

She spread star's cheeks apart and plunged the dildo into her ass. Star grunted as Savanna slowly pushed it in. This time it was easier because of all the lube. It didn't take long for Star to become accustomed to the new size in her ass and soon she was riding it better then a porn star. Savanna gleefully slammed into her several times. Star moaned and pushed herself against it. At last, she had her fill.

Star fell exhausted onto the bed. The slaves busied themselves unstrapping Savanna's dick and washing Star down with little white cloths and basins of water. At last Star was able to pick herself up and stagger off to rest for a while.

"Scorpio," Savanna said. "I want you to fuck Moonbeam right here on the bed where I fucked Star. I want to see you plow that big dick of yours into her tiny little cunt. Surely you can do that for me?"

"Rightly so, Mistress Savanna," Scorpio said. Moonbeam came over to the bed and lay near me, so that I could see her breasts and her soft nonviolated holes.

"Spread your lips," Savanna commanded. "Let Franco see how truly delicious you are. Let him see how much your little clit throbs."

Moonbeam spread her legs and held open her pussy. I nodded appreciatively.

"Scorpio, help her keep from having her clit throb too hard."

Scorpio kneeled over the bed and scooted her down a little ways. He buried his face in her delicious neck. Her fragrance was sweet. She spread her legs wide so he could enjoy lapping and sucking on the folds of her pussy. I watched, entranced.

His long curly hair fell across her legs. She wriggled her hips, eager to meet his darting tongue. He flicked and played and then set to work seriously sucking her cunt. She pushed into his face, writhing in the delicious sensations he was invoking in her.

Scorpio kissed his way up her body, stopping at her breasts to suckle on them for a moment, and then continued on until his lips met hers on the mouth. They shared several steamy kisses while her hand played with Scorpio's cock.

His cock grew under her firm grip. She pumped it as they kissed, their hips rolling together in a seductive dance. Scorpio was a tall young man and he had the size of cock to match his height. It was a true marvel, watching how big that cock could grow.

I marveled even more when I watched the length of it plunge into Moonbeam's cunt and stay there. She gasped as she was impaled. Scorpio kept his hips pressed against hers as he stretched backward, looking toward the ceiling. For a moment, it appeared as though he were studying the paintings on the ceiling, when in fact, he was probably relishing the sensation of his dick rammed to the hilt in Moonbeam's pussy.

"Is this what you want, Queen Savanna? To see this slave girl so full of cock that she doesn't know whether to scream or cry?"

"Keep fucking her, Scorpio. I will tell you when she is done. And when you are done too for that matter."

She slapped Scorpio's ass with the riding crop a few times and he set to work fucking the girl. Savanna orchestrated their every move. She told him when to thrust and when to pull out. She clapped her hands to speed up the rhythm and slapped his ass to get him to slow down.

Scorpio moved Moonbeam's legs so that they were over his shoulders. I could see everything from the angle I was on and couldn't believe how far he was getting that mammoth dick of his into that tight, snug pussy. It made me want to shoot my own load all over the place.

Scorpio rammed her quickly and Moonbeam squealed with delight, her breath coming out in jagged sighs.

"Fuck me harder!" she cried out. "Oh please. Sink that big pink meat stick into my cunt and ram it home."

Scorpio continued to pump away at her. Her toes clenched as she drew nearer to orgasm. Scorpio was pumping her furiously now, his back muscles taut and firm, his biceps bulging as he supported himself on the bed.

"More, Scorpio!" Savanna ordered. "Much more."

Scorpio continued to fuck her, alternating his rhythms until he found a new one for the slave girl. She moaned and shouted her approval, practically crying as she came again.

Scorpio pulled out and lay down on the bed, staring up at the canopy. Moonbeam climbed upon that freestanding structure and squatted down onto it. Her face had an expression of relief as she moved herself up and down. She lay across Scorpio, her hips working self magic with his dick rammed tight inside of her.

"God, I'm going to come again," she moaned as she slid herself faster along him.

She bucked and Scorpio held her hips as he pumped into her. A long, low wail hummed from her lips as she came again, held up like a puppet as he fucked her furiously.

When he saw that she had come, he pushed her roughly off. He sat up and forced her down on all fours.

Savanna went over and ran her hands along Moonbeam's tight round ass. Savanna's fingers slipped into her tight little honey pot. Savanna shoved her hand in as far as it would go and moved it back and forth. The woman's eyes rolled back in her head from ecstasy. Savanna stroked her asshole and then shoved one of her still-gloved fingers into it. Scorpio took the opportunity to ram his cock into her cunt. He fucked her slowly, watching his dick sliding in and out of her, pulling at her pussy lips. Her juices were coating his dick. He seemed lost in a reverie for a moment as he slid in and out.

Moonbeam had finally caught her breath and was looking around. She smiled sheepishly at Star, who had returned and was standing by the bed. Star crawled onto the bed and sucked on Moonbeam's tits. Savanna still had her finger in Moonbeam's ass. Scorpio kept fucking Moonbeam. They must have fucked like that for a long time. I don't remember much except that it was great to watch and that I was growing weary. I saw all this wonderful hot action, yet I was tied up. No one was even paying attention to me. If someone would only suck me or offer her cunt to sit on my cock. But the slaves were there to service Savanna and her perverted desires, and service they did.

Savanna pulled Scorpio's dick out of her cunt for a moment and sucked on it. She shoved it down her throat. Scorpio groaned with pleasure. Savanna deep-throated him for a while. He held her by the hair and fucked her mouth. It was deliciously erotic to watch because of their height difference.

Savanna put Scorpio's cock back into Moonbeam's cunt and pushed his hips against her. She bucked and screamed against him. At last, he shot his load all over her back. He forced the last little droplets out by milking his dick.

"Star, lick her clean." Star set to work licking Moonbeam's back. She lapped up the great sticky patches of come. She made her way from her back to her cunt. She ate out the girl who trembled with yet another orgasm. How lucky it must be to be a woman who comes so damn much. I could hold my own with any guy, but nothing like what a multiorgasmic woman was capable of.

Savanna was sucking Scorpio's dick.

"You aren't done yet, young stud. We need you big and hard to get ready for the next part."

She suckled Scorpio's balls and deep-throated his wilted shaft. She then stopped and tied his hands high up on the canopy where there were ropes dangling down. She had to climb on the bed to reach them and did the work quickly.

"That's better," she declared, as she set back to work sucking his dick. She had him positioned so that he could lean toward the bed. We faced each other. He looked down at my hard, throbbing cock and laughed.

"Bet you wish you were getting some of this," he teased.

"You know I do."

"Silence," Savanna said as she slurped and suckled Scorpio's dick. Star and Moonbeam were doing a sixty-nine, shoving their fingers rapidly into each other's snatches as eager tongues sought out their clits. Savanna stood on the bed and wrapped her arms around Scorpio's shoulders. She hooked herself onto him, sliding her cunt up and down his cock a couple of times before climbing off again.

She crawled over to the girls.

She positioned Star in front of Scorpio and Moonbeam in front of me. She directed them to lower their cunts onto our cocks at the same time. It was amazing, watching those girls sliding those steaming pussies up and down our shafts.

We weren't allowed to move, so the girls had to do all the work greasing themselves up and down our long poles. Moonbeam's pace quickened and her pussy lips clamped down against me as she came. Shortly thereafter, Star came too.

Savanna lay on the middle of the bed, rubbing her own pussy, ecstatic at the sight of her slave girls enjoying so much cock.

"Girls, come to me," she ordered. "Pay service to your Queen."

Star set to work licking Savanna's pussy while Moonbeam suckled on her tits. Savanna pulled Star's face into herself.

"That's a good job. Lick my little clit," Savanna directed. Moonbeam took first one ringed nipple and then the other into her mouth. Her tongue toyed and played with the rings, the nipples. Savanna rubbed her own tits and pussy, holding and helping the women give her pleasure.

"Now, go fuck the boys."

This time, I had Star pumping against me. She was royally juiced up from her session with Scorpio. Her cunt slid easily along me, just tight enough for some killer friction.

I thought I was going to lose my load for sure when she came, but I had a strong feeling I wasn't allowed to. I had to be strong and save my glory for Savanna. Star slid off of me panting.

When Moonbeam had her fill, she slipped away from Scorpio.

Savanna untied Scorpio. She lay on the bed as he rubbed his wrists to get the feeling back into them. His cock was still hard, pointing toward her like a divining rod.

"I want to feel a young, hard cock in my pussy. Make me come, Scorpio."

She didn't have to ask Scorpio twice as he mounted her and pumped her frantically.

Savanna's legs were thrown up over his shoulders and I could see his dick slamming in and out of her. He pumped her hard and deep with his big dick. She squealed and cried as she enjoyed him. She couldn't seem to get enough of him. She bucked and flailed against him, her face flushed, her forehead glistening with sweat.

She cried out as she came. He impaled her fully, letting her twitch and writhe on the end of his cock in ecstasy. His own face was flushed as well, and by his jerky movements I knew he wasn't going to last much longer.

Savanna sat up, taking Scorpio's dick into her mouth. He stroked it a few times with his hand and cried out as his jizz shot into her mouth. She drank his come, relishing every drop.

My balls were aching with the urge to come. I wondered when my turn with Savanna would be. Her tortures were plenty.

Her hand found my dick and stroked it. She wrapped her lips around my dick, teasing and toying with it.

"You want to come so bad, don't you, Franco?"

"Yes I do, Queen Savanna."

"You want to feel your hard cock deep inside my warm fleshy cunt, don't you?"

"Desperately, Queen Savanna."

She pulled away with a laugh.

"You are just going to have to wait." Savanna sat up and waved her hand at Scorpio, who stood at attention at the side of the bed.

"Scorpio, bring in Misha and Kiki," Savanna commanded.

We all waited patiently until Scorpio returned with two tiny women dressed in geisha outfits. They twittered shyly and fluttered their fans.

"Misha and Kiki, I need you to show Franco your special touches."

Misha and Kiki giggled, batting their eyes demurely. Silently, they folded their fans. They approached me and took little vials of oil from their pockets.

Quickly and deftly, they rubbed the oil over my throbbing body. They kneaded it into my shoulders and neck, my belly and balls, down my legs, and even lifted my feet to rub the sweet scent on my soles. They removed my nipple clamps and rubbed the soothing oil along my chest.

This wasn't a greasy oil, since it sank right into my skin without leaving a sheen. I wondered if it was some ancient aphrodisiac recipe, as my desire grew even stronger yet at the same time I felt an inner peace. Misha kneeled down at my feet and took my erection into her mouth. She played with it for a while as Kiki sucked on my balls. Savanna and the slaves watched hungrily from the sides. My head rolled back and my eyes shut as I savored the delicious sensations. It would be very hard not to come with these beautiful women working oily magic on my body.

"Enough," Savanna said, apparently realizing that I was nearing the end of my limit.

"I feel like playing some more," she said thoughtfully, as if trying to determine how she wanted to play this time.

She looked at Scorpio, who left again with the blond slave boy, Leo. They returned carrying a large wooden post and lots of white rope.

"Remove your clothes," Savanna said to Kiki and Misha.

The geisha girls silently removed their robes. They were slender with petite breasts and waists.

Scorpio set to work wrapping the ropes around the girls while Leo helped. He worked quickly, tying and knotting rope repeatedly so that the girls were covered in a harness of rope. Their breasts, squeezed bigger, took on an odd shape as they stuck out from between the ropes.

Savanna tickled Misha with a large plume feather. Misha twitched but didn't make a sound. Her obedience was stellar as Savanna tormented her first with the feather and then her flogger. Savanna's strokes grew steadily faster and harder as they lashed across the girl's arms and legs. The flogger met her belly and as with the other areas of contact, left long red streaks.

At last Savanna grew tired of Misha's silence. She turned to Scorpio, who waited expectantly.

"Up she goes," Savanna ordered with a wave of her hand.

For the first time, I noticed a pulley system leading up to the ceiling. Scorpio held a large clasp in his hand. He hitched it up to the loop at Misha's waist and then proceeded to hoist her up with the aid of another rope.

Misha swung in the air like a fly caught in a spider web.

Savanna turned her attention to Kiki.

This time, instead of using the flogger, she used a riding crop. She stroked Kiki lightly all over. She flicked her nipples. Savanna tapped Kiki's nipples lightly, a delicate pitter-patter. Kiki sighed. Savanna slapped her with the crop on her nipple. The pain caused Kiki to cry out.

"Silence," Savanna said. "I will not have you pollute the air with your weak, insignificant noise."

Savanna led Kiki to the post. She nodded to Scorpio, who set to work busily tying and untying knots until Kiki's arms were tied as she faced the post but her legs were free.

Scorpio left discreetly and returned with another strap-on dildo. This time, the dildo was created from crystal. It sparkled in the candlelight. I wondered how cold and glasslike it would feel inside the body.

Savanna's fingers played with Kiki's pussy, roughly pinching and massaging it. She pulled open Kiki's pussy lips and stuck her tongue in. Savanna's head was buried in the cheeks of that little ass as her mouth worked magic.

Savanna massaged that ass and then stood up. She raised her crop and landed it squarely on Kiki's left cheek. She brought down the crop again on the left cheek. Kiki couldn't resist crying out.

Savanna tossed down the whip.

"Is this what you want?" she asked as she forced the crystal cock into Kiki.

Kiki spread her legs wider, rolling her hips.

"Yes, my queen."

Savanna plunged into her again.

"I can't hear you."

"Fuck me, my queen. Please fuck me hard."

Savanna gripped Kiki's ass with one hand while the other played with Kiki's clit. She thrust into Kiki repeatedly until Kiki came.

Savanna pulled out her crystal cock, glistening now with Kiki's juices.

Savanna walked over to the dangling Misha.

"Scorpio, lower her."

Scorpio unwound the rope so that Misha was lower to the ground.

"Lick her juice from my cock." Savanna shoved the crystal cock into Misha's mouth.

Misha obediently licked until all the pussy juice was gone.

Savanna stared at me, her eyes burning with intensity.

"Do you like watching Misha suck my big cock?" she asked me.

"Yes, my queen," I said.

"Do you ache for me, Franco? Do you yearn to fuck me?"

"Yes, my queen. I ache for you desperately. I have waited and watched you. I have held back my orgasm in anticipation of sharing it with you." My balls were aching, I needed to come so badly.

"Perhaps . . . perhaps I almost believe you."

She handed her crystal cock to Leo, who put it away. She retired to the bed and lay back on it. Watching herself in the mirror, she played with her breasts for a moment.

"What do you think, Franco? Should I let you come in my cunt? Have I waited long enough to taste you?"

# CHAPTER 12.

S avanna stood up.
"Thank you. All of you. Each and every one of you. You have done a fine job so far this evening. Now, you may leave us alone."

The slaves came before her, one by one, and kneeled. Misha was lowered from the ceiling and untied. Kiki was released from the post. The slaves gathered up wayward bits of clothing and left.

Savanna hopped into the bed, watching me, as I stood helplessly tied to the bedpost.

"How do you feel, Franco? All tied up like that?"

"I want to please you. I want to be part of you," I said truthfully. In fact, the longer I was tied up, the more I enjoyed it.

As she sat back on the pillows, looking at me, I wanted her more then ever. After everything that had occurred that night, I still hadn't been given the opportunity to fuck my Savanna.

She took a nail file from her bedside and started to file her nails. They were long and had a French manicure.

"I ache for you, Savanna," I said, realizing that I was going to have to start talking.

"I don't feel like you ache enough, Franco."

"But I do. See how hard my cock is."

She didn't look at my erect dick. She continued to file.

"I want you to crave me, to know that you can't live without me."

"I already know that I don't want to spend a minute apart from you."

"But you must feel it. Really feel it."

"How can I tell you what I feel inside? How can I show you when my hands are bound?"

"I will know."

She finished filing her nails and smiled strangely.

"I will know," she said again.

She slid down the bed, her long, soft feet playing with my mouth.

"Do you remember me?" she whispered.

"Remember you?"

"Yes. I doubt you would. It was just a thought."

"Have we met before?"

"Maybe. Maybe not."

She wrapped her lips around the head of my dick. Her tongue did a little fluttering dance on the tip before she slipped her lips away.

She ran her tongue along my pole, up and down in long, languid strokes. I quivered.

She used her hand and mouth alternating rhythms until she found one that required me to summon all my strength not to blow my load in her mouth in that moment.

That moment.

In fact, the idea of the moment took me out of the moment long enough to pull back my urge to ejaculate.

She sat back and opened her legs. She toyed with her pussy.

"I bet this looks good to a hungry boy like you," she purred as she toyed with her clit ring. The flashing silver of her ring distracted me for a moment. I yearned to taste her.

"Bring it here so I can taste," I said. She closed her legs coyly and rolled around the bed until her ass was on the edge of the bed, not far from where my dick was pointing. Without a word, she crawled on her hands and knees and eased herself onto my hard cock.

I felt helpless and powerful at the same time.

"What a nice, big, hard rod you have," she said.

"I try to stay in shape," I said. I wasn't sure why I said that, I was at a loss for words.

Since my hands were still tied to the post, there was no way I could hold those delicious hips at all. They were lovely, half moons that swelled into another kind of half moon. Her cunt was hot and moist. She thoroughly enjoyed herself as she rode my cock. Back and forth she went. Sometimes she kept a rapid pace, and then she'd slow down to a rhythm where it felt like she was exploring the sensation of my dick in her cunt. She sped back up again, searching for orgasm.

She eased away from me, resting on her elbows. The very tip of the head of my cock was still in her pussy. With her legs spread wide open, I could see the sides of her pussy puckering out from the girth of my dick shoved inside of her. Even though she had just fucked someone else, I didn't see her pussy do that with him. I had been watching for it, too.

She pulled away from me and stood staring at me.

"How do you feel?"

"Fantastic."

"Do you want more?"

I nodded my head.

"Pardon me?" she asked.

"I would like more."

"More what?"

"More of you, Mistress Queen Savanna. Please let me fill your hot, aching hole with my cock."

"I'm tired of this position. We need something better."

"If you untied me . . ." I suggested. She leaned over and looked me in the eye.

"How dare you say such things?" she barked. "You need to be punished. Swiftly and immediately."

She went over to a dressing table and picked up a riding

crop. She snapped it in the air a few times. I winced as I thought about the sting it was going to leave on my ass.

She stood behind me. I clenched my butt cheeks together.

"Spread your legs," she commanded, tapping between my legs with the crop. As I spread them out, she slapped my inner thighs with the crop. It smarted, like bee stings. I spread my legs until she told me to stop.

With my legs so far apart, my balls were hanging free. My dick stood out like a divining rod, though I was starting to lose a bit of hardness due to the apprehension I felt.

She slapped my ass several times on each cheek with that damnable riding crop. It stung like hell, but it was good all the same. When she stopped, the stinging continued on for a bit, like a bite and then faded into a warmth of nerve endings tingling. It felt good. Savanna stroked the crop along my scrotum. It was unnerving—I hoped she wouldn't slap me there with that crop.

She crawled under me and started sucking on my balls, putting first one and then the other into her mouth. She licked them and sucked them and rolled them around in her mouth. She could get them both in and tugged and pulled on them. I stared down at her—in so much ecstasy that I probably would have fallen down if it weren't for the ropes holding me up.

She ran her tongue on along the underside of my dick and then got up.

She returned to whipping me with the riding crop. This time, there were harder, stinging blows. She also stopped and rubbed my ass cheeks every few minutes, before she'd begin a new pattern. The massage of her hands was welcome relief to the tired, sore muscles.

She untied me.

But not for long.

She firmly tied my arms and legs to the bedposts. Very businesslike, she put a blindfold on me. She stood beside me and I wondered what she was going to try next.

There was a rustling, in the corner of the room. Had more people come to this room? Were there people there or not? My skin prickled, as I had the uneasy sensation of being watched.

I didn't say anything that time and let Savanna toy and tease my nipples.

"You like having your nipples played with," she stated.

"Yes, Mistress Savanna." She ran her long fingers down the length of my torso.

She pinched my nipples again and walked back over to her little table of goodies. She found some clamps. When she came back, she was holding them like castanets.

"You're going to love this, big boy," she cooed as she fixed the clamps to my nipples. She turned the little screws until they tightened. She turned them more, and I winced. Another cruel turn, and I cried out.

"Oh!" This set of clamps was more intense than the first set she had placed on me.

"How dare you speak," Savanna said, and turned both the screws a little tighter. It was intense: a crushing pain in my nipples that soon subsided to a dull throbbing, warmish sting.

She was sucking my dick again. I had no complaints with

that at all. Then—I felt her tight hot pussy wrapping around my dick like she was a virgin.

"God, Franco. You're so big."

"You make me big. Bigger then I ever imagined," I said, which was really only a half lie. I know in my teen years my dick was bigger, or maybe I was just thinner. I don't know. I just know that I was blessed with a good tool and it worked properly most of the time, so I couldn't really complain.

She controlled her pussy, using it to maximize pleasure for both of us. She lowered herself in short shallow strokes as if she were a puppet dancing off the end of my dick. She took the length long and hard and deep. She lowered herself as far as she could.

She sat there for a moment and then tried to lower herself down a little more.

She jiggled her hips a bit, maybe to get her clit in on the action. I wished I had my hands: I could have rubbed her hungry clit for her while she fucked my dick.

She rode me like that for several moments, calling out names. She stopped for a while and I felt as though she had sprinkled something on me. I thought I caught the whiff of herbs of some sort and then there was a splash of something that maybe I should call a spray, since there was moisture.

"What are you doing?" I asked. There was no reply but her toneless humming.

"Don't worry. I'm back. Did your cock miss my cunt?" she asked.

She squatted back on my dick and rode it like she hadn't been fucked in a week. At last, she shuddered and moaned. She fell forward, nearly dragging the blindfold from my eyes. Laughingly, she tore it off.

"No worries here," she said.

As I was able to see her, it seemed like she had shifted in some way. How in the space of a few minutes she seemed one way and now seemed another.

I didn't know what to make of it. She seemed happier. More fulfilled.

"OK, pony boy. I'm saddling up and getting me some nice white pony cock for breakfast."

Savanna set to work untying my bindings. My hands and feet throbbed joyfully as the circulation returned to them. Savanna took my wrists, one at a time, and rubbed them gently.

"I remember so many things, Franco," she said dreamily, massaging and kissing my hands.

Her eyes were distant as she spoke, as if she were watching a scene unfold beyond my vision.

Her lips met mine and she sprawled on top of me, hugging me. Hungrily we kissed, all games and pretenses pushed aside. Now it was just me and Savanna, mind to mind, flesh to flesh.

After all I had been through this night, I was finally beginning to unravel the mystery of Savanna. Gone were her playthings, her people, her toys. There were no ropes or whips to invoke power over me. Now it was man and woman.

I rolled her over and pinned her down, palm to palm, as I

kissed her. With every kiss, I ached to know what was in her mind, her heart. Our connection was strong, as though we had kissed a thousand times before with passion and abandon. After watching her all night being taken and serviced by her slaves, I relished the chance for my turn.

My mouth found her breasts and I playfully toyed with her nipple rings. I stared with astonishment at her beauty.

"Savanna," I sighed as I nuzzled into her breasts. "Savanna, they were right."

It seemed like one of those stories you'd hear from someone you didn't know very well. A beautiful woman luring a man to her arms. Yet it had happened to me. Somehow out of all the men in this universe, in this club even, Savanna had been waiting for me.

"Why?" I asked her, kissing her gently on the lips.

"Why what?" she asked.

"Why did you pick me?"

She laughed.

"My dear silly Franco, I didn't pick you."

"What?" My feelings were hurt.

"Fate picked us long ago. We have our destiny to follow." She broke her hands away from mine and cradled my cheeks in her hand. "Don't worry your mind with such things. Let us explore each other."

She wrapped her legs around my hips and drew me into her. My pole parted her flesh with easy force. She was warm and inviting. A little sigh escaped from her lips as she hugged me to her.

"My Franco . . . my Franco . . ." she muttered.

I pushed into her harder, and lifted her hips a bit. Pushing myself up more, I was able to get better traction. I fucked her harder. She held on to my biceps. For a while, I didn't think of anything but Savanna's flesh wrapped around mine. It was easy to be in the moment as I fucked that beautiful woman. She whispered and sighed in my ear, but I know not what she said. My body was all-consuming, every nerve-ending on fire. The culmination of the night's events was happening right here and right now. All the teasing and tormenting she had subjected me to were forgotten as my cock pumped in and out. She tensed up and made a sound like an "oh." My dick slipped around in her as she came with gushing force. My cock was pushed out with an expulsion of ejaculate.

"Oh!" She said again in the strange little voice. She grabbed at my dick and shoved it back in, pumping it against that sweet spot. She gushed again and laughed.

"Franco. See what you do to me."

We kissed, wrapping our arms and legs around each other. Savanna rolled me over so that I was on my back. As I looked up at her, I noticed our reflections in the mirror affixed to the top of the canopy. Her smooth, muscular back, my happy flushed face, her long legs tangled around mine. It was like watching a porn movie.

As she sat up and rode my cock, I noticed a shadow in the corner of the mirror. At first, I thought it was some sort of curtain, but upon closer inspection, I came to realize that it was a person. Someone was hiding above the bed, in a corner of the domed ceiling, almost blending in with the paintings. The flashes of images I had noticed all night now made sense.

The huddled figure was cloaked in robes and there was a strange plastic look to his face. His arm was moving rapidly and it wasn't hard to determine that he was jerking off. Savanna continued to fuck me, to kiss me, to ride my pleasure pole. I closed my eyes and ignored the Phantom of the Opera.

She rode me long and hard, enjoying wave after wave of pleasure. Our bodies played in harmony, as if we had been making love our whole life. We knew where to touch, to look, to caress, how to send each other into joyful bliss. I had never experienced so much emotion in this physical act. Never knew that there could be emotion. My mind was filled with brightness and joy, my flesh singing as I never knew it could sing. The poor Phantom was trapped playing with himself, voyeuristically longing for love. I had found love. I had found lust. I had found the woman I had had been searching for my whole life. My melancholy was satiated. My loneliness was over.

Or so I thought, in that moment.

I wanted to believe, in that moment.

I turned Savanna over and she balanced on her hands and knees. My dick thrust into her doggy-style. At first, I relished the sensation of this new angle, and slid my dick slowly in and out. As my excitement grew, my pace picked up. Before long, I was fucking her harder than I've ever fucked anyone in my life. The bed shook with my force and she was merciless to move at all as I held her hips. One of my hands grabbed and kneaded her juicy butt while the other one kept our angle at the maximum pleasure zone.

It didn't take long for me to come. I wanted to last longer, but it just wasn't possible. The moment came and went so quickly, yet I can still remember it. The sensation of fucking Savanna was unlike any I had before or since. My mind stopped as pleasure took over. My nerves were awash in a sea of swirling, tingling sensations.

We collapsed together on the bed and I glanced up to watch us happily snuggling in each other's arms.

We were perfect together. My dark hair with her blond hair. My muscular body embracing her lean taut figure. My loins finally felt content. My mind was content. Blissful in my contentedness, I dozed.

CHAPTER 13.

When I opened my eyes again, I was struck by the smell of incense permeating through the room. I was lying spread-eagle on a king-sized canopy bed. I looked up and saw myself reflected in the large mirror on the ceiling of the canopy. I smiled as I remembered watching Savanna and me writhing and twisting, our flesh connecting and reconnecting.

"Hurry up." Savanna stood at the foot of the bed. She had put on another dominatrix outfit. Leather straps laced around her neck like snakes, winding and writhing along her flesh until they curled at the stilettos she wore on her feet. She had a studded leather g-string between her legs. As she put one of her stiletto feet on the bed, I could see her pussy lips spreading. I yearned to taste her sweet nectar once more. Her hands held a flogger, which she snapped toward me.

"They are waiting. We don't want to waste the night."

I quickly pulled on my leather pants, hopping as I followed her out the door.

She was a flash of long blond hair and black leather as her beautiful bottom led me toward another room. I wondered just how many rooms this club must have. I felt like I had been wandering for a lifetime and yet my adventure was still not complete. I had found Savanna, as everyone had told me to all night. Now what was I to do? What was the plan? What did she want with me?

The next room we entered was guarded by two tall, broad, black men. They both wore leather loincloths and black leather armbands. Various tattoos adorned their bodies. They nodded at me as I slid past them.

The room was one of the most amazing fetish rooms I'd ever seen. It was enormous and there were scenes going on all over the place. I saw cages and stocks and strange types of chairs and tables and various other pieces of equipment. It made the cage room in the other part of the club look like child's play.

Savanna stopped at one of the sets of stocks. Long, black curly hair hung from the neck hole, the owner of the face unseen. It was a girl in a long white nightgown. I realized that it was Christine, from the Phantom-of-the-Opera room. Savanna grabbed a handful of hair. She pulled the girl's head up. Christine's pretty blue eyes were wide with fearful adoration.

"Miss . . . Mistress Savanna . . ." She smiled. Savanna put her face close to Christine's.

"Do not look me in the eye, wench," she said. Christine averted her gaze.

Savanna massaged Christine's hair and scalp roughly. Christine kept her eyes down. Savanna pulled Christine's hair.

"You've been a naughty little girl, haven't you?" Savanna said.

"No, mistress, I only just . . ."

"You were singing again, weren't you?"

"Yes, mistress."

"And you know what that means."

"Yes, mistress." Savanna walked around the stock, unhooking her flogger from her belt. She pulled Christine's nightgown up around her waist. Christine wore knee-length pantaloons with many ruffles.

"Franco, come here." Savanna waved me over. "No . . . closer."

I stood beside Savanna.

"Yes?"

Savanna cracked the whip against my thigh. It stung and I rubbed it.

"Yes, mistress . . . my queen," I whispered.

"Tell me, what do you see when you look at Miss Christine's ass?" She stood staring at Christine's white pantaloons.

"I see . . . I see, underwear. Big puffy underwear," I said. Savanna nodded.

"Yes, that is what we see. I do not want to see underwear. I want to see her naked ass." Savanna snapped her whip at me again. I approached Christine. I took her pantaloons by the elastic waist and pulled them down. I heard her gasp.

Her ass was beautiful. Two juicy, plump apple cheeks that ended at the base of a back that was probably just as killer. My cock grew hard at the sight of it. I arranged her nightgown higher along her back and caught a glimpse of her large breasts through the sheer material. I made her step out of her pantaloons and hung them nicely on the stock next to her head. I returned to Savanna's side.

Savanna flicked me with the whip again.

"Warm her up," she commanded.

"What?" I asked

"Rub her ass. Make her want me."

Well, she didn't have to ask me twice. I went over to those luscious apple cheeks and started to knead them beneath my fingers. I pulled and pushed her fleshly mounds together and apart. I stared at her warm dark holes appearing and disappearing as I massaged her ass.

"Pinch her," Savanna said.

I pinched Christine lightly along her ass, quickly like little beetles skittering along her flesh. I increased the pressure and slowed down the pinching, relishing her soft flesh between my fingers. I massaged and pinched her until Savanna told me to stop.

"Come kneel beside me."

I returned to Savanna's side and knelt down on the cold, concrete floor. I watched with fascination as she began to flog Christine. Her strokes were even, rhythmical and as the sharp sting of her flogger echoed through the room, other people stopped what they were doing and came over to watch. I recognized a few faces from my previous adventures. Faces that I had played with or watched playing with others.

At last Christine's ass was a bright red. Red streaks created a crisscross pattern along those pretty apple cheeks. Savanna hooked her flogger back onto her belt. She stepped closer to Christine to appreciate her handiwork. It was a work of art, the red streaks against pale flesh. Her ass was even more beautiful. I yearned to plunge my hard cock right between her folds.

"Come along, Franco," Savanna said as she pushed her way through the circle of people who had gathered to watch her. She walked along until she came to a woman tied to a table. I recognized the woman as Dr. Frankenstein's monster, Agatha. Not a monster at all, but a beautiful creation. The creature was shackled to a table, her arms spread wide. Her legs were slightly bent and shackled at the ankle. The table was more like a birthing bed or something with an indent between her legs so that someone could stand there and fuck her. The creature had huge tits and her pussy was spread wide for all to see. She was sucking the cock of a tall, dark man who stood above her. Several other dark men stood around her, cheering her on. I stared at her damp pussy lips, wondering how many dicks had slammed into her that night.

"Franco. You must try my new toy," Savanna grinned. She took a riding crop from her belt and flicked it in the air. It made a loud cracking noise. The men around Dr.

Frankenstein's monster looked at her. Their eyes were wide when they saw who wanted their attention.

"You may all leave now. I want to play with my new toy," she said. The men took off like a flash. I watched as Savanna walked over to the table and stood on it. She kneeled over the creature's head and slid her g-string to the side.

"Beautiful creature of the night, show me pleasure," she whispered throatily to the creature as she sat down on her face. Savanna's face was pure pleasure as the creature licked her. Savanna turned to me.

"Come over here," she said.

I went over to Savanna. Her cheeks were flushed as she squatted over the girl and her busy tongue. Savanna grabbed my pants and unbuttoned them. Within minutes, she had unzipped my fly and had my cock in her mouth. She was a goddess, my Savanna. How she could suck and lick. She ran her tongue up and down the length of my ever-hardening shaft. She sucked the tip noisily. She spit on my dick like a dirty slut and rammed it down her throat. I fucked her mouth for a while as she squirmed and moaned on top of the creature. She pushed me back.

"Fuck her now." She pointed. "Fuck that steaming hot cunt. Look at her, how she wants you."

The girl's legs were wide apart and I could see her glistening cunt. Her clit was large and hard, her hole still open from whoever had been pumping into her before we arrived. I took my cock from Savanna's mouth and plunged it into that sweet darkness. The creature moaned. I pulled my large dick out, nice and slow, so she could savor every inch of it. I pushed it back in again, this time right to the hilt. She hitched her breath but before she could breath again I was slamming into her with a fury. I stared at Savanna's ass while I fucked the creature. Agatha's head was bobbing with my every stroke, sucking on Savanna's clit. Savanna turned back to look at me.

"Slower, Franco. You must savor the pleasure."

I slowed my strokes down, though I just wanted to ram this girl. I couldn't believe that I even could get it up again after all the fucking I'd done all night, but here I was. Faced with beauty and the beast. Yet the beast wasn't beastly at all. In fact, she was beautiful.

Savanna stood up on the table and turned to face me.

"Stop," she commanded. I thought I was going to die. Stop? Stop? I stopped.

Every time I thought I was growing used to her forceful ways, it was like starting over again.

Savanna stroked my hard shaft with her long fingernails. Teasing me mercilessly.

"Surely you aren't ready to come just yet?" she asked. I swallowed. I could see that this was going to be another endurance test of some sort. I hoped I was up to it. She toyed with one of her nipple rings as she fixed me with her beautiful gaze.

I stood back from the table as she straddled the creature's torso. Savanna played with the creature's enormous tits. She stroked them and massaged them, pulling on the nipples until they stood up straight on their own. She lowered her mouth to them, sucking first one and then the other. The creature stared at me, longing for my cock again, I'm sure. I resisted the urge to stroke myself as I watched the beautiful women kissing and rubbing their breasts against each other.

"Shove your dick in her pussy again," Savanna ordered. She crouched over the girl, her body in line with the girl's as I shoved my hard cock back into that delicious creature's pussy.

"Fuck her hard." She sucked on the creature's tits while I fucked with long hard slow strokes.

"Faster," Savanna gasped. I picked up the pace, staring at Savanna's ass right in front of me. I held on to Savanna's hips for support.

"Now, quick, shove it in my ass," Savanna commanded.

I slid my cock from one hole to new, tighter warmth. I thought I was going to come right then and there, but I managed to hold off. Savanna was deliciously tight as I slowly ground into her. I noticed her hand had gone down to the creature's pussy and she was fingering her. They both moaned and groaned with twin pleasure. I was moaning and groaning myself.

I pulled out my cock so that I could see Savanna's gaping asshole. A delicious sweet hole beckoning with possibility and pleasure. Goosebumps shivered up my spine as I plunged back into her again. She was pushing against me, harder and harder. I heard her squealing and laughing, kissing and talking dirty to the creature below her.

"Harder," she ordered. "Slower and harder."

I rammed her to the hilt and my own fingers slid down to her clit. I teased her clit as my cock rooted for home. Suddenly

I felt her clenching against me, throbbing with orgasm. She moaned and sighed, shuddering on top of the creature. I kept fucking her, slow and hard as she had commanded. She went limp for a minute, gasping. Sweat glistened in little beads on her back. Suddenly, she tossed her hair.

"Enough." She kicked me back with her heel. My cock slid out and was in the cool, unrelenting air once more. I yearned to feel the warmth of her ass, her cunt, her mouth. I didn't care what. I wanted to feel her wrapped around me.

She pressed her hand under my chin and drew her mouth toward me. As she kissed me, her tongue ran along my teeth. She drew my tongue into her mouth, sucking on it. I wished it were my cock again. My cock was so hard; I swear I could have burst any second. Instead, she bit my tongue and pushed me back.

"Save it. There is more work to be done. Much more work."

A sweet voice filled the air. I looked over to the platform stage, and Christine was singing her song. The one written for Savanna. The Phantom was playing the piano, and Christine's beautiful voice carried over the moaning and groaning of pleasure.

Savanna watched, clasping her hands together with delight.

"She has a most beautiful voice," Savanna sighed. "To think, they wrote this song just for me."

I nodded. The few hours that had passed since hearing the piece first performed had ripened the performance. The piano and voice danced their duet, causing everyone in the room to stop what they were doing and focus on the performance.

Over by the platform stage, I noticed Alice in Wonderland and Little Bo Peep. They had their arms around each other and were clearly mesmerized by the beauty of the lush, plaintive song.

After Christine finished singing, she left the stage to a polite round of applause. Classical music played from somewhere and soon the stage was filled with tiny young ladies in tutus.

"I love the ballet," Savanna sighed. She rested her head on my shoulder and looped an arm around me.

"Don't you love the ballet, Franco? The fluid movements, the pretty costumes, the tragic stories?"

"The ballet has always pleased me. Actually, I enjoy musicals of all sorts. Broadway, opera, ballet . . . music inspires me."

"Me, too. I often wonder if in another life I danced or sang."

"You have a beautiful voice," I said, remembering her low, sultry Celtic song. Even though she wasn't really singing as you would on a stage, it had been clear there was talent in those vocal cords.

"I studied singing for a while. All kinds of dance, too. Even ballet. I guess I love to be center stage." Savanna grinned.

"Who, you?" I teased her with sarcasm.

"Oh, stop, Franco. We all had our dreams as children. Some of us grow up to live our dreams, others have to find new ones."

"Did you follow your dreams, Savanna?"

"I'm here with you now, am I not?" Her face beamed as if she were a child. There was wide-eyed innocence there. For a moment, but only for a moment.

It was that glimpse of innocence that I saw in my Savanna, in that moment, that I've held in my heart to this day. We all have a dual nature. Some of us more than others.

When the ballet number was over, there was more applause. Dr. Frankenstein walked onto the stage and spoke into the microphone.

"Ladies and gentlemen, thank you all for coming out tonight. We hope you are enjoying this celebration of fall, of the world between worlds, of Halloween."

There were cheers and claps from the audience.

"Our biggest thanks goes out to Savanna, our Mistress, our Queen of the Night."

More cheers erupted from the audience.

"Savanna, please come up on the stage."

Savanna disengaged herself from me and went up on the platform.

"Savanna, I wanted to officially present you with my creation. I hope you enjoy her."

Dr. Frankenstein stood proudly as Agatha came onto the stage. She was wearing a strap-on dildo.

"Your present pleases me, doctor." Savanna smiled. "She is a vision of perfection."

Dr. Frankenstein blushed and removed his glasses to wipe them. Savanna planted a kiss on his cheek. She went over to Agatha and looked her over.

"Yes, I've seen this beautiful creature in action. You've done a fine job."

She gave Agatha a hug.

"I'll be seeing you in my chambers later." She grinned. The crowd laughed.

"I want to thank everyone for coming out tonight. This has been a fantastic celebration. Now please, enjoy what is left of tonight, for tomorrow is quickly upon us."

There was more applause as people scattered to resume the play they had started. Savanna took my hand and we made our way through the crowd.

CHAPTER *14.*

O ur long winding path returned us to that cavernous palace where I first laid eyes on Savanna. It was strange to come back to this large, hollow room when all around me there were rooms packed with people. An entire club full of people were dancing and laughing and exploring each other.

Here, it was just Savanna and me.

Savanna took my hand and led me over to her throne. She sat back on it, her legs spread to either side. Her pussy was open and glistening. My eyes closed as I thought of how sweet she felt clamped around my cock in that other life.

"Don't just stand there, Franco. Service me."

I knelt down before Savanna and buried my face between her legs. My tongue quickly found her little pleasure nugget and I tapped on it persistently. Her fingers gently toyed with my hair. When she finally spoke, it was in a faraway voice.

"I used to dream of a time, Franco, when I would be everything I wanted to be."

I lapped and circled her clit. I could barely hear her; it was more like she was talking to herself. I didn't pay much heed to what she was saying as I was trying to dance to my own song in her pussy.

"It's funny. How you can have it all and yet feel incomplete. Why is it that our work doesn't define the whole person? Why is it that we have to be so many different people all rolled into one?" she mused.

I moaned a response and the vibration of it sent her twitching.

"Ooo, do that again. Hum on my clit."

I hummed on her pussy, flicking her clit with my tongue. She spread her legs impossibly wide as she pushed her pussy more into my mouth, as if craving the vibration way up inside of her as well.

I licked and sucked her, humming so that my vibrating mouth could pleasure her more. She succumbed to my power for a moment. Then she sat up and pushed me away.

"We must have wine," she said. "We must have a feast."

She patted the little stairs leading up to her throne.

"You may sit here."

I sat at her feet.

She rang the little bell and within a minute, Star and Scorpio arrived.

"You may prepare red wine and a variety of snacks," she instructed.

"As you wish," Star bowed.

Savanna dismissed them.

"You do like red wine, Franco?" It was more of a statement then a question.

"Yes." I licked my lips, still tasting her pussy juice on them.

"Excellent." She glanced up at the television sets, watching a few of the antics taking place in the various rooms. Her eyes gleamed with voyeuristic pleasure.

"Would you like me to take care of your aching pussy?" I asked her as I turned around toward her again. My fingers massaged her thighs as I spread her legs wide open once more. She sank back in her throne, her head thrown back on the cushy red velvet padding on the back of the chair.

That chair was probably more comfortable than my bed at home. At any rate, I suckled on her pussy until the return of the slaves.

Delicious treats were brought in. There was enough food to feed an army. There were meats and deserts, fruits and vegetables. Many of the trays were laid on portable stands. Desmire presented us with a platter of wonderful-looking treats.

Savanna plucked a strawberry tart from the desert tray and popped it into her mouth.

"Delicious." She sighed, savoring the sweet taste of fruit and custard.

She took another strawberry tart and licked at the glaze coating of the strawberry with her long pink tongue. She offered it to me and I licked it as well. She smiled, one of those knowing smiles couples have with each other to show they are thinking something warm and pleasant. There was a connection between us. A static charge, like clothes sticking together when they come out of the dryer. It was so easy. This exchange of energy was a happy harmony. It started to dawn on me that maybe there had been something to all this, after all.

Savanna could possibly be my soul mate. The thought elated me greatly and I picked up the strawberry and held it between my teeth. Savanna's lips pursed out and slurped the strawberry from me. She chewed it as she kissed me. The smell of strawberries filled my senses. To this day, when I smell strawberries, I think of that moment. That magical moment when everything made sense. When I believed everything was going to be OK.

The bald slave, Star, indicated the wine goblets.

"Would you like me to pour the wine now, Queen Savanna?" she asked.

"Please do. And hurry. I don't want to keep my handsome man waiting."

As the wine was poured from a stone jug, I noticed there was a steam rising from it.

"Hot wine?" I asked as the scent of oranges and cinnamon filled my nose.

"Sort of . . . mulled wine. A deep red wine with cinnamon, cloves, oranges and other wonderful fall smells. Don't you love it?" She leaned over the table and sniffed the air.

"I find it deliciously enticing. Like you," I said. The smell reminded me of something, but I couldn't place my finger on it. Something about holidays and never seeing family and all that. An ache started to leach through my happiness moment.

"Franco. Come, you must try it. It is a delicious concoction." She pushed a glass toward me. She lifted her glass in a toast.

"To my handsome Franco. I treasure you by my side every day."

I didn't say much after that. I didn't say much at all. I had a little talk with myself in that strange world between happy and melancholy. I reasoned with myself, the paradox of my existence.

"I hope to be with you always, Savanna." I raised my glass and clinked it with hers. "I hope we can work something out. I've barely met you and I feel this . . . thing."

"A lot of men find me hot," she sighed.

"Maybe so. But this is more then hot, Savanna."

As I sipped on the wine, the pungent scent of something else stirred a memory. After I had about half the glass, I suddenly remembered where I had smelled the wine before. It wasn't a Christmas or Thanksgiving memory haunting me. It wasn't a lost pet or a girl that wouldn't return my calls.

No, it was the smell associated with three very strange and sexy witches trapped in the catacombs of this club somewhere. Their strange words and wild and wicked costumes flashed through my memory. How their beauty lay under the masks. Their little talks came back to me. As memories of them sucking and fucking me and my friends floated through my head, I remembered, too, the whole person of their existence. They were the ones making the potion. They were the ones who propelled the night forward.

The brew I held in my hands was the potion. I closed my eyes. I was doomed. I had already drunk of the mixture. Savanna was watching me intently, her eyes shining with secrets.

"Is it good, Franco? Do you like it?"

I nodded as I struggled to finish the rest of the rich brew. She put her hand over mine. I realized as she did so that I was only fooling myself. There was no spell. There was no long-lost love or anything else. It was a clever treasure hunt designed to make a customer feel he is special. She probably had already played these games with others that night.

In considering how this was all a façade, everything was a fake Halloween billboard, right down to this potion, I fell out of the game for a while, disillusioned. There were no potions. There were no spells. My disillusionment grew into more disillusionment. I fought the clutches of melancholy and scrambled for the moment.

Eventually I realized that I have to be responsible for me. If I dug Savanna, then that was fine. However, if I didn't dig her, but just wanted to fuck her, well, I had to figure that out, too. I had fucked her already and yearned to fuck her again. I could die happy knowing I'd fuck her every single day of my life until I dropped dead. The problem with a lady like Savanna was that you never knew what she was going to say or do.

When there was only a mouthful of wine left in my glass, I clicked it against Savanna's glass.

"Here's to us. Here's everything we ever wanted and everything we ever hoped to be."

I finished the wine, tilting my head back to drain every drop. Savanna was watching me intently. It was almost like she was waiting for me to turn into some sort of boogeyman. I didn't believe though. I didn't believe the potion had power.

I didn't want to believe the potion had power.

There was no magic. There was no witchcraft. The potions were as fake as the masks on the people down stairs. It was oranges and cinnamon and a few green herb things for good effect. No more, no less.

Satisfied with my self-analysis, I tried to relax and enjoy the rest of my time with Savanna. Relaxing wasn't possible. It wasn't on the schedule.

My fingers felt strange, as if they were growing warm. A tingling sensation passed through my body. As quickly it had come, it was gone. Like a wave or a ripple. However, it left me with a really big boner.

As I dreamed my little dreams, Savanna summoned her team.

"Bring me the bed, and the equipment."

The slaves pushed in the large canopy bed on wheels. When the mammoth wooden structure reached the center of the room, they fastened the braking system. The bed was gorgeous. The pillars had gargoyles carved into them that turned into giant claw feet at the bottom. On the top of each post was a massive gargoyle head, complete with open mouth and long glaring teeth. The eyes flickered with orange-flamed lights inside. The canopy was a massive display of curtains and drapes tied back with ropes.

Once more, Star and Scorpio tied me to the bedpost. Once more, I was forced to watch Savanna enjoy the pleasures of her servants. Agatha had joined the team of Star and Desmire. The three slave girls ran their fingers along Savanna, stroking, prodding, and pinching. Savanna grinned evilly at me.

The bald slave girl, Star, took a dildo from the table and returned to Savanna. She pulled Savanna over to me. Star stood behind Savanna and spread her pussy lips open so that I could see her clit and her gaping hole. I struggled against the ropes, craning my neck to try to lick Savanna's sweet hole. Star pulled Savanna back just beyond my reach. I could smell her hot, juicy cunt throbbing with anticipation.

Star plunged the dildo into Savanna's steamy cunt. She thrust the dildo in and out of Savanna with long, slow, deep strokes. Savanna held onto the bedpost for support. The bed shook as Savanna wriggled under the dildo. Star licked Savanna's juicy pussy as she pushed the dildo slowly in and out of that hot pinkness. It was agony to watch that woman flicking Savanna's sensitive clit with her skilled tongue.

As I watched that tiny little clit get bigger and harder, I wanted go over and claim what was mine. I wanted nothing more then to yank my head up and hold that trembling clit between my teeth and flick it with my tongue. The bald-headed woman seemed to be doing a good job at it. Savanna wriggled her hips, throwing her head back so that her blond hair was streaming down her back. Her dark eyes glanced over at me. She saw me staring, my cock a rock-hard pole. It grew, stretching longer, aching as my mouth and tongue ached. Ached for that soft sweet flesh. There was no need for a dildo to be sliding in out of her when my cock would do as well.

But there was to be no Savanna for me as the teasing continued. It was worse this time, being tortured by the teasing. I thought it would be worse watching Savanna coming over and over again with other people when I yearned to fuck her. Now that I had fucked her, it was far worse to watch her enjoy others. I knew the magic of her cunt and I wanted it back.

Agatha walked up to Savanna, wearing a cock harness. Savanna grabbed the plastic shaft and stroked it, as if it would feel pleasure. Savanna licked it and sucked it, staring at me.

Soon, both women had mounted Savanna and were double fucking her with their strap-on dildos. It was one of the kinkiest, most arousing sights I'd ever seen. Two beautiful women, one bald, one a sewn-together creature, with huge fake dicks, plunging in and out of Savanna's ass and pussy. They pumped together in unison, taking long, pleasurable strokes in time to Savanna's commands.

I wanted to scream that they should use my big hard cock. Touch my hard pulsing dick. Stop using the fake cocks and ride my real one.

But I remained silent as they played their little games.

When Savanna had had enough of their double-penetrating antics, she commanded them to leave her. She stood up and went over to a side table where Scorpio and the tall black man from the dungeon were waiting with towels and wet cloths.

They washed her carefully and gently from bowls of warm water. She regarded me with amusement.

"I want you," I said softly. "I want you and only you."

Savanna laughed.

"We shall see about that."

She clapped her hands together a couple of times and Scorpio, Desmire, and Star untied me from the post. However, then they tied me to the bed, my arms and legs splayed out and fastened by ropes to the pillars. I watched as the slaves worked quickly and efficiently. I wondered if I would ever learn how to tie ropes so rapidly and firmly.

Savanna sat in her throne, sipping on a glass of wine. She regarded me thoughtfully.

"I know what you need. I know how to see your strength. How to appreciate the fine specimen of man you are and can be."

"Come to me, Savanna. I want to share pleasure with you."

My cock was hard and pointing straight up in the air.

"My handsome Franco . . . such a big hard cock you have. Will you save it for me?" she asked, giving me a sly look.

Scorpio and the black man brought in a young petite girl. She was so thin you'd think that she would blow away in the wind.

They each took an arm and a leg and hoisted her in the air. Without a word, they planted her firmly on my cock.

The girl yelled with pleasure as my cock impaled her to the hilt. She was tight and warm as my cock pushed through her flesh. They moved her up and down, very slowly at first so I could relish every inch of her tight little hole. Watching her held by the two tall muscular men made her seem even more helpless. The idea of her helplessness combined with my own excited me. My cock was so hard it was painful. Her little pussy lips were stretched to the hilt as she slid up and down my massive dick.

They pumped her up and down faster, picking up speed. The girl was gasping for breath as they rapidly fucked her on my cock. Savanna was watching me with a smile on her face. The girl was wet and her juices slipped along my pole. When I tried to thrust my hips up to meet the girl's tight pussy, a sharp sting landed on my thigh.

"Don't move." Savanna's voice controlled me but it was Star who had slapped me with the whip.

"We control the pleasure, not you," Savanna said.

I stopped moving my hips. But it was difficult. The urge to fuck was so primal, so strong, and this girl's cunt was so deliciously tight.

They moved the girl faster and soon she was yelling. Their strong arms moved the girl up and down, up and down, and my cock stayed big and hard. She twinged and wriggled, the pulses of her orgasm slipping and sliding on my cock like hail pellets in a storm.

"Oh, god, I can't take any more!" the girl cried out, as she came again. Her head rolled back as she gasped for air. Scorpio and the black man pushed her down one more time, fully impaling her on my cock. It took every ounce of strength I had in me not to come. The girl collapsed in a heap. They carried her limp, spent body out of the room.

I lay in wait of what would happen next. I dozed for a moment, lamenting the lack of warmth around my hard throbbing dick and catching my breath from the sudden removal of my pleasure.

When I opened my eyes again, there was Savanna. Her dark eyes gazed down on me from the foot of the bed. She smiled as she saw me looking at her.

"Did you enjoy, that Franco?" she asked, crawling catlike up the bed.

"Most definitely," I said. My cock was still hard as a rock. She looked at it.

"Are you ready for more? Can you take any more?"

She lowered her head down until her breath was hot on my cock.

"You've been such a naughty boy, Franco, that I'm not sure I'm ever going to let you come again."

Her grin was wide. Almost too wide in the flickering candlelight. Shadows danced across her face. Her tongue reached out and flicked the end of my shaft, very quickly. One little stroke and she turned back to me as the sensation hung in the air like a person poised on a tightrope.

My cock ached. My balls ached. She knew it. It was in her eyes, the way she grabbed the base of my shaft and held it firmly. She was powerful in how she stood there, looking down on me.

Her strength was so omnipresent that I almost felt fearful of her. She lowered her face to mine and looked me in the eye.

"You need to earn it, Franco. You need to earn me."

"What should I do? What do you want?"

"Play the games and you will see. It will all come out in the end."

I kept my mouth shut but I wanted to point out that I had already played many games to earn her. I had watched her fuck and suck so many people in the few hours we had been together. She had tied me up and tortured me with whips and women, yet she still had more sadistic torments in mind. She was determined to have me prove my desire for her, over and over again. As she decided what to tease me with next, I had a suspicion that no matter what happened or what I said, I would never be able to prove to her that she was enough.

Maybe there had been something from the past that came into this, haunting her. Maybe I reminded her of someone she wanted to get revenge on. Or maybe she just got off on having a man tied up and doing her biding.

Savanna sashayed over to her table of treasures and picked out a long red tapered candle. She picked up a lighter and clicked it. The flame shot up quickly.

"That should be you, Franco. Quick to be at my attention, whenever I want you. Whenever I'm ready."

I nodded.

"The flame burns bright when it is here. But it can be snuffed out in a heartbeat."

"Yes, I know, Savanna," I said softly, my mind racing, wondering how she was going to torture me next.

Suddenly, the bondage seemed too much. I didn't feel like I was playing a game in the funhouse anymore. Fear and paranoia rippled through me. I pulled against my restraints.

"What's the matter, Franco? Afraid you will come too hard?"

She lit the candle that was in her hand. She held it up, admiring the flame.

"Pretty flame burns so bright. It lights our world with its eager growth. Our energy feeds it. Do you know that, Franco?"

"Energy doesn't feed a candle, Savanna. Fire burns from oxygen."

"We have the oxygen, Franco. And we have the energy too. The energy makes the candle burn brighter and stronger. You can control the dance of the flame. Watch and see."

Savanna looked down at the flame. As she came closer to me, the flame flickered wildly.

"That's just you moving and breathing on it that makes it dance so."

"Perhaps. But why didn't it just go out then, if I'm moving and breathing."

"Probably has a good hold on that wick."

As I looked toward the candle, the flame shot higher and held steady. Savanna moved toward me again and as the flame grew higher, it didn't flicker at all.

"How do you do that? Is it a special candle?"

"No, it isn't special at all. It is us. Our energy."

I closed my eyes and thought about the candle flickering madly as it had before. When I opened my eyes the candle was flickering again. Savanna was standing beside me.

"See how the flame responds to your desires?" Her face glowed with knowledge. "We cast off energy. The candle tells us, Franco, that we are meant to be together."

"But we all cast off energy. I'm sure the candle would flicker for any two people."

Savanna shook her head.

"No. You can believe that if you want, but the reality is, that you and I together are special. Or at least our energy is."

She tilted the candle slightly and a drop of wax rolled off. It seemed to fall through the air in slow motion before hitting my chest. It burned for a moment and then stopped. It didn't hurt as much as I thought it would.

She covered my body with tiny pinpricks of candle wax. She would drip the wax onto my body and then lean down close to blow her hot breath against the cooling wax. Sensations of pain and pleasure rolled together into a wonderful eroticism.

As the wax dried on me like droplets of blood, I looked like I had been attacked by someone in a horror movie. Or maybe I more resembled a sieve.

Savanna stepped back to admire her handiwork.

She laughed and then turned the candle vertical. Slowly, she walked backward away from me.

"Look at the candlelight, Franco. See how the candle is sad it is leaving. So sad it just might decide to go out."

The candle flickered out. She put down the candle and came back to me.

"You look so . . . lonely, all tied up like that." She patted me on the face, much like a mother might to a sad child. It was strange. This whole night was an oddity I would never forget.

She disappeared to her table again and this time returned with a paddle.

"Franco has been a naughty boy."

She tapped the balls of my feet with the paddle. It woke up my circulation and soon my toes were buzzing with an unusual sensation. Slowly, she dragged the paddle along my legs, giving tiny slapping raps as she did so. The paddle slapped against my thighs. She lightly tapped at my erection, batting that massive rod back and forth in some kind of demented game. I didn't mind it. I didn't think it was the best sensation in the world, but it was part of my punishment and there was nothing I could do.

After she tired of smacking my penis around, she worked her way up to my shoulders with the little paddle. She used the tiny little slaps. All my waking nerves were tingling with a joyous anticipation. It felt better than Christmas morning, for now I knew what that big present in the corner was. There was no doubt in my mind that Savanna and I would be together. At the very least, I should be able to get her out on a few dates, I thought.

I imagined Savanna in my one-bedroom apartment.

"Franco, are you paying attention?"

Her words were angry and sharp as she walked away again. I was startled. I hadn't even heard her talking to me. It was as if I had been sucked into a magical little world. It made me wonder how long I had been lost in my own thoughts.

She returned with a crop.

"You aren't making this very easy. How am I supposed to see if you are a good boy when you keep being so very very bad?"

She slapped me along the legs with the riding crop. Her wrist jerked gently as she performed little slaps.

"Oh for god's sake, Franco," she said, exasperated. She put

down the crop and brought back another item from the table of delight. It was a large leather mask. There were no eyeholes. Before I could protest, she slipped the mask down over my head. It pretty much covered my face and I was rendered blind to her beauty. Now that I couldn't see, she resumed her riding-crop torture session.

From the way she held the crop, to the various techniques she used, she had me trembling with an exquisite pleasure.

She untied one arm and one leg. Thinking I might be free, I tried to wriggle myself over.

No such luck.

"Where do you think you're going?" she asked.

"Nowhere. I'm not going anywhere at all. I just thought that . . ."

"No. You will do what I say and when I say. Roll over this way."

She hitched up my arm to the post so that I was lying on my side with both arms and feet all tied up.

She rubbed my exposed ass with strong, firm hands.

She parted my ass cheeks until I was nervous with vulnerability.

She slapped those ass cheeks several times until I moaned. She rubbed my ass cheeks in a pinching massage. She pulled my ass apart and put her face into it. She wriggled her tongue around my asshole. I had never had that done to me before and it made me feel good.

She tongued my asshole for a while. Her tongue was warm and wet. After I overcame my initial apprehension, I sank into the pleasure she was giving me.

She slid off the bed.

Soon, my ass was assaulted with a flogger of some sort. I could feel many strands hitting me when she kept her flogging firm. Conversely, there was a featherlike quality to the touch of the leather as she dragged it along my ass.

She flipped and flopped it gently along my cheeks.

A pair of strong hands held my ass open so that the lashings hit their mark. Once in a while my ass cheeks would be spread to receive a fine slapping.

My ass surely must have been growing red from all the flogging. I was so contorted from the ropes and the bed. Finally, when I thought I couldn't take any more of the flogging, it stopped.

I was untied, released from my bindings. My wrists and ankles ached. My mask was removed and I had to blink several times to readjust my eyes to the dim lights.

Savanna had more treasures in store for me. She had the slave girls rub oil and soothing lotions on my wrists and ankles. Savanna herself spread oil along my chest and cock with long, smooth strokes.

Her hand slipped up and down my cock. I was still so hard. I didn't know it was possible to be hard for so long. Especially with all the flogging and such.

It was truly amazing to me how much my cock could endure.

I was so weak, I didn't know or understand what to do next.

"You must join us. We love to have our parties. What better night than this one for a party?"

She rang her bell and the slaves all returned.

Without any encouragement from Savanna, the slaves started to hug and kiss each other. Soon leather outfits were being unzipped and unbuckled. Clothes were falling to the ground all over the place.

They kissed and hugged.

They formed a chain of moving, writhing bodies. Sucking and hugging and fucking each other in one long, undulating snake. Savanna took me by the hand

"Come, let's go watch this wonderful time while we drink some wine."

She returned to the throne and I to her feet. She retrieved the canister the wine had come in and set to work pouring us two new cups. As she raised her glass, she said,

"Franco. I hope you have enjoyed your evening here."

For a moment I thought she was telling me my time was up, it was all over and I was out the door.

The cold light of day would make this strangest of nights seem like a wild fever dream. I couldn't concern myself with that for now.

"What would you like, Franco?" Savanna asked as her gaze traveled toward the writhing, undulating bodies before us.

"Is this another one of those esoteric questions, or do you mean right now?"

"What is your deepest darkest desire? Right now."

"You know what it is."

"Say it, say it out loud."

"I want your lips pressed to mine as my cock invades your warm pussy and I want us to remember that moment forever."

Savanna smiled.

"You remember that moment. You will remember that moment," she said.

I did remember that moment. When I had taken her on her bed. How she had kissed me and moaned my name as my cock slid into her. I treasured that moment, and being greedy I wanted that moment again.

"Shall we join the others?"

I nodded.

"Whatever you desire, my queen."

We joined the undulating pretzel on the bed.

Happy moans and shrieks filled the air.

There was an air of urgency as I found Savanna's pussy and lapped at it happily. Around me, I saw cocks entering cunts and mouths sucking on nipples.

I slid Savanna onto my cock.

As I was thrusting into her, one of the slave boys, Leo, the blond one, climbed on top of her. He fucked her tight asshole frantically. I could feel him pumping through the wall of her uterus and, as strange as the sensation was, it felt great. His muscles gleamed in the candlelight, his face in intense concentration as he slammed his dick in and out of her asshole. Savanna's mouth found mine and we kissed as her cries filled my throat.

Leo gave one final thrust and then pulled out, spraying her back with his come. The slave girls eagerly licked it off with loving tongues.

Savanna sat up and rode me harder. I felt her pussy clenching me as she came. No sooner had her orgasm subsided then she eased my cock out of her cunt. Savanna slid onto her back and slipped onto my cock. This time I pushed into her asshole with ease. I thought I was going to come right on the spot. Scorpio thrust his cock into her cunt and started pumping her.

"Harder!" she cried.

He pushed into her harder, thrusting to the hilt. He was large and I couldn't move at all while he was inside her.

It wasn't long before Scorpio came with a shout.

I turned Savanna over and fucked her asshole doggy-style. When I was ready to come she pulled away and took my cock in her mouth. I pumped into her pretty face furiously, and at last I relinquished myself to her.

For several minutes I lay in a reverie, half in and half out of consciousness. I was finally spent. Exhaustion consumed me and it would have been easy to slip into a comfortable sleep.

But there was to be no sleep for me that night.

Around me, the slaves gathered up their clothes and toys and set to work putting everything away. As two of the slaves made the bed, I was forced to stand and start looking for my clothes. Savanna held her arms out as Star and Scorpio bathed her with a wet cloth from the basin. They scrubbed her quickly and efficiently. Gone were the gentle, seductive touches and glances. Everything was businesslike, as the room was put back into order.

Savanna returned to her throne, wearing a red silk kimono. She was more beautiful then ever as she resumed her spot as ruler of her people. The canopy bed was wheeled away, as were all the tables of food and wine and toys. Ropes and chains were wound and sorted. Whips were hung on hooks on the back of one of the traveling dressers. The air was that of a carnival being torn down. I slipped on my shirt, and had a little more trouble pulling on my tight leather pants. I sat on the steps at Savanna's feet to pull on my boots. As I finished zipping them up, Savanna finally spoke.

"What did you think of your evening, Franco?"

I turned to look at her. She was watching me intently.

"I've never had such a night," I said honestly.

"I see."

"I've never felt so connected to someone."

"Someone?"

"You. I feel like I've known you forever."

"I feel the same way, Franco."

I took her hand and kissed it.

"I want to get to know you better, Savanna. I want to see you again."

"You will, Franco, you will."

"When? Can we go for breakfast? Surely you must be hungry?"

Savanna laughed.

"My dear Franco. I am full. I am content. Don't worry, you will see me again."

My heart wanted to believe her, but in my soul, I knew she was lying.

Although, maybe she wasn't.

I stumbled through the maze of corridors, alone and exhausted. On one hand, I was elated with my adventure. My heart sang as I realized that Savanna was the woman I had secretly desired. She had the qualities of my elusive trophy wife. Perhaps I had formed my fantasy woman in her image the whole time, a hangover from another life.

On the other hand, a sense of dread crept up on me. Exhaustion suddenly filled every pore of my body and my mind seemed unable to make sense of all that had happened. My nerves sang, stretched to the shaky limits of pleasure and pain. My heart pounded, loving the adventure I'd had, but knowing, on some level, that it never would happen again.

Not the free and easy seduction of the Halloween rooms.

Not the anticipation and elation of meeting my soul mate.

My friends were hanging around the lobby, when I emerged, spent and speechless from the catacombs. They slapped me on the back.

"So? How did it go?" they asked. "Where did you go?"

"I found Savanna," I said.

"We figured as much. That's why we waited for you. We wanted to make sure you didn't get scammed or anything."

"No, I didn't get scammed. Not for money, anyway," I said. "What about you guys?"

"I stayed with the mermaids. I'm probably more shriveled then a raisin after sitting in those Jacuzzis for hours."

"I went back to the diner. I wanted to see the roller-skating meat locker lady you told us about. Man, she was something sweet."

As my friends and I made our way out into the morning sun, I saw Savanna around every corner.

Every car that passed us by, every blond woman in a café window, spoke to me of Savanna. In the glint of the sun on a window to the shadow of darkness in the alley, she haunted me, day after day.

It has been a very long time since that night. A time of endless dreaming and wondering. If we were soul mates, as she seemed to think we were, why would she cast me off? Weren't we meant to be together?

As time went on, it came to me. Maybe I had abandoned her in a past life, and that was why she was punishing me now.

My queen was making me wait.

Again.

And so I waited.

And I will continue to wait. I know that she will find me one day. I know that my Savanna will come back to me.